Praise for

The Rainy Night Stalker

The strength of *The Rainy Night Stalker* lies in its protagonist, Moon McFadden. The blend of her vulnerability—haunted by the trauma of her parent's murder—and her steely determination to use her psychic abilities for justice creates a heroine both deeply human and otherworldly. The emotional toll of Moon's work is palpable, especially as she grapples with the impending death of her Aunt Maisie, the one person who understands her gift. The parallel loss of family and the terror of facing a killer obsessed with her adds depth to her character and grounds the supernatural elements in a very real emotional struggle.

The pacing of *The Rainy Night Stalker* is relentless, from the discovery of the first victim to the final showdown. The narrative pulls the reader into the mystery with each new clue, building suspense with the constant ticking of the clock toward the next rainy night. Moon's escape and subsequent fight for her life in the wilderness are heart-stopping, with the author delivering taut, cinematic action that brings the reader to the edge of their seat.

But what truly sets *The Rainy Night Stalker* apart is the atmospheric writing. The rain itself becomes a character, adding an oppressive, melancholic mood to the story. The imagery of rain-slick roads, foggy fields, and darkened cabins creates a haunting backdrop that perfectly complements the dark, twisted narrative. Shannon's use of the rain as both a literal and symbolic element ties the entire story together, adding layers of meaning to the killer's ritualistic murders.

At its heart, *The Rainy Night Stalker* is more than just a thriller. It's a story of loss, survival, and the lengths one woman will go to for justice. Moon's ability to "hear" the dead is not just a plot device—it's a metaphor for the way trauma echoes through our lives, and how confronting that trauma is often the key to overcoming it. As Moon whispers to the dead, she speaks not only to the victims she's trying to help but also to the ghosts of her own past.

With a gripping plot, complex characters, and a chillingly original villain, *The Rainy Night Stalker* delivers on every front. Fans of paranormal thrillers and psychological horror will find themselves hooked from the first page, and Moon McFadden is a heroine they won't soon forget. This is a must-read for anyone looking for a hair-raising, emotionally resonant story that lingers long after the final page.

—**Lee Anderson**, best-selling author of *What Happened at Sisters Creek*

THE RAINY NIGHT STALKER

A THRILLER

DEBBIE SHANNON

ISBN: Paperback 978-1-948981-16-3
ISBN: Ebook 978-1-948981-14-9

Printed in the United States of America

Book cover designed by Robin Locke Monda
https://www.robinlockemonda.com/

Book interior designed by David Provolo
https://reedsy.com/david-provolo

Author photograph by Sharona Jacobs
https://www.sharonaphoto.com/

First edition

Published by Fogbow Books, LLC, New York.

To my sister, Patty,
for all those times we scribbled plot ideas
on cocktail napkins in foreign bars,
discussed scenes while swimming laps,
pinched names for characters from airport
announcements and old cemetery gravestones,
and a thousand others—
this is dedicated to you.

You've always had my back. This is the one!

La pluie nous a débués et lavés,
Et le soleil desséchés et noircis.
Pies, corbeaux nous ont les yeux cavés,
Et arraché la barbe et les sourcils.

Rain has unsmirched and washed us
And the sun has dried and blackened us;
Magpies and crows have carved out our eyes,
And torn off our beards and eyebrows.

—François Villon, *Ballades des pendus*

Chapter One

She was there to help her ex-boyfriend bury his mother in an unmarked grave. Mae "Moon" McFadden waited in her county-issued Dodge Grand Caravan at the cemetery as a chilly June rain poured straight down stripping petals from headstone flowers leaving the stalks like skeletons.

She checked her phone. St. Peter & Paul at 10:00 a.m. It was the right cemetery and the right time, but she didn't see any other cars. Moon shifted in her seat. She dreaded being anywhere near a cemetery.

She could see the dead.

She watched the ghost of a woman kneel in the dirt in front of a new headstone. The ghost traced her fingers across the engraved name, then leaned forward and kissed the stone. Moon watched other departed souls wander the grounds pointing at various headstones or staring up at the gray sky as though it held the answers. Even when she didn't see them, Moon could feel them. She knew how each person buried there had lived and died. Thankfully, none of the departed realized she was there, or they would have clustered around her van to try and communicate with her.

Rain patterned the windshield. Moon took a deep breath to steady the butterflies. Finally, Matthew pulled up and parked behind her. Seeing him in the side-view mirror, her heart skipped. Matthew Benson. They had been high school sweethearts. Prom king and queen with a romance that trickled into college. It had been ten years since she had seen him. She watched him get out of the car and huddle under an umbrella. He looked the same. Blond curls. Dimple smack in the middle of his left cheek.

He caught sight of her in the side mirror. Moon straightened in her seat and checked herself in the rear-view mirror. She wore her long, dark hair in a loose bun at the base of her neck. The one side had lost gravity, and a wayward curl tickled her cheek. A gentle mix of her mother's African American and her father's Scottish genes, she had light brown skin and dark almond-shaped eyes. Freckles peppered the bridge of her nose. She looped the runaway curl behind her ear, pressed her lips together, and got out of the car.

"Hey." She opened an umbrella and walked over to him. She reached under his umbrella and hugged him. "I'm so sorry about your mom."

"Thank you. I appreciate you being here."

"Where is Julie?"

"Let's not talk about that right now."

Matthew opened the back door of his rented Buick Lincoln and pulled out a shiny wooden box. As they trudged through the wet grass, the departed spotted Moon and walked in her direction. Unseen by Matthew, a half dozen souls followed closely behind them. Puddled water here and there shimmered black and gray. They all made their way over to where a man stood under a small green tent beside a wheelbarrow filled with dirt. The man, Jack Phillips, was tall and lean. Everything about his face was vertical. Deep creases in his cheeks made his thin mouth appear as an em dash in between parentheses. He held a shovel, and at his feet was a deep, shoebox-sized hole in the ground.

"Where's the headstone?" Moon asked.

"Julie and I are still arguing about which type to get."

They closed their umbrellas and ducked under the tent. Matthew shook the man's hand.

"Mr. Phillips, you know Mae McFadden."

"Yes."

"Hello," Moon said, extending her hand.

Mr. Phillips looked at her hand, cleared his throat, then gave her a curt nod. He had blue eyes, though they weren't aimed at her but at the ground. Moon slipped her rebuffed hand into her raincoat pocket but kept her gaze on Mr. Phillips. Living in a small town had its disadvantages. People knew Moon and her grandmother and aunt, and many had long considered them outcasts. Some thought they were evil. Still others believed they were crazy. Some in town thought they possessed mythical powers. What they didn't know was that Moon inherited the ability to see and communicate with the dead from her grandmother and aunt. As a young girl, Moon often sat in the dark stairwell late at night with her face pressed against the balustrades, listening to the lovestruck women who snuck up from town looking for answers in the tarot cards her aunt revealed. Moon learned from an early age that people often distrusted things they didn't understand.

"Shall we begin?" Mr. Phillips asked, still not making eye contact.

Moon looked around to see if anyone else was coming. Matthew nodded to Mr. Phillips who then balanced the shovel against his leg and pulled a small Bible from his pocket.

"I'd like to start by reciting Psalm 23." Mr. Phillips opened the Bible and pulled on a ribbon bookmark. The well-worn pages fluttered open. "Yea, though I walk through the valley of the shadow of death, I will fear no evil—"

Moon held up her hand. "Hang on a second. Can we have a minute?" She pulled Matthew aside.

"What are you doing?" Matthew whispered.

"Why am I the only one here?"

"There's a good reason, I promise. I'll explain everything to you later. Trust me."

He gave her a look. That look, from those soft blue eyes the color of jeans that had been washed a thousand times. That man could radiate charm at will. He motioned for her to follow him back over toward Mr. Phillips. The departed gathered respectfully behind the couple with their hands folded and heads bowed, and Mr. Phillips resumed. Matthew stood close to Moon as though they had both swallowed magnets.

After reading a few verses, Mr. Phillips closed the Bible and put it back in his pocket. Matthew stepped forward and knelt beside the grave pit. He reached down to place the wooden box on the bottom of the pit. He stood and brushed dirt and wet grass from his pant legs. Mr. Phillips handed Matthew the shovel. He scooped dirt from the wheelbarrow and poured it into the hole. A hollow thud ascended as earth clapped the lid of the box. One of the departed, an old, distinguished-looking Black woman in a pink flowered dress, came forward and shuffled over to the grave pit, leaned over, and peeked inside.

Matthew held the shovel out to Moon. She hesitated but took the shovel from him and scooped some dirt. She glanced down into the hole. The old woman nodded encouragement. Moon shook the dirt from the shovel into the grave, then handed the shovel back to Mr. Phillips.

"I'm sorry for your loss, Matthew," he said.

"Thank you."

Moon and Matthew walked back to their cars. When they reached her van, she closed her umbrella, and they stood face to face under his umbrella. Her cell phone vibrated in her raincoat pocket. She reached in and read the text.

"Can I buy you lunch?" Matthew asked.

"I can't." She flashed the phone. "I've got to go to work."

"Oh, gosh, I'm sorry."

Moon took the keys from her pocket. "When someone dies, I go to work."

He embraced her for a moment, then kissed her cheek and opened the door for her. She got in and rolled down the window. He leaned in on his elbows.

"Dinner then. I'm staying at the Hilton. I'll explain why you're the only one here."

"That sounds nice. I'll call you when I'm done."

She plugged a GPS into the cigarette lighter and entered the address from the text.

"Seriously, a GPS? I didn't think they made those anymore. Why don't you just use Apple Maps on your phone?"

"What can I say? I'm old school."

"Okay, old school. I'll see you later."

He took a step back, and she rolled up the window. It was then she noticed that his cologne had brushed her raincoat. It was a scent memory from long ago yet still present—fresh and sexy with hints of lemon, Italian bergamot, and cedarwood. She took the cologne in with a deep breath then turned over the ignition. As she drove away, she glanced in the rear-view mirror. Matthew was standing in the rain circled by the departed. They all watched her pull onto the side road that led to the highway.

Moon dialed her boss, Police Chief Larry Quinn, as soon as she turned onto the side road that led to the highway.

"We got us one," Chief Quinn said. "You'll see the cars four miles up Whiskey Hollow Road."

"Yes, sir."

She drove east on Route 17. The rain was relentless, and she found herself trapped in the vortex of a semi as it barreled down the highway. The wipers slapped at the spray with little effect. She tried to slow down to get away from the semi, but a pickup truck was on her tail, and there was no hope of passing. After suffering through miles of near-blind driving, she took the exit that led to Whiskey Hollow Road.

Although this wasn't too far from home, she had never traveled this particular country road. Asphalt soon turned to mud and gravel that snaked up the hill. The rain turned to a frayed and raveling mist, but the sky remained gray and discouraging. Small rivulets flowed diagonally from ditch to ditch. As she rounded a curve, she spotted the line of black and white cruisers and pulled off to the side of the road behind Chief Quinn's car.

Moon got out of the van and opened the back hatch where she kept her crime scene gear in a duffel bag. As she pulled items from the bag, she heard growling. She spun around and saw the wind rustle the tall grass across the ditch. The growling grew louder. As the grass parted, she saw a big mean farm dog, its ears laid back against its broad head. The dog was emaciated, and the hair on its hackles was raised. Its head was lowered, but its eyes were locked onto her. It snarled, then wrinkled its nose and opened its mouth wide, baring its teeth.

She averted her eyes and stood perfectly still. She had read somewhere that making eye contact with dogs was a sign of aggression. She remembered a story her father once told her about the time he and a friend were out deer hunting. They had taken a break and were sitting on a log on the edge of a field eating a sandwich when they saw a German Shepherd chase a deer across the field. The friend lifted his rifle, took aim, and shot the dog.

"Why did you do that?" her father asked.

"The dog was ruined. He had turned—got a taste for blood. If it chased deer, it'll chase humans."

"That's a damn shame. That was a good-looking dog. I wondered who owned it."

"I owned it. That was my dog."

Moon wondered if the dog staring her down had ever tasted blood. She swallowed hard. She could feel her heartbeat in her ears. She took a deep breath and gathered her gear. She closed the back hatch and slowly backed away from the ditch with her eyes on the ground. Once she had crossed the road, she glanced back at the field. The dog seemed to have melted back into the tall grass.

A policeman waved to her from behind yellow crime scene barrier tape about 30 feet away. She hopscotched over a puddle and paused under an old red maple tree just before the yellow tape. She kept her eyes on the ditch as she slipped a hairnet under her bun and over her head to her forehead. She pulled the hooded overalls over her black slacks and blouse. She stepped into rubber boots and looped the camera bag around her neck, then punched gloves into her pocket and clipped a tripod to her belt loop.

Her eyes swept the area. A gust of wind caused a handful of leaves to cartwheel across the road. After the heavy rain, the air was weighted with the smell of ozone and worms. There didn't seem to be any neighbors for miles. No sounds of traffic. It was something she missed from her days in Manhattan. She craved the constant hum of energy.

Moon had been back in the small upstate New York town of Clivesville a few years. The city covered 3.3 miles and was bisected by the murky waters of the Chemung River that slithered west to east through the middle of the town.

Clivesville seemed to have safely cupped itself within the narrow hands of a vast range of hills deeply scarred with ridges about 40 miles above its junction with the Susquehanna River. Home to the Fortune 500 company MacKinley, Inc., it was also home to blue-collar factory workers, working-class teachers, firefighters, and police officers, and to white-collar engineers, attorneys, researchers, and physicians. It was also home to sex traffic ringleaders disguised as dentists, white supremacists and militia groups, pedophiles, and kitchen meth lab operators. The nearby Amish built sturdy roofs and carports for the townies. The countryside was filled with McMansions enfolded by meticulous landscaping, wild lilac trees, and rolling pastures. Farther down the road were rusted trailers scattered throughout the hollows like thrown dice, their summer lawns littered with deflated snowmen leftover from the holidays, angry dogs chained to trees, and ravaged car bodies cast onto cinder blocks. The countryside was peaceful, idyllic even, but at times, danger buzzed the air. The serenity of an afternoon hike in the woods could be shattered by the sound of gunfire. Was that a responsible sportsman target practicing at the local gun club? A hunter out of season? A group of beer-drinking buddies in a nearby field target shooting the neighbor's cat with an AR-15?

Aunt Maisie was Moon's only living relative. When Maisie got sick, Moon quit her job in Manhattan as a forensic photographer, sold her apartment on the Upper East Side, and moved back home to take care of her. Moon wasn't used to small-town silence. She closed her eyes and listened to the murmur of police voices beyond the crime scene tape in the nearby field. And the wind. She cast one last look over her shoulder at the ditch, then ducked under the yellow tape.

Moon trudged up the hill about 40 yards alongside the muddy path made by the police to the field on the edge of the woods. By the time she got to the top, her calves were burning. Police Chief Quinn and District Attorney Richard Mendoza huddled side by side on the edge of the field. Their umbrella canopies made a figure eight.

In his late 50s, Chief Quinn was well-built and tanned from hours in his Lowe fishing boat stalking smallmouth bass in Keuka Lake. He rarely wore his uniform. Instead, he preferred to wear jeans, a button-down shirt, and on chilly days an old navy cardigan that looked as though it had left Ireland before the famine. The permanent crease between his eyebrows made him appear unapproachable, serious, but he was the first man to rush into traffic to help an old lady safely across the street.

District Attorney Mendoza sported silver temples and a strong body. He had a deep voice, a reassuring fireside chat voice. He had just stepped into his 60th year and had lost very little to time. He looked to be the type who played football or some other sport in college, and his current gym habits kept his body in shape.

Chief Quinn waved Moon over. Three policemen stood a few yards away on the edge of the field. One of them was bent over with his hands on his knees studying the ground. Moon took photos of everyone standing on the edge of the field. She always took photos of the spectators knowing that many times, the perpetrator would return to the scene to observe the police and even offer to help in the investigation. It also allowed her to identify any reluctant witnesses who could be identified and interviewed at a later date.

"Who's that with Newman and Patterson?" Moon asked, snapping another picture of the bent-over man.

"That's the new kid, Stevens," Chief Quinn said. "He was the first responder and secured the scene."

Stevens threw up, and the other two policemen placed their hands on his back.

"Is he going to be okay?" Moon asked.

"He'll be fine," Chief Quinn said. "He just needs to get his sea legs. A hiker found the body while crossing the field."

"Was the body moved or anything altered?"

"Nope." Chief Quinn gave a slight smile like he appreciated the question. He flipped a small spiral notebook shut and tucked it and his mechanical pencil into his shirt pocket. "She's all yours."

Moon snapped on surgical gloves in a puff of talcum powder. Latex gloves have a particularly offensive smell caused by residual chlorine that gets trapped in the molecules of the latex. Moon hated the smell of latex because she associated its scent with the dead. She pulled a Canon EOS 5D Mark IV DSLR camera with a wide-angle lens from the camera bag. She scanned the waves of hay and turned in a 360-degree circle to get an idea of the overall scene using a three-step approach. Before she began shooting, she always took in the entire crime scene. She thought, why here? Why this field? She started photographing at eye level in a clockwise direction working from the outside perimeter of the scene toward the body. As she tightened the circle, she replaced the wide-angle lens with a normal lens and snapped mid-range photos. She shined a flashlight on the ground at an oblique angle. Even in the daytime, this was a good way to catch evidence.

Moon had a feeling that she was traipsing through a battlefield where the wrong side had triumphed. She spotted something white in the middle of the field among the tall stalks. It was the naked body of a woman. As she spiraled closer, she switched lenses again, this time to a close-up lens. As she approached the body, Moon averted her eyes for a moment, more from the indignity. The victim lay face up in the trampled straw and mud. Legs akimbo. Her nipples and areolae had been removed from her breasts.

Moon studied the hay looking for traces of blood. Footprints. Anything. As she got closer to the body, she took pictures of the victim from five angles—both sides of the body, both ends of the body, and straight down from overhead. She started from the head working her way down to the feet. She snapped pictures of the torso, breasts, and ligature marks. The bottom of the victim's feet had cut marks. There was an abrasion on her chin and the front of her shoulders. She snapped on a macro lens and took close-up pictures of the wounds. Moon crouched down and snapped pictures of both the victim's profiles including her ears which are as unique as a person's fingerprints.

She took photos of the woman's face and focused on the eyes. Many people believe a person's eyes are a window into their soul. The eyes are the most sensitive part of the human body. In life, the pupils are round and equal in size. Once a person dies, the muscles that control the pupils relax, causing them to lose their symmetrical shape. The eyelids become flabby. If someone opened them, they would remain open. After death, the eyes no longer react to light, touch, or pressure. A dead person's pupils will be dilated. Moon looked at the woman's cornea. That clear part of the eye will become milky or cloudy within a half hour to several hours after death. The degree of change in the eyes after death depends on many factors: temperature, air currents, humidity, and weather. If someone was experienced in reading the condition of the eyes postmortem, they could pretty accurately pinpoint the time of death simply by looking at the person's eyes.

Moon needed a moment alone with the victim. To be still. To observe. To listen. To let unseen things in. She crouched down in the tall stalks beside the right side of the woman's face, which was drained of everything, pale as birch. The victim's empty eyes were frozen on the gray sky, and her mouth was open in a silent scream. Moon snapped a photo. She peered over the camera and watched as the dead woman slowly turned her head and gazed directly at her. She saw a vision of the woman running naked through the woods with her wrists zip-tied tightly behind her back. Tree branches slapped her body. A lock of her long beautiful honey-colored hair was ripped from her head and dangled from a branch. When the woman looked back at whoever was chasing her, she tripped on a tree root. She fell hard onto her chest and chin. She struggled to get her footing, to get up and run. She heard footsteps and the snapping of branches just a few feet away.

"I've got you now," the male voice said. His steps, his voice, were unhurried. Proud. Smug.

The victim's eyes left Moon and drifted back up to the sky.

Chapter Two

After taking all the pictures and measurements she needed, she waved the coroner over. Dr. Lloyd Babbitt was in his early 50s and short and stocky. His head was as bald as an egg, the dome stippled with freckles. A thick mustache hid his upper lip. He lived in his Levi's and his time-kissed cowboy boots. Lloyd had three loves in his life: his job, his beer, and the Buffalo Bills—depending on the day, not necessarily in that order.

Moon joined the men on the edge of the field. They watched Lloyd examine the body. Moon motioned for Chief Quinn and Mendoza to take a few steps away from the officers.

"Her wrists were zip-tied behind her back as she ran away from the killer through the woods," Moon said. "She tripped and fell hard. She tried to get back up, but he found her."

"Did you see his face?" Chief Quinn asked.

"No. I heard his voice, though. That's all. I'll let you know if I get anything more from the photos."

After a few moments, Lloyd waved to the officers. Newman and Patterson joined him in the field with a body bag. Stevens stayed behind. After the victim and surrounding ground cover were secured in the body bag, Lloyd joined Moon, Chief Quinn, and Mendoza.

"What have we got?" Chief Quinn asked. He watched Newman and Patterson carry the body bag down the path to the road. Stevens walked behind them at a distance.

"Her body temperature is 91 degrees," Lloyd said. "The average temperature last night was 68 degrees, leaving us with a time of death around 10:00 p.m. last night. She has a rope burn along her armpits and neck. The burns and the abrasions on her back would suggest she was dragged. Ligature marks on her wrists indicate restraint. Tortured, obviously. Because of the extensive bruising, I'd say the abuse had been repeated over a period of time. I'll see what I can get in the lab, but the UV light showed no semen. We'll test for blood, semen, saliva, and other bodily fluids, but as far as I can tell, this guy left behind nothing. He knew what he was doing."

"What are the chances of getting any DNA?" Mendoza asked.

"We'll see. DNA lasts as long as saliva does, which can be 4-15 days at room temperature, longer in the cold. This rain can quickly and easily wash surface DNA all away. I'll let you know how much evidence I can get in the postmortem."

Lloyd made his way down the path to the awaiting van that contained the body. All autopsies performed in upstate New York were done either in Rochester or Binghamton. Lloyd would make the hour-long drive to Binghamton.

"As soon as I saw the victim, I knew there might be a connection to the Catskill murders," Mendoza said. "Same M.O."

"How do you know about murders in the Catskills?" Moon asked.

"There have been two murders in the last month just like these in Sullivan County. Madelaine Spencer is the District Attorney there. She phoned me and talked to me about the murders. Those victims in the Catskills were found in fields with the same body parts missing. I can't believe that's a coincidence. I've been in touch with Janet Brown who is the special agent in charge of the FBI's field office in Albany. They're bringing in someone from D.C. to help us with this case. His name is Detective Stuart Bauer. He's one of the best FBI profilers in the country."

Mendoza looked down and pushed the muddy ground with his toe.

"What are you thinking?" Chief Quinn asked.

Mendoza looked out at the field where the mangled body of a beautiful woman had lain. "Cases like this make me want to throw in the towel. I think about my house on Sebago Lake, and a retired life in Maine sounds better and better to me. I could occupy my mornings fishing and spend my afternoons kayaking. I could light a fire in the evening and pour Loretta, my darling wife of 30 years, and myself each a glass of Barolo. I'm thinking after we nab this S.O.B., I might call it a day. That's what I was thinking."

"Sounds like a nice plan," Chief Quinn said. "Until then, we've got work to do."

Moon drove back to the police station and parked the van in the employee lot in the back. She took the elevator to the basement to her small, windowless office. The hall was short and narrow. The only other rooms down there were an unused office and a storage room. She got along well with the police officers, but she preferred to be apart from them while she worked. She needed the quiet and the darkness. It allowed her to calm her mind and focus.

The only furniture in her office was an old, battered executive desk, a wooden office chair, and an antique floor lamp. She had found the abandoned desk in the storage closet. It had been on its side and shoved to the back. She persuaded a few guys in the office to swap out her metal desk for the old wooden one. It was enormous, taking up nearly the entire wall in her office.

She dropped her purse in the bottom drawer and turned on her computer, then transferred all the digital photographs into Amped FIVE software for editing and storage. All digital photos were saved as they were originally captured, entered into evidence inventory, and tracked. She scanned them all, pulling those that needed to be enhanced. Some needed to be cropped or brightened, or the contrast adjusted, and color processed.

She studied the photos and made copies of any that needed adjustments. She never removed any information. When submitting these altered photos for courtroom use, she knew the original photographs must be available for comparison. She was often called to court to show and describe any enhancements that were done and why.

Down in the belly of the basement, Moon lost herself in the photos. She cleared her mind and watched the pictures come to life like a movie. To everyone else, they were crime scene photos, but Moon was often able to see beyond the still photos—to see what the victims saw.

After several hours, Moon felt brain numb. She unwound her bun and teased her fingers through her hair. She closed down the computer and drove home. She slipped into shorts and a T-shirt. She pulled her hair up into a ponytail, stepped into Skechers, and went for a long run. The afternoon sky spat a cold, light rain that felt refreshing. She loved the smell of the air when rain fell on the asphalt. The rhythmic pounding of her feet on the road and the back and forth swinging of her ponytail allowed her mind to wander. Within minutes, her body fell into a familiar pattern, and all she heard was the *puck, puck, puck* of her stride and her steady breathing.

At spots in the road where trees grew close to the curb, she ducked under the branches that bowed with the weight of the water on their leaves. She left the road and climbed a hill along a well-worn hiking trail. The great arms of the ancient pine trees flapped in the gentle gusts. She took a deep breath and filled her lungs with perfumed air. A tree had long fallen across the path and was barnacled with moss.

Her stride never broke as she leapt over the tree. The forest floor had a certain scent when it rained. It reminded her of a winemaker's note. She once was told by a sommelier that the Pinot she had ordered was redolent with upturned forest floor, morning dew, and mushrooms.

Just as the trail looped sharply to the left, everything became pitch black as though night had immediately fallen. Startled, Moon stopped running and stood still on the path. It was raining hard, and Moon had a difficult time seeing where she was. The well-worn trail she was just on, the trail she ran on nearly every day, was choked with thick brush. As she tried to move forward, her ponytail tangled in a branch, and she yanked it loose. She heard a noise. Someone was in the woods behind her. Whoever was back there was walking toward her.

That was when Moon realized she was seeing what today's victim had seen. She was in those woods reliving her horror. Moon looked back to try and identify the killer but could see no one. She heard him gaining on her, so she moved in the opposite direction and tripped over a tree root just as the victim had done. Moon landed hard on her hands and knees, but because her hands weren't tied behind her back, she was able to scramble to her feet. She forced her way through the trail until it dead-ended, hopelessly clogged with a thicket of dense bushes and shrubs. She heard the killer's footsteps behind her. Unhurried. Proud. Smug.

She looked back and caught a glimpse of a shadowy figure that had floated into view between the evergreen branches. She spotted something rise—a flash of metal. It was the barrel of a rifle aimed at her. She heard the chick-chick sound of the rifle loading.

"I've got you now," the male voice said.

Moon turned away from the man, lowered her head and shoulders, and threw her whole weight against the thicket like a running back. She exploded through the brush onto the trail where it exited the woods into their backyard. The vision was over, and the sun shone once again. The pouring rain was gone, replaced by the light mist.

Moon sprinted for home and didn't look back. She raced across the grass up onto the back porch and through the screen door that led to the kitchen. She pushed inside and slammed the door behind her with her back. Maisie was at the stove frying chicken.

"You all right?"

"Yeah." Moon leaned against the door and let out a deep sigh.

"You hungry?"

"Starved, but I'm having dinner with Matthew."

"Oh, that's right. Have a good time."

"I'll bring back dessert."

Moon wiped sweat from her forehead. She went to the dining room window and parted the lace curtains. She stared at the entrance to the trail for a moment. After seeing nothing out of the ordinary, she let the curtain flutter back into place.

Chapter Three

oon left the shower feeling rubber-legged and spent. She threw on a light blue sundress and tan high-heeled sandals. The rain started up again as she drove to the restaurant. Splats of water hit the windshield as she drove. She found a parking space about a block away from the restaurant. It was then that she realized her umbrella was back home on the dining room table.

She made a run for it. She skidded to a stop in front of Three Little Red Hens restaurant and paused under the awning long enough to shake the water from her hair and arms then went inside. She let her eyes adjust to the dimly lit room. Gray glaze-painted walls, yellow and blue hand-blown glass pendant lights, and rococo molding above the large bar mirror gave the place a Parisian, bohemian feel. The restaurant smelled of freshly baked bread, garlic, and sizzling meats.

She spotted Matthew sitting at the end of the long mahogany bar. He wore dark jeans, a white dress shirt, and a charcoal gray blazer. She stood still for a moment and admired him. The shape of a memory sharpened and suddenly transported her back to a not-forgotten summer when "they" were "we." The trembling passions of first love. She had fallen headfirst into his heart. It was perfect—long, hot days that melted into cool nights. They had just graduated from high school and had the summer to themselves before each of them left for college. He was going to study finance at Boston University. She had been accepted to The George Washington University. The school's Columbian College of Arts & Sciences offered a Master of Science degree in crime scene investigation and forensic photography.

They had two precious months before they would need to go their separate ways. They spent them at his parents' cottage on Seneca Lake swimming and boating, driving through the countryside, and hiking the gorges. One afternoon, they hiked a trail to the top of a hill. They left the trail and wandered deep into the woods where they came upon a waterfall. At the bottom of the falls was a round pool of clear, ice-cold water. The slate rock banks alongside the pool were flat, warm, and dry—the perfect place to come for a picnic. That became their secret place. They often brought a bottle of white wine and a bag filled with crusty bread, cheeses, and fruit. Matthew tucked the bottle of wine in the cold water under a stone along the edge of the pool. One afternoon a week before they were to head off to college, they went to their secret place and made love beside the waterfall.

She took a deep breath bringing her back to the present. Matthew did a double take when he finally noticed her and waved her over. He stood and offered her the empty barstool beside him. He motioned to the hostess who signaled one minute with an index finger.

"Wet becomes you," he said. "Our table is just about ready. How was your day?"

Moon shook her head. "Unless you want me to ruin your dinner, I suggest we change the subject. I've got one we can talk about. Why was I at the cemetery this morning and not your wife?"

Matthew smiled and glanced at his watch. "Under a minute." He nodded to the hostess. "Our table's ready. This discussion deserves a bottle of wine."

They followed the hostess to a table. A young waitress with black earlobe gauges handed them menus. The green and black leaves of a vine tattoo peeked out from under her shirt collar. Her lips were as red as backup lights.

"Can I start you with a drink?" she asked.

Matthew flipped the wine list open. "Let's have a bottle of the Smith & Hook Cab."

As soon as the waitress left, they opened their menus.

"You look beautiful," Matthew said, studying his menu.

"Don't."

He snapped the menu shut. "Can't a guy compliment a friend? Are you seeing anyone?"

She smiled and looked down at her watch. "Under a minute. No one special since I moved back."

"How's Aunt Maisie?"

"Better. She's in remission." Moon rapped her knuckles on the tablecloth. "I like being with her. We get each other. And I like living in that big ol' house again."

"Everyone knows that big purple Victorian house just outside of town on top of Grasshopper Hill. It suits you both."

Moon closed her menu and placed it on the edge of the table. "Talk to me. What's going on?"

Matthew sighed and pulled on his napkin. "My marriage isn't turning out the way I had hoped it would."

The waitress came back with the wine. She presented the bottle, uncorked it, and handed the cork to Matthew. He sniffed it and nodded to her. She poured a little into a glass. He held the base on the table with his index and middle finger and swirled. He lifted the glass and tilted it to inspect the legs and color. He brought his nose into the glass and then tasted.

"It's very good. Thank you."

The waitress poured them each a glass then set the bottle on the end of the table. Matthew handed her his menu.

"I'll have the Chilean Sea Bass," he said.

Moon handed her the menu. "The same."

As soon as the waitress was gone, Matthew swirled the wine some more. Stalling. Moon waited for him to say something.

"Julie and I have had our ups and downs," he said. "More downs than ups. After my father died last year, I've been thinking a lot about my life. Taking stock. Did I make the right choices? Where is my life headed? Am I happy and fulfilled? Are there things I missed out on? It seems as though I'm on a fast-moving train, destination unknown."

He took a sip of wine and let it linger in his mouth before swallowing. His eyes never left the glass. "Now that Mom is gone, I feel as though I'm at a big T in the road. I have to make a decision about which way to go."

The waitress brought a basket of rolls and butter. Moon lifted the cloth covering the warm bread and pulled out a roll. She carved a small amount of butter from the butter dish and spread it onto her plate, then buttered a section of her roll and took a bite. She waited for Matthew to say something. She sat back and listened to the smooth Parisian jazz playing in the background that mingled with the din of muffled chatter, cutlery chiming on plates, and occasional laughter.

"The short answer to your earlier question—the reason Julie wasn't here with me today is because she didn't want to come. She said, 'Funerals make me sad.' Seriously, who likes going to a funeral? But it's my mother, for God's sake."

Moon reached across the table and took his hand.

"She's not the same woman I married."

"People change. Trying to change them back is an exercise in futility."

"Of course, in reality, neither of us is the same. We've both changed. But we haven't changed together. At some point, we went in vastly different directions and grew apart. There are times I don't even know her anymore. And…I think she's having an affair."

Moon released his hand. "What makes you think that?"

"A gut feeling. Sometimes you just know. New outfits. New perfumes. Weekend vacations with her girlfriends." He air-quoted 'girlfriends.'

"Have you had her followed?"

"No."

"You should. If anything, it would give you peace of mind."

"I suppose. As for why I asked you, it's because I wanted you to be there. You knew my parents well. They loved you. Dad was buried in California. Mom had lived in Florida for the past 15 years, but she had planned to be buried next to her parents here. Back home. I asked you to be with me because I knew you would be there. I could always count on you. And, I wanted to see you. I needed to see you."

Moon looked around the dining room. She leaned in. "I'm not going to be your mistress."

"I wasn't asking you to be. That said, I have a confession to make. Through all my ups and downs, professional and personal, do you know who kept showing up? You. Moon McFadden. Voted most likely to remain in my dreams long after I let her go. That'll go down as the worst mistake I ever made. You're my favorite regret."

He raised his glass and they clinked.

"I'm leaving for Boston in the morning," he added. "To go back and get my shit together. I've got a lot of thinking to do."

The waitress brought their meals and refilled their glasses. They spoke of old times and smiled until their cheeks were sore. After they finished their dinner and lingered over coffee and dessert, they stood under the awning outside the restaurant. Matthew opened his umbrella.

"Where did you park?" he asked.

"At the end of the block."

He put his arm around her waist and brought her under the umbrella. "Shall we?"

They ran down the block and stopped on the sidewalk in front of her car while she plucked the keys from her purse. They rounded the front of the car and paused for a moment by her door.

"Thank you for dinner," she said.

"It was the least I could do. It was so good seeing you. Moon—"

"I know." She touched his cheek.

"You remember that time we got caught in the rain walking home from the park?"

"Of course. When we got to my porch, you stood in the rain and sang to me. You held your arms out and sang 'Just the Way You Are' at the top of your lungs."

Matthew shook his head. "Gotta love Bruno Mars. Really silly, huh?"

"Really romantic."

He nodded. "You okay to drive home?"

"Yes, I'm fine."

"You had half a bottle of wine. Do I need to get out a breathalyzer?"

She smiled and shook her head. She opened the car door, got in, and placed Maisie's to-go dessert box on the passenger seat. He motioned for her to roll down the window. She cranked the window open.

"You are the one person on earth who still has a window crank."

"Cranks are standard on a Chevy Spark. Like I said, I'm old school. I like the crank."

He cocked his head and smiled.

She smiled back. "What is it?"

"Nothing. I'm always home when I'm with you." He leaned in and kissed her cheek. "Text me when you get home."

"Will do. Have a safe flight."

She put the car in drive. This time when she pulled away, she didn't look in the rear-view mirror. She didn't have to. She knew he was watching her leave.

Chapter Four

The struggle with evil by means of violence
is the same as an attempt to stop a cloud,
in order that there may be no rain.
—Leo Tolstoy

At 10:00 p.m. that same night, it was raining hard. He only hunted during dark, rainy nights. The ones he hunted were all the same—young, beautiful women, who, if he met them out in the real world, wouldn't give him the time of day let alone date him. He needed to take them down a notch.

Seth Jacob Woodman lived alone in a one-story ranch-style cabin 20 miles outside of Clivesville in the town of Groverton, New York. No hope of getting cell service. Not a neighbor for miles. He loved the silence. People who chose to live in such remote locations liked it that way. They didn't want you in their business, and they sure as hell wouldn't pry into yours.

The cabin was built in a U shape with a bedroom at the end of each wing. A kitchen, dining room, and living room were located along the bottom part of the U. In the center of the U between the wings, an open grassy courtyard had been built around an old sturdy oak tree. The back of the courtyard faced 15 acres of shadowy forest. Before each hunt, Seth turned the flood lights on in the courtyard. When everything was ready, he opened the sliding glass doors and went inside. A Tupperware container was on the dining room table along with a surgical gown, hair net, and gloves. A clean towel had been draped over the back of a chair.

He walked down the hallway to the windowless bedroom in the east wing to retrieve his prey. He unlocked the door, and before he entered, flicked the light switch on the wall outside the door. The shiver of a single light bulb dangled from the ceiling by a wire above a bed. On the bare mattress, a naked woman lay face down. Her legs were spread and her ankles were tied to either bedpost. She was gagged and blindfolded. Her wrists were bound behind her back with zip ties. As he approached her, she whimpered and cowered away from him.

"I'm going to get you out of here," he whispered. "I will let you go. I promise."

He untied one of her ankles from the bedposts and bound it to her other ankle, then released that from the bedpost.

"If I didn't think you'd run or try to kick me, I'd free both of your ankles. You wouldn't do that now, would you?"

The woman let out a muffled cry, but he ignored her. He lifted her off the bed and flung her over his shoulder. He carried her down the hall, through the kitchen, into the dining room, and out the sliding glass doors into the courtyard. He walked through the courtyard to the edge of the woods and set her feet on the ground. He cut the rope from her ankles but kept her wrists bound behind her back. He stood in back of her and ran his fingers through her long blond hair, soft as loon feathers. With his hands on her shoulders, he positioned her to face the woods, then removed the blindfold but kept the gag in place. She looked momentarily stunned, standing in the dark in the pouring rain. She turned to see his face, but he wore a camouflage hunting mask that covered his head and neck.

"You're free," he told her. "Go. Run."

He pointed forward, and she turned back toward the trees. The flood lights from the courtyard lit 30 feet into the black woods. She ran as fast as she could through the heavy brush. Seth ambled back to the courtyard and stood just outside the sliding glass doors. To the left of the doors was a canvas awning protecting a patio table and chairs. He pulled the mask off his head and placed it on the table. He flipped a cigarette from a soft pack, and as he struck the match, the flame reflected off his dilated pupils. He cupped his hands around the cigarette and touched the flame to the tip, then drew the hot smoke into his lungs. The tobacco crackled, and a curly ribbon of smoke rose from the tip of the cigarette up into the awning. Two streams of smoke whistled from his nostrils.

Seth had been ignored by attractive girls all through high school. He grew up hating them and nursed fantasies of cruel revenge. He had had violent urges since then and fought them. He bought certain types of magazines and indulged in internet bondage videos. He thought he could keep the urges in check. But fantasy doesn't come close to the real deal. Once you've tasted the real thing, well, fantasy just won't cut it.

When he was finished with his cigarette, he crushed the butt in a glass ashtray. Also on the table was a short ski rope looped and secured with a snap hook. Seth attached that hook to a carabiner on his belt loop. He picked up his .243 Winchester and adjusted the spotlight he had mounted to the rifle. He screwed a .308 suppressor on the end of the rifle barrel. The spotlight and silencer weren't legal in New York, but he didn't give that too much thought.

He pulled the mask back down over his head and neck then crept into the woods. He stood still for a moment, listening to her fumble.

His pulse quickened. He moved in the direction of her whimpering and spotted her about 40 yards into the woods. She had gotten herself hopelessly tangled in the thick brush. He liked to watch them try to escape. He finally took aim and pulled the trigger.

He pulled the body from the woods and loaded it in the bed of his truck and drove several miles across the country roads. Once he found an open area that pleased him, he pulled over and carried the body into the middle of the field where the rain would wash her clean.

After returning home, he stuffed the gown, hair net, and gloves in a cotton bag he left on the patio table. He entered the house and placed the bag on the stack of logs in the fireplace. He took a long hot shower and dressed in navy silk pajamas and Brooks Brothers burgundy velvet slippers.

In the living room, he took a long-handled candle lighter from the mantel and lit the cotton bag. Lost in his own solipsistic musings, he plucked a Waterford crystal tumbler from a curio bar cabinet and poured himself a double Rémy Martin XO. He turned on the stereo turntable and placed the needle on an LP—"The Hunt", Mozart's String Quartet No. 17 in B-flat major. He took a sip of the cognac and let the essence of late summer fruit and jasmine linger on his tongue.

He sat down on the sofa in front of the fireplace and crossed his legs. The heat from the fire and the cognac were soothing. He turned his head to the left to admire his precious artwork on the wall in the dining room, hung safely away from the heat of the flames.

Chapter Five

The next morning, Mendoza and Moon took a seat in the back of the conference room at police headquarters for the briefing. It was 7:00 a.m.

Mendoza handed Moon a cup of coffee. "Any luck with the photos?"

"I think so."

Chief Quinn leaned against the wall by the door with his hands on his hips. Lloyd Babbitt sat in the front row.

"Do you know who's sitting next to Lloyd?" Moon asked.

Mendoza nodded but held up an index finger to pause the conversation. Chief Quinn coughed into his hand, and everyone immediately stopped and watched him stride across the front of the room and stand behind a podium.

"Good morning. Before we begin, let me remind you all that what is said here in this briefing is confidential. I don't want any of these details to leave this room. If the press gets wind of anything, it could hinder our investigation. Do I make myself clear?"

The officers nodded.

"We were able to match yesterday's victim with a missing person report on a Ms. Margaret Bender. Ms. Bender lived in Alfred, New York, was single, and lived by herself. She worked in the admissions office at Alfred University. Her parents had the unenviable task of positively identifying her late last night."

"I'd like to introduce someone who has experience in these cases—psychological profiler Detective Stuart Bauer. Detective Bauer is one of the best profilers in the country. He heads the Behavioral Analysis Unit at Quantico."

Chief Quinn motioned for Detective Bauer to come to the front of the room. Detective Bauer stood and walked to the podium. He appeared to Moon to be in his mid-30s with short dark hair and a cleft chin. When he turned and looked up to take in the room, Moon noticed that his light brown eyes looked as soft as a Disney fawn. Looking more like someone who had stepped out of the glossy pages of a men's magazine, he wore a cream-colored knit shirt that hugged his fit physique. His navy slacks and shiny black dress shoes without socks completed the appearance. He might have even been considered handsome if his furrowed eyebrows hadn't made him look so angry.

Moon suddenly saw an image of Stuart on a city street at night. He was chasing a man down a dark alley. He called out for the man to drop his gun. Instead, the perp raised his gun, and Stuart was forced to fire his weapon. As he approached the bloody body on the ground, he saw that it wasn't the perp he had been chasing, but a kid with a cell phone. Moon blinked and came back to the present.

"Thank you, Chief Quinn," Stuart started. "Unfortunately, I do have experience in cases like these, specifically the two cases in the Catskills. Like this one here, those killings occurred on rainy nights. I believe this killer is a male in his late 20s or early 30s. I say male because most female serial killers are more likely to kill by drowning, poisoning, or suffocation. Males are happier using brute force, and this certainly fits the bill. I believe he's white. Serial killers tend to kill within their own race, and all the victims to date, that we know of, have been white. Unlike typical serial killers who may live at home or have no job or a menial job, this one is educated."

Bauer stepped out from behind the podium and paced the room.

"We have his M.O.—the type of victims he's choosing, how we think he overcomes his victims, and the time and place these killings occur. More revealing is the killer's signature. *Why* is he doing this? What is that thing that fulfills him emotionally? A killer's M.O. may change as he develops skills and comes up with better, more successful methods of execution. His emotional reasons, however, will stay the same. Finding his emotional core reasoning is the key to finding who he is."

Moon leaned toward Mendoza. "Your guy knows his stuff."

Mendoza smiled and nodded. "You know it."

Stuart continued to pace the floor. "The fact that the victims all had been tortured and their areolae removed has been kept from the papers. The precision of the excision around the areolae suggests someone who is experienced with knives. Because of the heavy rain, we were unable to get any usable tire tracks or shoeprints at any of the crime scenes. He knows enough about DNA to know that the rain makes retrieving it and any forensic evidence difficult if not impossible. We don't know how the killer is choosing his victims or why, but there is some connection. These murders aren't random. They might seem random, but serial killers pick their victims with a purpose. This one is no exception. There will be more victims. We're looking at a few days of dry weather, which, if our theory holds true, may buy us a little time to brainstorm."

Chief Quinn returned to the podium as Detective Bauer took his seat.

"Thank you, Detective. That's it. We'll schedule another briefing when we have more."

Everyone stood to leave the room. Mendoza, Moon, and Detective Bauer followed Chief Quinn down the hall to his office. Mendoza made the introduction.

"Stuart Bauer, I'd like you to meet Moon McFadden. Moon is our forensic photographer, but she also works with us as a consultant."

"Nice to meet you." Moon shook his hand.

They filed into the office and took seats. Chief Quinn sat behind his desk. He handed Mendoza the files containing the autopsy reports and the crime scene photos taken of the Catskills victims. Mendoza skimmed through them, then handed the files to Moon.

Moon opened a file. The first victim's name was Christine Krohmalney. A beautiful woman even in death. Her shoulder-length dark brown hair draped across her face. Moon flipped to the autopsy results. Christine had a bruise on her left temple, the blow probably knocking her out immediately. Moon checked for levels of histamine. When tissue is injured, the damaged cells release inflammatory chemical signals that stimulate the blood vessels to widen increasing blood flow to the injured area. Mercifully, Christine's histamine levels were very low which suggested that she was already dead when the killer performed his handiwork.

Moon opened the next file. The second victim, Sandra Thompson, had been in the field a while before her body was discovered. Magpies and crows had pecked at her eyes and flesh. Her lips were gone, exposing her teeth and gums, which left her with a ghastly smile. Sandra's histamine levels were low as well.

In addition to the removal of Sandra's flesh by animals, Moon noted the number and types of insects that had clustered on her skin. Insects are found in and around a decomposing corpse. Knowing the life cycles of the insects can determine the time of death, the time between death and the discovery of the body, and whether or not the corpse had been moved.

The first recorded incident of forensic entomology where insects were used in a criminal investigation was in thirteenth-century China. After a farmer had been found murdered, all the suspects were asked to put their sickles down on the ground. Only one sickle attracted blow flies to the trace amounts of blood on the blade that wasn't visible to the human eye resulting in the murderer's confession.

As soon as death occurs, the cells in the body start dying and enzymes begin to digest the tissue from the inside out. Bacteria and other gases attract the insects almost immediately. They lay their eggs, and the developmental process begins. Knowing the life cycles and the types of insects present, forensic entomologists can determine how long the body had been dead.

Moon ran her fingers over the image of Sandra's mutilated face. Stuart looked away.

"The killer hunts his victims," Moon said.

"I thought the same thing," Stuart said. "Did you find any shell casings or spot something specific in one of your photos?"

"Not exactly. He sees a beautiful woman who is open and warm. He spots their self-confidence a mile away."

Stuart looked over at Mendoza who shook his head.

"Given the removal of the areolae, we may be dealing with a lust murderer," Stuart said. "Removing parts of the breast could mean the killer wanted to defeminize his victims. The posing of the victims post-mortem could suggest the killer had an obsessive fantasy. It wasn't enough just to leave their bodies in a field. Typically, lust murderers, who often torture their victims before killing them, have a compulsion to act out their fantasies with the body. Finally, given the two locations, we need to recognize that this murder here could be a copycat of the ones in the Catskills. Or, there may be two killers working together."

"No. That's not it," Moon said.

"How can you be so sure?" Stuart said. "It's worth a consideration."

"Only if you want to waste precious time." Moon turned to Mendoza. "There is only one killer. Once he finds his next victim, he becomes completely obsessed with having her. He stalks her and immobilizes her. By the time she comes to, she's bound and gagged. When he's done torturing her, he waits for a rainy night to set her free at the edge of the woods. Then he hunts her for the thrill of the chase. I dated a guy once who hunted deer. Once the animal is down, it's common to take a rope, similar to a water ski rope, and tie it around the neck of the deer to drag it out of the woods. I think the killer did the same thing with his victims. Unfortunately, not all his victims were killed cleanly by the gunshot. He looped the rope around their necks and dragged them out of the woods. Death by asphyxiation only takes a few minutes, but that's an eternity when every cell in your body is screaming for oxygen."

"Wait, how in the hell do you know all this?" Stuart asked.

Moon kept her eyes on Mendoza. "The killer has two houses—one somewhere near here and one in the Catskills. Both are remote. He must have some science background to know to use the rain to wash away DNA."

"I don't understand," Stuart said.

Moon slid the files back to Chief Quinn but kept her hand on Sandra Thompson's file.

"There are two victims here," she said.

"There have only been three victims that we know of," Stuart said, "the two in the Catskills and this one here. There was only one victim found at each of the crime scenes."

"I don't know what to tell you. Here, there are two."

"Stuart, we use Moon's skills in several different areas," Mendoza said, "some of which are unconventional." He side-glanced at Chief Quinn. "It's not something we advertise. Moon has certain… abilities."

"Oh, my God." Stuart bolted out of his seat. "Are you kidding me? What are you saying? That she's some sort of fortune-teller? Some two-bit card reader? A pay-by-the-minute phone psychic?"

"Excuse me?" Moon shot him a look.

"I'm not about to work with some carny barker."

Mendoza stood. "That's enough." He ran his fingers through his hair. "Janet warned me that you could be an ass. She never said just how big an ass."

Moon shifted in her chair to face Stuart. "Look, for what it's worth, I don't want to work with you either. I know you're a bitter man, but it's not my fault your marriage ended over what happened."

Stuart spun around. "What did you say?"

"The kid in the alley."

"How the hell do you know about that? Hey, I'm talking to you."

"No, you're yelling at me."

"The two of you, knock it off," Mendoza said. He turned to Chief Quinn. "This was a bad idea. Stuart, no one outside this room knows about Moon and what she does for us here. I hope I can trust you to keep this a secret."

Stuart stared at the floor and sighed. "I won't say anything. Believe me."

The phone rang, and the Chief answered. "Chief Quinn. Yeah. Christ. All right." He replaced the receiver. "They found another body in a field outside Addison. Same M.O. I need you both to play nice and come with me."

Chapter Six

Out beyond ideas of wrongdoing and rightdoing,
there is a field.
I'll meet you there.
—Rumi

Moon followed Chief Quinn and Lloyd Babbitt through the country roads. She glanced in the rear-view mirror and saw Stuart's car behind hers. They turned onto Hardscrabble Road which crooked to the left. A policeman flagged them over. She parked the van behind Chief Quinn's car, and Stuart pulled in behind her. As she rounded the back of the van, she glanced over at Stuart, who averted his eyes. Moon pulled on her overalls and grabbed her camera gear. They both headed to the field without looking at each other.

While Chief Quinn took notes from the first responding police officer, Moon stood at the edge of the field and scanned the entire area, turning her body in all directions taking in the countryside. The previous night's storm finally wore itself out, surrendering to the clear summer morning—brilliant, green, and warm. The tall trees that fringed the edge of the open field looked like slender eyelashes. It was such a peaceful place. The verdant field was dotted with daisies. Such a cheery flower. Fluffy white cumulus clouds rolled across the deep blue sky. Large round bales of hay were scattered here and there throughout the field. A real-life Van Gogh painting. Too beautiful a place for such defilement.

She screwed a lens onto her camera, then shielded the top of the lens from the sunlight with her hand and shot a series of photos turning in 360 degrees from the edge of the field.

Stuart pointed to the field with a snicker. "You do know that the body is over there."

"I am using a 15mm fisheye lens, Detective Bauer," she said while snapping photos. "All wide-angle lenses have what's called barrel distortion, which causes the center of the image to bulge out. That's because the field of view is wider than the image sensor, so everything looks squeezed to fit the edges of the frame. Any straight lines that don't pass completely through the center of the image will be rendered as curved lines."

She stepped in front of him and continued to snap photos.

"Most normal wide-angle lenses will correct for this barrel distortion. These are known as rectal-linear lenses. This fisheye lens, however, does not correct for that barrel distortion. Instead, it embraces it."

She lowered her camera and faced him. "And that's the lens I want here." She went back to shooting the area. "When I use a fisheye, I can get a different view of the entire crime scene. Even though this crime scene appears to have a lot of straight lines, I'm using a full-frame fisheye to get a super-wide view of the area. This allows me to look at the scene in a different way."

Stuart took a step toward her with his hands on his hips. "I'm not sure how useful snapping a picture of the woods behind us will help you when the body is in the middle of the field in front of you."

Moon unscrewed the fisheye lens and replaced it with a wide-angle lens from her camera bag on her hip. "Have you ever seen the movie *My Cousin Vinny?*"

"Not my type of flick."

Moon continued to snap photos as she stepped into the field. "Well, in the movie, the inexperienced lawyer, Vincent LaGuardia "Vinny" Gambini travels to a small southern town with his fiancée, Mona Lisa Vito, to represent his cousin in a murder trial. Mona loved to take pictures of just about everything she saw which frustrated Vinny to no end. But lo and behold, one of Mona's many photos just happened to capture a clue that held the key to solving the case."

"What does that have to do with anything?"

Moon rolled her eyes. "All right, I'll give you another example that might make things clearer for you. A forensic photographer in Florida was at a crime scene and took a bunch of photos." She reached into her camera bag and switched the wide-angle lens for a normal lens. She began to walk in a spiral around the perimeter of the crime scene, snapping shots of the surrounding field and patterns in the grass, all from different vantage points.

"The purpose of a forensic photographer, Detective, is to document what is here and where it is in relation to the scene, whether or not there's an obvious connection to the crime. So, this photographer in Florida is in the dead man's house, and he's snapping pictures of the inside of every kitchen cupboard and refrigerator. Seems crazy, right? The dead man was in the living room. Later on, they found a receipt for a six-pack of beer matching the beer that was in the refrigerator. Relatives of the victims said that he didn't drink beer. The team went to the convenience store where the beer had been purchased and saw the victim on the surveillance tape. Apparently, he had picked up a hitchhiker and purchased beer for him. They came back to the house where the hitchhiker murdered the man. With this evidence in hand, they were able to indict the hitchhiker and charge him with murder. The seemingly random photograph of the beer inside the fridge led to the arrest and conviction of the murderer. Case solved."

She stopped walking and turned to face him.

"Everything I record through photography—an assault scene, blood spatter patterns, shoe or tire prints, or a victim's injuries, or the contents of someone's kitchen cupboards—can successfully communicate more about crime scenes and the appearance of evidence than a written report ever could. One of the most important reasons forensic photographers capture the entire crime scene and evidence is to later use them in court. What I am able to see in those photos further adds to the story behind every crime scene."

She lifted her camera and snapped a picture of him.

"Detective Bauer, I don't question how you do your work. Stop mansplaining how I should do mine."

Chief Quinn stifled laughter and kept his eyes on his notepad.

Moon tightened her spiral, advancing close to the body. She stood completely still and closed her eyes.

"I'm here," she whispered. "If you have anything to say, please tell me. I can hear you. You know who I'm looking for. Tell me anything you can remember. Anything at all. Talk to me."

Her eyes snapped open. She turned and saw the naked victim standing by the edge of the field beside a hay bale. Her body was intact just as it had been in life. Her breasts were flawless and uncut. Moon walked across the field toward her. She stopped a few feet from the woman and waited for her to speak. When she didn't say anything, Moon tried to break the ice.

"I'm sorry this happened to you."

The dead woman seemed confused. She looked around the field then at a point somewhere in the distance.

Moon took a cautious step closer. "What's your name?"

On the opposite side of the field, Stuart stared at Moon and scratched his head.

"I don't get it," Stuart said. "Who is Moon talking to?"

Chief Quinn looked up at Stuart without moving his head. "I'm going to let you figure out how stupid that question was."

Stuart folded a stick of Big Red gum into his mouth. "Oh."

"I'm surprised you're still asking questions after the way she handed you your balls."

Moon took a few steps closer to the hay bale and stopped. "Do you know who did this to you? Anything you remember would be helpful."

The woman's eyes scanned the area again. A wave of terror washed over her face when she caught sight of her own lifeless body in the middle of the field. Moon stepped in front of the woman to block her view.

"He's not here. You're safe. No one can ever hurt you again."

The woman looked downcast, then suddenly focused on something on the ground before looking up at Moon.

"What is it?" Moon asked.

The woman looked down at the object on the ground again, then stepped behind the hay bale. Moon hurried toward the woman and rounded the hay bale, but she was gone. She scanned the ground at the base of the hay bale and found what the dead woman was looking at. Moon aimed her camera and snapped a picture.

"Chief Quinn, can you come here?" Moon studied the camera's display.

He and Stuart joined her next to the hay bale.

"Look." Moon pointed at a Skor candy bar wrapper nestled beside a hay bale.

Chief Quinn picked it up with tweezers and placed it in an evidence bag. "It could be nothing, but it might be the first mistake the killer made."

"I think this is significant," Moon said. "At least that's what I think the victim wanted us to know."

Moon made her way clockwise over to the victim's body. After taking several photos, Moon crouched down and leaned in close to the woman. She touched her arm and suddenly saw an image of the woman kicking the killer in the stomach.

Moon sighed. "We will find him. I promise."

She stood, took a picture of the victim's right foot, and walked over to Chief Quinn, Lloyd, and Stuart.

"Lloyd, can you please bag her feet as well as her hands?" Moon asked.

Lloyd nodded and entered the field to examine the woman.

"The pattern is different with this one," Moon said. "In addition to everything else that was done to her, she was stabbed on the right side of the neck which could suggest our killer is left-handed. There's one more thing. Her second toes are longer than her big toes."

Stuart shifted his weight from one leg to the other and put his hands on his hips. "So?"

"So, before she was murdered, she kicked the killer in the stomach with her right foot. She scratched him. You'll find the killer's skin cells under her right second toenail."

"How could his skin cells be under her toenail?"

"The killer was naked."

Moon shot Stuart a look over her shoulder on the way back to the van. A cutting wind kicked up and tugged at her hair. She glanced up at the granite-gray clouds that had racked up, thick and low and heavy as they encroached upon the blue sky. Daylight began to extinguish, and it wasn't even noon. The air was weighted with the rain that was about to fall. She unlocked the van and got behind the wheel. She closed and locked the door and put her key in the ignition but didn't turn it on. The killer was somewhere out there, and it felt as though he was gaining on them.

People who have had near-death experiences have often reported seeing their whole lives flash before their eyes. When Moon touched the woman's arm, she not only got a glimpse of what the killer was going to do to her, but she also saw the woman's life pass before her own eyes. A wave of anguish overtook her. Moon thought of the woman's parents, undoubtedly wondering where their beautiful daughter was. She imagined that they may have felt anxious when their repeated phone calls went unanswered. Those parents, sick with worry, driving to the police station to file a missing person report. The agony of not knowing. Trying desperately to push the unthinkable from their minds. Later that afternoon, they will get a call from the police. The dreaded call in their hearts they knew was coming. They will make the long drive to Binghamton to identify their daughter. Their only child. Their gorgeous daughter, who loved horses and Newfoundland dogs, and pistachio ice cream, and whose favorite color was cobalt blue, the color of the Spanish tiles she fell in love with when the three of them vacationed in Barcelona four years ago. Their lives will never be the same. Their family will never be the same.

The dark clouds, laden with the promise of rain, seemed to fold themselves down around her spirit. She pressed her forehead against the steering wheel and wept.

Chapter Seven

The following morning, Moon met her friend, Holly Sherman at a local farmer's market. She found Holly standing in front of one of the bakery stalls inspecting the pastries. Holly wore a lemon yellow sundress as bright as her smile. The flood of morning sunshine cast golden patches upon her long black hair. Holly noticed Moon and waved her over.

"Chocolate croissants?" Holly asked.

"Oui, s'il vous plait." Moon handed Holly a cup of coffee.

"We'll take two, please," Holly said to the woman behind the counter. She handed a croissant to Moon, and they made their way toward a nearby picnic table.

"I saw Matthew," Moon said.

"Matthew Benson? You're kidding. How did that happen?"

"He was in town to bury his mother's ashes. He asked me to go to the cemetery to be with him."

"How's the wife?" Holly took a sip of coffee. "What does she look like?"

Moon took a bite of the croissant and shrugged. "I have no idea.

She wasn't there."

"I see."

Moon took a sip of coffee. "I can feel your look. There's nothing to see."

"You haven't seen the man in ten years, the guy you thought you'd spend the rest of your life with, well, except…"

"Yeah."

"I'm sorry."

"Thanks."

"And Matthew just happened to ask you out of the blue to help him bury his mother. Without his wife. That doesn't sound odd to you?"

"Not really. He said he and his wife are having problems. I feel bad for him. He's my friend, and I care about him. That's all." Moon finished her croissant and stood, brushing crumbs from her jeans.

"So you say."

They made their way back into the market and wandered from stall to stall inspecting all the farmers had to offer—raw honey, cheeses, fresh eggs, and jams. They stopped at a vegetable stand. Holly picked up a bundle of fresh basil and smelled it. "How did Matthew look?"

"Damn good."

Holly paid for the basil and dropped it into her canvas bag. "Do you still love him?"

"Let's just cut to the chase." Moon shrugged. "I will always love him. You never forget your first love."

"Do you think he still loves you?"

"Yes, I think so."

"We've all known each other since we were kids," Holly said. "It's hard for me to picture you with anyone else. You two always seemed right together."

"It wasn't meant to be. What's going on in Boston has nothing to do with me. Besides, even if there was a chance for us sometime in the future, he's there, and I'm here."

"Distance is nothing when one has a motive."

"So said Elizabeth Bennett."

"Just saying."

Moon gave Holly a playful nudge. She spotted a man throwing a clay pot at the next stall.

"Look at those," Moon said, pointing to several flower pots with sunflowers. "Wouldn't they look great on your porch steps?"

"They would. Sunflowers are my favorite."

"I know."

"Okay, I'll get them."

Driving home later, Moon thought about what Holly had alluded to at the market—that Matthew wasn't the only man she thought she'd spend her life with. The other man's name was Daniel Hoffman. They had met at an art gallery in Tribeca. She remembered that they had both been admiring a watercolor landscape painting. They came at it from different angles and were so taken by the painting that they bumped shoulders. He spilled his wine on her shoes.

"I apologize." He snapped a handkerchief from his pocket. "How clumsy of me." He bent down and began wiping her shoes.

"You don't have to do that. Please, stop."

He stood and smiled at her. She felt her breath catch in her throat. She cleared her throat and pointed at the soiled handkerchief.

"A handkerchief," she said. "Classy."

"I'm old school. I like a handkerchief."

"You wiped my shoes with it. The least I can do is wash it for you."

He folded it and stuffed it in his pocket. "I wouldn't dream of it. But what you can do is let me buy you a drink afterwards."

"Deal."

They left the gallery immediately and found a small wine bar around the corner. They talked until two in the morning. From that evening on, they were inseparable. Daniel worked at a hedge fund in the Chrysler Building. He was a native New Yorker having grown up on the Upper West Side. He had dark, wavy hair, brown eyes, and a neatly kept beard and mustache. He wore round silver-framed eyeglasses. It wasn't long before he had introduced her to his parents, Josh and Barbara Hoffman, and his three older sisters. By the end of that year, they planned to move in together.

Daniel made dinner reservations one evening at a restaurant on West 65th Street. Moon had a gut feeling he was going to propose. Because she had worked near the restaurant that afternoon, she planned to meet him there. The hostess led her to their table where she ordered a glass of Sauvignon Blanc. As she sipped her wine and waited for Daniel to arrive, she found it hard not to smile. She was so happy, she thought she might burst.

Daniel was late. She looked at her phone but wasn't worried. It was early June and the weather was sunny but very windy. Still, Daniel was never late. She texted him without getting a response. She became edgy when her subsequent phone calls all went straight to voice mail.

The hostess seated a middle-aged couple at the table next to Moon. They settled into their seats and leaned toward one another as if to share a secret.

"I can't believe it," the man said.

"Those poor people. The crane sliced that apartment building in half."

A wave of nausea washed over Moon. "Excuse me, I couldn't help but overhear. What happened?"

"A crane fell in Midtown and struck an apartment building," the man said.

"Where in Midtown?"

"56th and 2nd."

Moon threw $20 on the table and ran out of the restaurant. She hailed a cab that was able to take her to 57th and 2nd. They could go no further because the police had cordoned off the entire block. She pushed her way through the crowd on the opposite side of the street and saw that the center of Daniel's building had been crushed by what was left of the mangled crane. Construction was underway at an apartment building a block away. She would find out later that the crane wasn't properly secured to the apartment and broke away from its anchors. The poor worker in the crane's cab fell with the crane into the building.

Moon turned away from the rubble and the crowds and the flashing police lights. She stood in front of a coffee shop on 2nd Avenue and looked up at her reflection in the storefront window. Just then, she saw a man's face staring back at her in the window. She turned to see who it was. It was Daniel.

"Am I seeing you because you are alive or dead?"

"Moon—"

"Just say it."

"It was my time."

"No." Moon began to sob. She pushed her way through the crowd and away from the building. Daniel followed her.

"It's okay."

"How can you say that? How can it be okay if we're not together?"

People did a double take at Moon who looked as though she had lost her mind and was waving her arms and ranting to no one. They whispered to one another and moved away from her. She stopped walking and bent over with her hands on her knees. "I want to go with you. Please, Daniel. I want to be where you are."

"You can't. Not yet."

"Excuse me, Miss. Can I help you?"

A police officer stood beside her. Moon straightened up, and Daniel was gone. The police officer held her while she cried on his shoulder. They stood in the doorway of a corner deli. The police officer waved to the deli manager for some water. Once Moon gained control, the police officer handed her a bottle of water.

"Are you going to be okay?"

"Thank you. I'm okay now."

The police officer hailed her a cab, and she got in. Until the day she moved from New York City, she avoided that block. It was simply too painful for her to see the remains of the building, and later on, the repairs.

Forensics found very little of the victims in the section of the building that had been destroyed. They found Daniel's class ring still attached to his severed hand. Within 24 hours, Josh and Barbara had a memorial service for Daniel at their temple. They insisted Moon sit with the family in the front row. After the service, the Hoffmans hosted mourners at their apartment to sit Shiva. Platters of food that guests brought filled the dining room table.

"Moon, can you come with us for a moment?" Josh asked.

She followed him and Barbara down the hall into the library, and they shut the door. They handed her a small box. She opened it and gasped. Inside was Daniel's class ring.

"We want you to have this," Barbara said. "You may not know this, but Daniel had planned to propose to you that night. They never found the engagement ring. We wanted you to have his class ring. It's a poor substitute, but hopefully, in time, you'll be able to look at this and remember the good times you shared with him and be reminded of how much he loved you."

She slipped the ring onto her middle finger. She was too choked up to say anything. They hugged her and rejoined their guests. She stayed behind in the library waiting, praying Daniel would appear to her, but he didn't. After a few minutes, she left the room and joined the other mourners.

Chapter Eight

Moon's heavy sigh brought her back to the present. Thinking about Daniel made her feel a little melancholy. She decided to spend a few hours at work which always helped focus her mind. After several hours of categorizing photos, she left work, went to the supermarket, and headed home.

Moon walked into the house from the garage with an armful of grocery bags, passing through the open concept living room/dining room and entering the kitchen. The Victorian house was built in 1874 in the Queen Anne style. The exterior of the house had been painted purple with pink and cream trim and was adorned with a prominent turret on the front of the house and a sprawling wraparound porch. The roof was steeply pitched. The most unique house in Clivesville, it had the look of a gingerbread castle.

The first McFadden to leave Scotland for the United States was Harris McFadden. It was 1852, and he was 19 years old and had $20 in a stitched-up pocket. He had worked with his father, Alastair McFadden, building ships in Glasgow along the River Clyde until one early morning at the shipyard, his father was struck in the head by an improperly torqued wire cable and died instantly. Harris was the oldest child of six. While his mother and siblings were taken in by family members, he knew he needed to make real money in order for his family to survive. That meant only one thing: going to America.

The ink was still wet in the Ellis Island record book when Harris hopped a train and headed west to Pennsylvania to work in steel manufacturing. It was that cheap, high-quality steel that was used to make railroad tracks and fueled the boom that would by 1900 give the United States the largest rail network in the world. That steel also made building tall skyscrapers possible. Harris worked hard and climbed the business ladder. He sent money over to Scotland and brought his family to Pennsylvania to live with him.

Harris McFadden shadowed a Scottish-born industrialist, Andrew Carnegie, following him to Pittsburgh to work at the Edgar Thomson Steel Works. By the time he reached his early 30s, he had become a manager, securing the McFadden fortune for years to come. He married Elizabeth MacKinley whose family founded MacKinley, Inc. in Clivesville. They lived in Buffalo while Harris ran the Buffalo Steam Pump Company before retiring to Clivesville where he built the beautiful purple Victorian house on the hill.

Moon set the grocery bags on the kitchen counter. The back door off the kitchen led to another grand porch. The door was open. Moon shouldered through the screen door and stood on the porch, leaning against the wooden railing and taking in the evening sky. The sun had just dipped below the horizon. Civil twilight. The underbelly of a large cloud overhead glowed orange. She stared at the sky, not in reflection but in more of a suspension of thought.

Moon stepped off the porch and rounded the corner of the house. She found her Aunt Maisie in her garden in the side yard. She wore an old painting T-shirt and cut-off jeans. Maisie's long hair, the color of soft smoke, was in a loose braid and draped over her right shoulder.

Her well-worn Mets cap was pushed back off her forehead. She wore noise-canceling headphones over her baseball cap, so she didn't hear Moon open the door to the fence that surrounded the garden. Moon watched her aunt for a moment. Maisie was in her element. She sat on a towel and plucked weeds from around the tomato and zucchini plants while softly singing the Beatles song "Blackbird."

Moon stepped forward and tapped her on the shoulder. Maisie pulled her headphones off and draped them over her neck.

"You're home. Good. Help me up."

Moon held out a hand and pulled her to her feet. Maisie removed her gloves and brushed the dirt from her shorts.

"This is the last summer I'll have this garden," Maisie said.

"You love to garden."

"Ah, it's been so rainy the last few seasons. It's too much work. Most of the weeds I pull just break above the root and grow back in luxurious mockery. I think next year I'll take down this fence and fill the side yard with weeds—goldenrod, yarrow, and milkweed for the monarch butterflies. You know how much I love monarch butterflies. Besides, I spend too much of my time weeding. I'm done. The weeds have won. Besides, weeds are good. Weeds attract bugs, bugs attract birds. We'll get our produce at Wegmans. How was your day?"

"Don't ask. I'm going up to change. I'll be down in a few minutes."

As they came inside, Maisie banked right into the kitchen, and Moon headed back through the dining room. She plucked a grape off the vine from the bowl of fruit on the table and popped it in her mouth as she crossed through the living room. She climbed the opulent wooden staircase and headed down the hall to her room. She slipped out of her clothes, then knotted her hair in a covered rubber band and stepped into the glass shower stall. She stood under the showerhead and let the hot water wash away the day. She dried off and pulled on yoga pants and a T-shirt. She stood before her dresser and inspected the half-dozen glass bottles nestled on a decorative mirror. She picked up a purple bottle and removed the glass stopper. As soon as she breathed in the familiar scent, she was transported back to her childhood. The bottle was filled with Old Spice aftershave. It was what her father always wore. He wore it because that's what his father wore. That sweet-spicy smell would always remind Moon of her father, and of that time in her life when everything felt connected and whole.

Moon replaced the glass stopper, went downstairs, and joined Maisie in the kitchen. She had already rooted through the grocery bags and stood belly-up to the counter, thumping up crust for pie. Some sort of stew bubbled in the hefty cast iron skillet on the stove.

"What's for dinner?" Moon asked.

"Skillet surprise."

Moon shook her head as she pulled a huge bag of cat food from a cupboard. She hoisted the bag onto her hip and headed out the back door. She stood on the back porch and rattled the bag. The backyard extended about 60 feet from the porch. Beyond the backyard, a field of tall grass grew at the edge of the hundreds of miles of woods. The grass blades swayed as unseen creatures made a beeline toward her. No sooner had she stepped off the porch than a dozen cats ran from the tall grass and wove in figure eights around her ankles.

She lugged the bag across the yard toward a small shelter she had built by the field of grass. The shelter resembled a pool house for the colony of feral cats that roamed the fields. It wasn't much, but it kept them safe from the cold and storms. She filled several steel bowls inside the shelter and brought the cat food bag back inside.

"Whatever's in that skillet surprise smells amazing," Moon said.

"Thanks. It's a lovely mess, but it will go down well."

Moon plucked a large ceramic pitcher from the top of the refrigerator and filled it with water. She went back outside and brought the pitcher back to the shelter. She emptied the water bowls and filled them with fresh water. She walked back to the house and set the pitcher on the porch. She stood still for a moment in the yard, taking in the evening. The sky was in flux from pale lavender, pink, and orange just above the trees to a deep indigo blue high in the sky. A smattering of stars flickered on. It was quiet except for the chirp of crickets and Maisie's pan rattling inside the screen door.

Then she heard the rumble of the train about half a mile away. Moon turned and gazed past an ash tree and up at her bedroom window. The tree had been planted by her grandfather when Maisie was a girl. One of the fastest growing trees, an ash tree can grow 18 to 25 feet in a decade. Now that Maisie was 54 years old, the tree was nearly 100 feet tall.

After her parents' funeral, Moon was sent to live with her Aunt Maisie—a woman she barely knew, a woman wholly unprepared to raise a 12-year-old child. Her father couldn't wait to leave Clivesville after high school. He had disowned his mother and sister because they were, in his words, mental. The truth was, they were gifted. They read tarot cards for lonely housewives and made soaps and lotions. They had dreams that came true, and they saw and spoke with the dead.

Moon had only been to Clivesville twice for her grandparents' funerals. The small town got nearly 200 days of cold rain or snow a year. Even during those few visits, she missed the warm weather and the high blue skies of Virginia. That blue was her favorite color.

Nights in the big old house were cold when Moon moved in. There wasn't much wood for a fire. Maisie had lived in only one section of the big house for years. The other unoccupied rooms in the rambling house hung in darkness as if in a buried city. Cobwebs fluttered from the ceilings like shrouds. The intricately carved balustrades of the wooden staircase leading to the second floor seemed to sulk with shame at their lack of polish.

She and her aunt wore layers of clothes inside just to keep warm.

While walking home from her new school one afternoon, Moon spotted the freight train that cut through town. The last three cars were piled high with coal. As she climbed the hill to her house, she realized the train tracks zig-zagged over the hill in back of her house before making their way down into town. She walked across the backyard through 30 feet of woods to the tracks and spotted a large oak tree beside the train tracks. A sturdy branch grew out over the tracks. It rang in her head like a bell. She knew how to bring warmth into the house.

Moon made a note of the times that the train carrying the coal came through the hills into town. One of those times was each Tuesday morning just before dawn. At 12, she was already a veteran to hardship which tempers fear. Moon found a long iron rod and a burlap satchel in the unused tool shed on the side of the house. She hid the rod and satchel in the back of her bedroom closet.

The following Tuesday morning, she dressed well before sunrise, slung the satchel across her body, and grabbed the iron rod. She opened her bedroom window and tossed the rod to the ground. She climbed out the window, cupped her hands around the ash branch, and made her way hand over hand across the branch to the trunk. She shimmy-hugged the tree trunk until she was about three feet off the ground then jumped. She snatched the rod, hiked through the field, and cut through a corner of the woods to the train tracks. There, she stood behind the large oak tree beside the tracks. She waited, unseen, for the engineer to pass then climbed up the many tree burls to the thick branch that hung out over the tracks. She sat on the branch, and with her bent knees, lowered herself backward so she was dangling upside down directly above the train cars as they slunk by. She held the rod close to her chest and took a moment to close her eyes and feel the tickle of the breeze on her face.

Finally, Moon opened her eyes and spotted the last three coal cars.

She lowered the rod and positioned it directly over the train. As soon as the coal cars were under her, she lowered the tip of the rod, scraping it across the top of the coal piles. Nuggets of coal sailed from the top of the pile to the ground on either side of the tracks. After the train had passed, she climbed down the tree and gathered the coal nuggets in her satchel. She returned home and filled a steel ash bucket next to the fireplace with the coal and lit a fire. Maisie came downstairs and looked at the fire then at Moon. She walked over to the roaring flames and stood in front of them with her hands outstretched. She never asked where the coal came from. Moon knew that she knew. No words were needed.

After that morning, Moon fetched coal once a week. By the time she had collected the coal nuggets into her satchel and headed toward home, the sun was about to rise. She stood quietly at the edge of the woods that were lovely, dark, and deep. She listened to the songbirds wake up. Almost every species has a companion call when they wake that says, "Hello, I'm here. Where are you?" She heard other birds sing back through the treetops as if to reply, "Good morning. Hey, I'm over here."

Her father had been an avid birder. He taught her about the different types of bird songs and the sounds they made like companion calls, territorial calls, male-to-male vocalizations, and alarm calls. He taught her that before she entered the woods, she needed to clear her mind of all thought in order to not alarm the birds. It took some time and practice, but she knew she was finally successful when she could walk into the woods and pass within five feet of a singing bird without it alarming. Being mentally clear allowed her to give the bird its space and still allow her to pass without disturbing or frightening it.

She learned that when most people walk into the woods, it was as though they projected concentric rings of disturbance. All the animals and birds cleared out in a V shape away from the danger, and the birds sounded their alarms. Blue jays are pretty skittish birds, but when they see a threat, they look right at it and make a call that sounds like *Sneeeek! Sneeeek! Sneeeek!*

Above all, Moon loved crows. The American crow has gotten a bad rap, but Moon appreciated their beauty and intelligence. Like many humans, crows create life-long friendships. They are monogamists and are virtually inseparable from their mates. In addition to their strong friendships, crows maintain a close, life-long relationship not only with their parents, but with their siblings, aunts, uncles, and grandparents. The family members roost together at night, especially during the cold winter months. In an extraordinary act of selflessness, the offspring will take part in the rearing of their parents' next brood. That's called cooperative breeding. They will help their mother by bringing her food while she incubates her eggs as well as their baby siblings once they've hatched. They'll continue to protect their siblings by guarding the nest against any potential predators while their parents are off feeding.

It's been said that crows have long memories and actually teach each other about dangerous individuals. And they never forget a face. When they see a predator like a cat or a fox or a human that had treated them badly, they will dramatically caw and dive bomb it. Each time the crow saw that human, not only would it caw at him and harass him, but it would teach other crows who had not witnessed the original negative event to dislike that individual as well.

The forest would remain silent for about 10-15 minutes after the threat had gone, then the birds would resume their singing. Moon felt at ease in the woods. It was a place that had always given her solace. She learned that when she got good at not disturbing the birds, she could walk through the woods and listen to them sounding the alarm when other predators like raccoons, foxes, or bobcats were nearby. That secondary alarm let her know something unseen by her was moving in a certain direction, and that something had spooked them. This allowed her to move away from the threat without ever being in danger. Birds are the sentinels—the eyes and ears of the forest.

Moon listened to the rumble of the train and watched the cats nudge each other at the food bowls to get their fill of kibble.

"Supper's on the table," Maisie hollered through the screen door.

"Be right in."

Fireflies flickered on and off across the field as though tiptoeing across the tops of the tall blades of grass. A cool mist cast a soft hue onto the backyard. She stepped onto the porch and picked up the pitcher. She glanced up at the sky. A pack of coyotes lived somewhere near the edge of the woods. She learned the variety of sounds and vocalizations they made as well. Often called "song dogs", coyotes can make up to 11 different sounds from a lone howl when one of them is separated and is trying to find his pack, to group yip-howls signaling their location, to woofs, growls, and yelps when one or more of them felt threatened. The moon was nearly full. When the moon was full, she loved to sit on the back porch and listen to them sing.

She thought about the killer. Where was he at that very moment? Was he looking up at the very same night sky? Or was he stalking his next victim?

Moon heard a barn owl hoot and watched it take flight from its perch in a nearby Norway spruce. Somewhere in the tall grass, a field mouse was running for its life.

Chapter Nine

After dinner, Moon and Aunt Maisie headed to the living room. They each had their own sofa that ran parallel to each other and perpendicular to the fireplace with a large wooden coffee table in between. On either side of the fireplace were built-in bookcases. They each fingered down a book and flopped onto their respective sofas. There was a knock on the front door.

"Moon? It's Stuart Bauer."

Moon opened the door and motioned for him to come in. "Aunt Maisie, this is Detective Stuart Bauer. Stuart and I are working together on these cases."

"Nice to meet you, Stuart," she said, looking him up and down. "I'll leave you two alone to discuss whatever it is you need to discuss. I'll just bring my book upstairs."

She took her time gathering her book and making her way up the stairs, giving Moon a wink and a nod.

"Can I get you something to drink?" Moon asked.

"Sure. Bourbon if you have it. Neat."

Moon flipped down two tumblers and poured them both doubles.

She poured a few drops of room-temperature water from a Ball jar into each glass, then joined him back on the sofa.

"What brings you out here?"

"An apology for starters. I'm sorry I acted the way I did. As the district attorney correctly noted, I can be an ass. And to let you know that you were right about the skin under the toenail. We now have his DNA. Unfortunately, it doesn't match anything we have on file. Not yet, anyway." He took a long sip and studied his glass. "I don't understand how you work."

"I don't know how I work either. Information just comes to me, sometimes in a dream or through a vision. Sometimes it's through conversations I have with the dead. I can feel the energy of an event long after it had passed. There are times when I look at a person and can immediately see things, important things in their lives. And then there are other times when I don't see anything. I don't have any control over what I see or when, which can be frustrating. I can't explain it better than that. I just try to keep myself open in order to take in whatever information I can get."

Stuart studied her for a moment. "That thing you said about what happened that ruined my marriage."

"I'm sorry. That wasn't fair of me. I saw an image of a shooting."

Stuart looked at Moon and nodded. "My partner and I stopped at a 7-Eleven late one night for a coffee and happened to interrupt a robbery in progress. The robber shot my partner and ran out the door. I chased him down the street into a deserted alley. I thought it was deserted. Somehow, the guy must have ducked somewhere. I saw what I thought was the shooter turn and point something at me. I pulled the trigger. It was a 13-year-old kid with a cell phone. What the hell was a kid doing in a dark alley by himself in the middle of the night? My partner spent a month in the hospital and pulled through. I was suspended, naturally. There was a trial. I was found not guilty. I didn't feel not guilty. Killing that kid affected me. It ate me up. I started drinking, brooding.”

Stuart took another sip.

“After six months, my wife left me. I came home one afternoon to find she had packed her things, the furniture, even the curtains, and left. Just like that. No note. So much for better or for worse. Anyway, I got the help I needed to get my head and my priorities straight. I got a divorce, then got my master’s degree in criminal justice at Penn State and applied to work for the FBI. I spent most of my time in the Behavioral Analysis Unit. Truth be told, I’m still processing everything. My therapist assures me these things take time. Enough about me. What’s your story?”

“My father grew up in this house. He went to Georgetown Law where he met my mother. I was born in Arlington, Virginia and lived there until I was twelve. That’s when my parents were murdered. After that, I was sent here to live with Aunt Maisie. I was named after her. Mae McFadden is my name.”

“Moon?”

“When I was a kid, I’d often climb out my bedroom window at night, shimmy down the tree, and head to the railroad tracks to play craps with the hobos for pocket money.”

“Feisty.”

“Afraid so. My young eyes could see the dice clearly by the light of the moon. The guys called me Moon Eyes, which was later shortened to Moon. Word got around town and the name stuck.”

“Nice.”

“I like it.” Moon folded her legs under her. “Have you always been able to profile?”

“I can look at a crime scene and see things others miss. I’ve always been able to tell things about people. I can tell when someone’s hiding something. I can sit in my car in traffic and tell you when the light will turn green. When I'm driving, I like to listen to the radio. I play this game with myself. Just before one song ends, I like to guess which song the DJ will play next."

"And you're right."

"Many times, yeah."

Moon smiled at him. "A lot of people are psychic."

"I'm not psychic."

"I'm not psychic, either. Technically, I'm a medium. A medium can be a psychic, but a psychic isn't necessarily a medium. Psychics can predict things, but can't tell you where they got the information. Mediums can not only predict what will happen, but they can tell you who brought you the message from the Other Side."

"The Other Side."

"Dead people. Forget the label. Every one of us is born with a particular gift. Intuition. A certain perception, maybe? Some, like you, can see things others can't see. Mendoza said that you can get into the mind of the killer. I would guess that you're an empath. That's why you're the best at profiling."

Stuart smiled and looked around the room. "Any dead people here now?"

Moon scanned the room and smiled. "None that I can see." She finished her drink. "Would you like a topper?"

"Sure."

She brought the glasses over to the bar and topped off their drinks. Stuart stood and went over to the fireplace and leaned an elbow on the mantel. Moon joined him and handed him his glass. As he ran a finger along the grain of the wood, his blazer parted. Moon noticed the gun in his holster.

"Does this bother you?" Stuart asked, motioning to the gun.

"Yeah. I have an aversion to guns."

"Understood." He buttoned the blazer. "How old were you when you realized you had a gift?"

"I was about five. My parents and I went to one of my father's colleague's houses for a holiday party. The other kids at the party were older. They were hanging out in the basement—like *That 70s Show*. While the adults were in the living room, I wandered down a hall and found a boy about my age playing by himself in a bedroom. He saw me standing in the doorway and asked if I wanted to come in and play. His name was Joseph, and he was making animals out of blue Play-Doh. It's crazy but the smell of Play-Doh is still one of my favorite smells. Anyway, we played for a while. I remember having so much fun with him. I heard my mother call my name, so I got up and went into the hallway. 'What were you doing in there?' my mother asked. I told her, 'Playing with Joseph.' I found out later that Joseph had drowned in the family pool five years earlier. After that, the dead would seek me out. I see them at funerals or whenever I visit anyone in the hospital. Later, when I majored in photography, I would see the dead come to life in my photos. I look at the pictures and see things that had happened like a movie played out before my eyes. That's why I decided to study forensic photography. I want to help those victims get the justice they deserve. If I'm going to live with this gift, I want to use it for good."

"Like Wonder Woman."

"Without the bracelets."

Stuart took a sip of bourbon and ran his thumbnail along a knot in the mantel wood. "Chief Quinn said you sometimes can pick up on things at the victim's residences."

"Sometimes."

"I wanted to know if you'd be interested in taking a ride with me to the victims' homes. Do that voodoo that you do so well. No is a perfectly acceptable answer."

"Sure."

"We can start with Margaret Bender's apartment in Alfred. Maybe take a ride out to the Catskills. They haven't identified the fourth victim yet."

"I'd be happy to come with you."

"There's something else you should know. It's about the photo of the second victim. You said you saw two victims in the photo."

"Sandra Thompson."

"Yeah. Her maiden name was Sandra Bauer. She was my sister. You were right about there being two victims. It didn't occur to me at the time. Sandra was three months pregnant."

Chapter Ten

On a foggy Wednesday morning, Harry Wilson sat alone at a conference table at Bannister's Funeral Home. He was making the arrangements for his mother's funeral. Betty Wilson had died the night before at the Sunny Fields Nursing Home. She was 83 and had pancreatic cancer. Harry waited for the apprentice funeral director to return from the office with the necessary paperwork. Fluorescent lights buzzed overhead, and a grandfather clock in the corner of the room ticked off the seconds like a metronome. He had known this day would come, but he was still shaken. Harry needed someone to help him make the last important decisions of his mother's life.

"Sorry about the delay," Seth Woodman said. "I had to change the toner."

"No problem."

Seth sat opposite Harry and slid a folder across the table. Seth was on the cusp of 25—young as far as funeral director apprentices go. He wore a charcoal gray suit, a white shirt, and a black and white diagonal striped tie. He looked like a strange mix of a gym rat and shy kid. He was big—six feet two inches tall and strong. He had an angular baby face that had been badly pockmarked by years of severe acne as a teenager, but his deep voice and big doe eyes put grieving patrons at ease. They thought, this man can be trusted. He will help me through this difficult time. Harry sniffled, and Seth handed him the Kleenex box.

"There are several options we can do," Seth said. "I'd like to ask a few questions if I may."

"Please." Harry honked into the Kleenex.

"Would you like a memorial service here at the funeral home? That would give your family and friends an opportunity to pay their proper respects. They could greet you, say a prayer, sign the guest book, and take a prayer card to remember your mother by. From all you've said, she seemed like an angel. I wish I had had the privilege of knowing her."

"She was an angel."

"Did you want an open casket for the calling hours?"

"Yes."

After finalizing the funeral details, Harry handed Seth a check and the signed contract. He leaned over and picked up a shopping bag that was at his feet and slid it across the table.

"It's Mom's dress, jewelry, and shoes to be buried in." He pointed in the bag. "I included her rosary beads. She got those on a trip to Rome with Dad. They were blessed by the Pope, you know. Can you make sure those are in her hands for the funeral?"

Seth stood and shook Harry's hand. "Of course, Harry. Leave everything to me. I'll take very good care of your mother. We'll see you Friday afternoon."

After he saw Harry out the door, Seth walked into the back of the funeral home. The prep room was cool and bright and smelled of chemicals. He placed the shopping bag on a counter. He hung his suit in a closet and pulled on surgical scrub pants and top. Over that, he slipped his arms into a thick water-resistant gown with cuffs at the wrists. The gown opened in the back with straps at the waist and Velcro tabs at the neck. He secured the Velcro and wrapped the straps around his waist tying them in the front. Over that gown, he slipped into a blue disposable gown with thumbholes at the ends of the arms. He stuck his thumbs through the holes and pushed on a pair of black Microflex gloves that covered his hands up to his forearms. Over those gloves, he wore blue Microflex Safegrip gloves. He secured a respirator over his mouth and nose to protect him from the fumes from the toxic levels of formaldehyde in the embalming fluid. He pulled a face shield in place and stepped into a pair of tall rubber boots. The thick treads helped steady him whenever the floor got wet from water, embalming fluids, blood, or other juices that sometimes oozed from the body.

He opened the middle door of a horizontal refrigerator and pulled out the drawer that held Betty Wilson's cloth-draped body. He wheeled the stainless steel hydraulic embalming table beside the drawer. Betty was a wisp of an old woman—no more than 95 pounds soaking wet. Normally, he would use a Hoyer lift to transfer a heavy body to the embalming table, but in this case, he gently lifted Betty's body and placed her on the table. He positioned the embalming table in the center of the room and locked the wheels in place.

Seth removed the cloth that covered Betty's body and noticed a scar on her lower right abdomen, suggesting an appendix surgery at one point. She had beautiful white hair that flowed out onto the stainless steel table under her head like a halo. Harry was right. She was an angel.

Seth got to work. He washed the entire body with a disinfectant solution and massaged it to relax the muscles and break up the rigor mortis. After that, Seth focused on shutting Betty's eyes. He pulled the eyelids up, dried them, then placed a plastic eye cap over the eyeball. He then stretched the eyelid over the cap. The backward-facing spines on the surface of the cap, like a cat's tongue, locked the eyelid in place. Since eyeballs sink in death, the caps gave an overall natural plumping to the closed eye. Once the eyelids were lowered, Seth secured them in place with a Vaseline-like cream called Stay Cream.

He placed cotton in the nose and ears. Of course, Betty was no longer breathing, but the cotton prevented microorganisms as well as flies from entering the body. If allowed, a fly will lay its eggs in a dead body. It takes only a day for those eggs to hatch into maggots. He inserted cotton down the throat to absorb any purging fluids. Some embalmers use a plastic mouth former to make the cheeks look fuller, but Seth always thought it pushed the skin outward too far making the person look more like a monkey than a human. Instead, he used bits of cotton to fill the mouth and cheeks more naturally.

Seth made a small incision near the right collarbone with a scalpel. He located the internal jugular vein and common carotid artery. He made a small incision in each. He inserted arterial tubes, one directed up toward the head and the other toward the heart. A drain tube was inserted into the vein to drain the blood.

Seth positioned the embalming machine next to the table. The machine contained a mixture of formaldehyde, glutaraldehyde, methanol, humectants, and other solvents and wetting agents. He connected one end of a hose to the embalming machine and the other end to the atrial tube directed toward the heart.

Seth adjusted the knobs on the embalming machine, but before he turned it on, he took a step back and marveled at his work. He wanted to make sure everything looked good. Family and friends would approach the casket from Betty's right side. During the viewing, to those in the funeral business, that side was called the "money shot." Seth wanted to make sure Betty looked perfect, well, as perfect as she could considering her condition.

Seth also admired Betty's areolae. They were large and pink and perfect. He knew exactly where they would go in his project. He opened the refrigerator and got out his insulated lunch bag. He pulled out a Tupperware container filled with sodium nitrate. He picked up a scalpel, carefully cut around each areola, and placed them in the container, covering the tissue with the salt. He put the container in his lunch bag and put it back in the refrigerator.

He closed the open cuts on Betty's breasts with purse-string sutures which are done to repair round surgical lacerations by running the stitches around the periphery of the wound. Once pulled, the sutures closed up the round cut similar to a purse tied at its neck using a string.

He then turned on the embalming machine. Fluid moved through the hose, through the atrial tube, and into the body. The embalming fluid pulsed through the arterial system forcing the blood out through the jugular vein.

After the embalming process was complete and Betty was dressed and ready for the funeral, he cleaned up the prep room and threw all the disposables in the biohazardous trash box and taped it shut. He placed the needles and scalpels in a sharp box. He washed up and changed back into his suit.

His boss and the owner of the funeral home, David Bannister, was due back from a house call. David was a friendly man with a round face and a ready smile. He often introduced himself to new clients with a warm outstretched hand. "I'm David Bannister, the funeral director you can lean on." That always broke the ice, got a chuckle, and put people at ease.

Seth removed his lunch bag from the refrigerator and sat down in the break room. He pulled a sandwich out of the bag just as David walked in the side door.

"How's it going, Seth?" David asked, disappearing down the hall.

"Good. Got Mrs. Wilson read for Friday. How'd the house call go?"

David returned to the break room with a brown paper bag containing his lunch from the refrigerator. He sat across from Seth and pulled a sandwich from the bag.

"Suicide." He unwrapped his roast beef sandwich and took a bite. "Farmer dove into his thresher. Chewed his left arm to his shoulder before the machine froze. He bled to death before anyone found him."

"How do you know it was a suicide?"

"The note was in his back pocket," he said with his mouth full.

"Need help bringing him in?"

"Already brought him around back. We'll get to him after lunch."

"Any news on those terrible killings?"

"Nah, Lloyd said there's nothing concrete, yet." David looked over his glasses into Seth's lunch bag. "Anything good in there?"

Seth smiled. "Ham sandwich and an apple. Same ole."

Later that evening when Seth returned home, he pulled the Tupperware container from his lunch bag, dated it, and put it in the refrigerator. It took five days to dry cure human flesh. He pulled on a pair of gloves and a respirator and removed a container with the oldest date. He opened the container and fished the areolae from the sodium nitrate with tweezers. He placed them on a paper towel and brushed off the excess salt with a small makeup brush.

He brought a bottle of surgical glue and the paper towel into the dining room and set it on the corner of the table. On the dining room wall hung a four-foot by four-foot white stretched canvas. On the canvas was an Andy Warhol-style dot portrait of Seth's face. Dozens of areolae and nipples in various sizes and shades ranging from dark brown to pink formed the dots that created his portrait. A transformation from pockmarks to bulbs of precious flesh plucked from beautiful women.

As a teenager, Seth tried everything to get rid of the severe cystic acne that covered most of his face. Nothing he tried seemed to work. He went to a dermatologist who prescribed creams, lasers, and light therapy. Seth tried taking isotretinoin, but it gave him nosebleeds, so he stopped. By his late teens, the acne had permanently scarred his face causing deep pockmarks.

For years he had to endure the whispers of pretty girls behind his back. He'd turn in their direction, and they would look away. Or they would openly laugh at him. He spent most of his acne-spangled teens and adult years devising ways to deflect stares—a downcast look, a palm darting up to cover the cheek. As an adult, he grew a beard to mask the deep scars. As fate would have it, he was very good at growing anemic, patchy facial hair. He had endured a lifetime of holding a 2-7 offsuit. Not anymore.

Covering the canvas was a clear plexiglass protective casing. He removed the casing and propped it against the wall. He took down the canvas and carefully placed it on the dining room table. He gently lifted the areolae from the paper towel and glued them onto the canvas, just so.

Chapter Eleven

Most mornings, Moon was in the gym clearing her mind and taking any frustrations out on the weight machines or the punching bag. After showering and dressing but before she headed to work, Moon drove down to the brick-lined main street in town, Beechwood Row, which ran six blocks long. She parked her car across the street from Ryan's Cigar Shop.

Clivesville was just waking up. She liked the quiet of her car when she sat in it alone. She took a few minutes to watch the town come to life. Jessica Goldwyn, the owner of the East Side Art Gallery glanced up and down the street, wiggled the *Open* flag into the flagpole bracket by the front door, and dashed back inside.

The mayor of Clivesville, Rita Verdier, exited The Magic Brew coffee shop. She was a tall, well-dressed Black woman with kind eyes and a quick smile. Moon watched her tuck her purse under her arm and take a sip of her coffee. She kept her eyes on the sidewalk as she hustled past Moon's car. Since the murders, Clivesville had changed. Funny thing about fear—it spread like a virus, infiltrating the collective mind where it clotted, blocking people from going about their normal day-to-day. Local playgrounds were closed until further notice as perfect summer days went unclaimed by children, imprisoned inside for their own safety. Men were the only patrons at the local wine bars and breweries as the women of Clivesville drove straight home after work and locked their doors. Even though there had only been a few families directly affected by the murders, everyone felt the pain. Broken hearts, swollen and sorrowful, knitted the town together as only dark times could.

Moon got out of her car, crossed the street, and entered Ryan's Cigar Shop. They sold tobacco products, newspapers, and lottery tickets. A life-sized wooden Indian Tobacconist Statue stood in the corner saluting the patrons. Walking into the store was like taking a step back in time. The shop had been owned by four generations of the Ryan family since the mid-1920s and was currently run by a classmate of Moon's, Tim Ryan.

The shop opened in 1889 and was a place where your great-grandfather would go to get his hair cut, purchase a steamship ticket, regale his friends with stories, and solve the world's problems. The store's tin ceiling and tile floors dated from when the first Ryan, Gordie Ryan, bought the place from old Mr. Ainsworth in 1926. A 30-foot-long mahogany and glass cabinet graced the wall behind the counter. The store smelled of newspaper ink and cherry tobacco.

It reminded Moon of her father, who smoked a pipe on occasion. She remembered walking with her father into Archie Cooper's Tobacconist in Alexandria, Virginia. The shop had snuggled itself into the middle of brick-lined King Street in the old part of town. Tobacco was Virginia's oldest industry, dating back to the 1500s. The owner, Archie Cooper, Jr., had been importing pipes and Scottish products just as his father, Archie, Sr., had done for over 40 years. Back then, tobacco was seen as having medicinal properties. Tobacconists were often consulted as one would a pharmacist today. Depending on the ailment, the tobacconist would blend several types of tobacco to ease their clients' maladies.

While Moon waited for the old woman at the counter to scratch off her lottery ticket, she took the opportunity to lift the glass lids on the large jars of loose tobacco and inhale. The woman at the counter wiped the shavings from her card onto the floor and walked out the door.

"Hey, Tim."

"Moon."

Tim placed a New York Times on the counter. She handed him a five and pocketed the change.

"See you tomorrow," he said with a wave.

Moon slipped the folded paper under her arm and headed for the door. She left the shop and walked a block west down Beechwood Row to Rigby's Diner, her shadow leading the way. In the bright morning sky, the crescent moon could still be seen balancing itself on the tips of the trees in a cartoon smile.

She entered the diner and took a seat at the table in the corner by the window and unfolded the paper. She looked up from her paper at the counter. The three men seated there glared over their shoulders at her. As soon as she made eye contact, they spun around and focused on their plates. Bart, the cook, stared at her through the open window behind the counter. He sported pork chop sideburns and his black hair was slicked back in a pompadour. On weekends, Bart worked at the local Indian casino as an Elvis impersonator. He lowered his eyes, disappeared from the window, and went back to the flipping hot food on the griddle.

Danielle came over to her table with a cup of coffee and a small pitcher of creamer. She was a thin woman in her late 50s with friendly blue eyes that belied the hard life she had forged. She wore a maroon apron over her white blouse and jean skirt. Wrinkles roadmapped across her face. Danielle had a husband at one time. People around town whispered that he was a no-good drunk—abusive. One night, Danielle came home to find that he had taken a shotgun out to the barn and killed himself. He had gambled their life savings and a second mortgage on their house she knew nothing about. Danielle lost her soul to liquor for about a year, then clawed her way back. She seemed happy, but she had the look of someone who had stared evil straight in the eye.

"Any news about the killings?" Danielle asked.

"We have a few promising leads."

Danielle pulled a pad and pencil from her apron pocket. "What'll it be today, hon?"

"Waffles with berries, please."

She scribbled in her pad as she turned toward the kitchen to stick the order in the round ticket holder. Moon sipped her coffee and glanced around the diner. The fluorescent light overhead buzzed. Shelves along the walls were littered with antique Pyrex mixing bowls in soft hues of coral, yellow, and cornflower blue. Antique-framed prints of the downtown area graced the walls.

Moon focused her attention once more on the paper. Within minutes, Danielle placed the plate of waffles on the table and refilled her cup. Moon folded the newspaper in quarters and stabbed a strawberry with her fork. Stuart entered the diner, walked straight to the counter, and slung a leg over one of the red leather and chrome bar stools as though he was mounting a horse. He greeted the men as Danielle poured Stuart some coffee.

"The usual, hon?" Danielle asked.

"Yes, ma'am."

"Stuart," Moon said.

He swiveled on his stool to face her.

"What are you doing here?" she asked. "Did you follow me?"

Stuart picked up his coffee cup and walked toward her table.

Moon gestured for him to have a seat. She folded her newspaper and slipped it into her purse.

"No. I'm having breakfast. It's the best diner in town."

"It's the only diner in town."

"I have breakfast with the guys most mornings. The guy on the end is T-Bone." Stuart leaned in and whispered. "His real name is Bobby. Named after his old man whom he can't stand on account of his skirt chasing, so he likes to go by the nickname." Stuart sat back in his chair and continued. "T-Bone works for the county paving roads in the summer and plowing them in the winter. The one in the middle is Tommy B. He's worked at the factory loading glass onto the production line ever since he graduated high school. And the guy next to him in the flannel shirt is Lorenzo. His family came from Naples, Italy when his father was a boy. Their family owns the pizza joint at the end of the block."

"Yeah, I know who they all are. I'm shocked that you do."

"Not hard. It's not a big town.

"Here's your usual." Danielle placed a plate of two poached eggs on toast with a side of bacon. She took a bottle of Tabasco sauce from her apron pocket and placed it beside his plate.

"Thanks, Danielle." Stuart shook the Tabasco bottle and winked.

"You have a usual?" Moon asked.

"I'm surprised we haven't bumped into each other here before. I'm early today." He unscrewed the Tabasco and sprinkled it over his eggs, then picked up his fork, and dug in. "Listen, if you're not busy, I thought we'd take a ride out to Margaret Bender's apartment after breakfast."

"Sure. I'll let Chief Quinn know."

Moon's hand trembled as she reached for her coffee. She never knew how her encounters with the dead would go, or if she was able to communicate with them at all. Some souls were pleasant and helpful.

Others were mean and resentful. She didn't blame them. Passing could be frightening and very emotional. And depending on how they died, the dead could feel a great deal of residual anger and lash out at the nearest person who could sense their presence. She never knew what to expect, and it always made her nervous. She would soon find out how Margaret felt.

Chapter Twelve

tuart and Moon arrived at the Herrick Academy Apartments just after 9:00 a.m. They entered the building and took the elevator to the second floor. He fished a key from a duffel bag containing evidence retrieval items, then ripped the crime scene seal with the key and unlocked the door. They both slipped on gloves and booties over their shoes and went inside.

The apartment opened into the kitchen and dining area. Stuart walked straight through to the living room. Moon wished she could have come alone. She wanted to take her time. The police had already gone through the house, but Moon had a feeling there might be something they missed. She took her camera from her bag, stood in the middle of the kitchen, and took in the room. The refrigerator magnets might have been from places Margaret had traveled—Nova Scotia, Vancouver, Italy, the Lake District in England, and Ireland. A ceramic plaque above the stovetop read "Martha Stewart Doesn't Live Here." She took pictures of both. Moon opened the refrigerator and found it full, as though Margaret had just come from the grocery store. A note on the side of the refrigerator suspended by a frog magnet was of The

Flexitarian Diet. She peered into the cupboards and took photos.

"What are you doing?" Stuart walked back into the kitchen.

"I'm getting to know her."

Moon made her way to the living room and sat down on the sofa. The room was quiet. You couldn't hear any traffic noise from outside. She jumped as the thermostat clicked and the air conditioner sighed like a final breath. She knew the killer wasn't there, but she couldn't shake the stab of dread. Margaret had been there in that room a few days earlier. If she had known her life was about to end, would she have done anything differently? If she knew she only had days to live, would she have tossed that diet in the trash and ordered a pizza? Would she have called friends she hadn't heard from in years? Would she have called her parents for the sole purpose of telling them how much she loved and appreciated them?

Instead, Margaret dieted and lived as though she had fifty years left to live. She should have had fifty more years. The lingering sense of dread was thick and cold. An icy shiver rushed down Moon's back. She had lived a lifetime of seeing the dead—of seeing their desecrated bodies. She knew how to manage her fear. She took a deep breath in through her nose and blew the air slowly out of her mouth in a hiss. Despite the cold jitters she felt, the room itself was cozy with sage-colored walls, warm wood floors, and a blue-green patterned area rug. The apartment smelled of apples and Murphy's Oil Soap. Moon felt a profound sadness that Margaret would never be back there, sitting in that lovely room.

Stuart popped his head into the room. "Are you getting vibes?

"Vibes?"

"You know what I mean."

"I told you, it doesn't work that way."

She stood and followed him down the hall to the bedroom. Margaret's bed was made. A digital clock on the nightstand read 9:27 a.m.

Moon sat down on the edge of the bed. A book, *Gone Girl*, was tented on the nightstand closest to the bathroom. A black dress hung on a hook on the bathroom door. She stood and walked over to the dress.

"It's strange. After we die, all that's left is our stuff being picked over, divvied up, or thrown away." She took down the hanger and held the dress at arm's length. "I'm guessing she wore this to a funeral."

"And you know this because?"

"Because of the wonderful things she does."

Moon held the dress up to her body in front of a mirror. "This dress is pretty. It's too conservative for a cocktail event. It says funeral dress to me. If she wore it, which I suspect she did, she would have put perfume on before she went out." She lifted the sleeve and sniffed the wrists. "White Linen."

Moon pointed to a prayer card on the dresser. "There." She replaced the hanger on the bathroom door and snapped a picture of the prayer card.

Stuart placed it in an evidence bag. "I'll check with the funeral home to see if we get anything."

Moon held the sleeve of the dress between her palms and closed her eyes.

"What are you doing?" Stuart asked.

She opened her eyes and ran her fingers over the fabric. "I can sometimes pick up energy from physical items. Sometimes the energy from an event can linger around a particular item long after the event has passed. It's as though the energy has imprinted on the item. Sensitive people like me can sometimes read that energy and know what happened."

She walked back over to the dresser and picked up a necklace that had been left in a ceramic bowl. "One time when I was about 15, I went to a girlfriend's house for a sleepover. She had some clothes that she had worn earlier on a chair in her room. When I moved them to sit down, I touched the belt that was still looped in her jeans. I immediately saw that her father had used that belt as a whip to punish her. My girlfriend had no idea that I knew about the black and blue marks on her back under her clothes."

She replaced the necklace and sat on the bed. "When I do pick up energy, especially from a victim, I know that I am reading it for a reason. I just have to figure out why the object is sharing that energy with me."

After inspecting the rest of the apartment, they headed outside to the parking lot. They stood just outside the doors to the apartment building and scanned the area. Moon took pictures of the two areas of the parking lot. Brick enclosures covered the parking spaces closest to the doors. They housed the higher-end cars. Half a dozen Teslas were parked near their wall chargers. The rest of the less expensive cars were parked in the uncovered lot farther from the door.

Moon shielded her eyes from the sun as she stared at the covered parking area.

"You see something, don't you?" Stuart asked.

Moon nodded. "There's a man over by the empty charging station."

"The fact that you're seeing him and I'm not means … "

"Yeah. That's exactly what it means. I'll be right back."

Moon walked over to the man. "Can I help you?"

The man looked confused. "You can see me? You can hear me?"

"Yes. Is there something I can do for you?"

"Extraordinary. I'm waiting for my wife to come home from work."

Moon waited for the man to speak again. He was bald with a salt and pepper goatee. He wore round wire-framed eyeglasses.

He looked down at the ground. "I wasn't the best of husbands. I had an affair at work with my secretary. I know, pretty unoriginal. I was consumed with guilt, but I couldn't stop myself. The stress led to my heart attack. I suppose I deserved it. What bothers me most is the fact that I took out a sizable life insurance policy six months before I died. My wife is the sole beneficiary, but she doesn't know about the policy. Each night when she comes home, I try to reach her. I want her to be able to cash in that policy and enjoy the money. It's the least I can do for her. I know this is also unoriginal, but the affair meant nothing to me. I loved my wife."

The man looked up at Moon and shrugged.

"I can help you," Moon said. She took out a piece of paper and pen from her purse. "What's your wife's name and apartment number? If you give me the insurance policy information or where she can find it, I'll make sure she gets it."

"Thank you. Her name is Jane Brusman. Apartment 415. I'm Josh Brusman, or I was."

"Moon McFadden. Nice to meet you."

"Please tell her that the insurance policy is in a blue folder in my office in the left-hand drawer of my desk. It's in the hanging file marked J."

Moon wrote the information. "Have you been here a while—waiting for your wife?"

He scratched his head. "I'm not sure."

Moon scanned the parking lot. "Did you happen to notice anybody else waiting for someone to come home? Watching the parking lot?"

"A man stood behind those trees for a while, then he stopped coming around."

"Can you describe him for me?"

"He only came after dark. He walked into the parking lot and stood behind those trees inside the brick fence surrounding the lot. I didn't pay much attention."

"Thank you. I'll make sure your wife gets this information. For what it's worth, you weren't the only one having an affair. She was, too. The architect designing your house in Darien, Connecticut. Kevin Portman."

"Oh."

"I'm sorry."

Moon walked over to Stuart.

"I'll be right back," she said. "I need to go back inside and slip this under a door."

She dashed inside, and a few minutes later, joined Stuart in the parking lot.

"What did he say?" Stuart asked.

Moon turned to look at the man, but he was gone. "He saw someone watching the parking lot from behind those trees. Let's go take a look."

They walked across the parking lot and stepped behind the trees.

"From this angle in the dark, the killer could see Margaret, but she wouldn't necessarily see him," Moon said. She motioned to a mature oak tree with a wide trunk. They stepped behind the tree and stood with their backs to the brick wall. Moon spotted something at her feet and elbowed Stuart.

"Our guy has a sweet tooth," Moon said, snapping a picture.

"Bingo." Stuart picked up a small Skor candy bar wrapper off the grass with tweezers and placed it in an evidence bag. "Nice job."

They headed back to the police station and found Chief Quin alone in his office sitting at his desk. His elbows were propped on the desk, and he cradled his forehead in his hands. The only light in his office came from the banker's lamp on his desk, casting a green glow across his face. As soon as he heard them, he motioned for them to sit down.

"They've identified the fourth victim," Chief Quinn said. "Her name was Rachel Mariner. She worked at the Elmira Airport as a ticket agent for Delta Airlines. She was single and lived by herself in Horseheads."

Chief Quinn took off his glasses and massaged the bridge of his nose. Just then he looked much older. The creases around his mouth bowed into a frown.

"Please tell me you two have something, anything. I'm catching hell from Mendoza who's catching hell from the governor." He sat back in his chair and stared at the ceiling. "The press is badgering me for any nugget of information they can get out to the terrified public."

Chief Quinn rose from his chair and walked into a small bathroom behind his desk. He came back with a glass of water and sat down at his desk.

"Oh, and the updated forecast calls for rain in three days. Without anything to go on, it's going to take a miracle to stop this guy."

"We just came back from Margaret Bender's apartment," Stuart said.

"I hope you have a miracle hidden up your big city crack." Chief Quinn pulled a packet of Alka-Seltzer from his desk drawer, ripped it open, and dropped two tablets into the water.

"We found a Skor candy wrapper outside the apartment, which could tie the third and fourth victims. It's something."

"We think Margaret may have gone to a funeral," Moon said.

"A funeral. Great." Chief Quinn studied the fizzy water and sighed. "You two want one of these? They're good for you."

Chapter Thirteen

eth Woodman was the only child of Hazel and James Woodman. They had lived in a grand historic house on West Church Street in Elmira. Hazel was a stay-at-home mom—a woman who let her husband dictate everything, because that's the way God had intended things. She was a slight woman who wore lipstick and pearls no matter where she went. James was a serious man with a receding hairline that made his forehead appear to have horns. He was a well-known and respected physician who was set on his son becoming a doctor and eventually taking over the practice without any regard for Seth's dreams or what he wanted to do with his life.

As a young boy, Seth was made to come straight home from school. He would climb the stairs to his bedroom and crack open his textbooks. It wasn't long before he was distracted by the sounds of boys playing outside. He closed his books and pressed his forehead against the windowpane to watch the boys play soccer in the next-door neighbor's backyard.

"Have you finished your homework?" Hazel would say from the doorway. She'd then enter his bedroom and straighten the papers on his desk.

"Yes."

"Then come help me set the table."

On workdays, James came home at 6:00 p.m. sharp. Hazel would greet him at the door with a scotch, neat. He'd collapse into his La-Z-Boy and sip his drink until supper was placed on the table at 6:20 p.m. During dinner, James would drink wine with his meal.

After dinner, the three of them would retire to the living room. James would sit in his chair, sip his brandy, and barricade himself from his family behind an open newspaper. When he was finished with the paper, he'd remove a section, then folded the rest of the paper and draped it neatly across the arm of the chair. He'd crease that separate section down the middle.

"Come over here, son," James said. "Stand here and read this."

Seth would sigh and look to his mother for support, but she'd keep her eyes on her knitting needles. He'd then slowly stand and walk toward his father. James would hand him the section of the newspaper, and Seth would begin reading.

"The p-p-p-ol-ol-ol—"

"Spit it out, boy! The police. You can overcome this if you would only try harder. Start over."

As soon as James noticed that Seth was left-handed, he forced him to use his right hand. He'd watch, thin-mouthed, as Seth fumbled his pencil or struggled to use scissors. He bought Seth a right-handed baseball glove and played catch with him in the backyard.

"Left-handedness is a sign of weakness," James would say, tossing a ball. "You'll thank me later on. The whole world is right-handed. You don't understand now, but you will."

When his father wasn't around, Seth used his left hand for everything.

Hazel was devoted to her husband and Jesus Christ. She dressed conservatively and looked down on any woman she perceived to be indecent. She never missed an opportunity to point this out to Seth— while driving to get ice cream, while on the way home from church, or while walking through the aisles of the grocery store.

One afternoon, Hazel pulled Seth close to her behind the grocery cart and pointed. He had just turned twelve.

"Do you see that woman, Seth?" Hazel whispered into Seth's ear. "Do you see those shorts she's wearing? That type of woman right there is inviting trouble. That's a hussy if I've ever seen one. You steer clear of the likes of women like that. It's obvious they only want one thing."

"What's that?"

"They want to have sex with men. Dirty, filthy sex. You mark my words. Sex is disgusting. It's wrong. Those who have sex are branded with the mark of the beast. It will only lead to disease, and *it* will fall off." She raised her eyebrows and looked down at his jeans when she said the word *it*.

Seth had no idea what she meant by *it*, but he soon understood. That summer, a young couple, Dan and Sabina Johansen moved in next door. Dan had been hired as a ceramic engineer at MacKinley, Inc. The couple had moved to Elmira from Oslo, Norway. Dan was a thin athletic man with a narrow face. He was well-dressed and wore his salt and pepper hair in a disconnected pompadour. His wife, Sabina, was the most beautiful woman Seth had ever seen. She was tall, a few inches taller than her husband, with long, softly curled hair somewhere between blonde and dark honey that draped over her large breasts. Seth's parents had invited Dan and Sabina to dinner one evening to welcome them to the neighborhood. Seth sat across from Sabina at the dining room table.

"How do you like school?" she asked him.

He was so flummoxed by her, he nearly burst into tears.

"Seth has a slight stammer," Hazel said.

Seth smiled and nodded and kept his eyes on his plate for the rest of the dinner.

A few months later, James hosted a cocktail party for his fellow Rotary Club members and their wives. Among the guests were the Johansens. Seth observed them from the corner of the living room. He watched Sabina drink her martini. Each time she took a sip, she rolled her head back and shook her hair ever so slightly. Seth's breath was caught in his throat. He had to struggle to keep from staring at her.

As more and more people arrived, Seth escaped to the kitchen. He grabbed a flashlight from under the sink and pushed his way out the back door. He crossed their backyard into the Johansen's backyard. He stood with his back ramrod straight against a tree looking from side to side. He crossed the yard to their back door. He turned the doorknob slightly, expecting it to be locked. The door eased open, and Seth crept inside. He prowled through the house, taking in all the sights and smells. He took down a framed picture from the fireplace mantel. The couple had been photographed on a beach somewhere warm. Sabina wore a red and white polka-dotted bikini. Her hand was behind her neck as she mugged for the camera. Her perfect breasts struggled to be contained within the bikini top. Her cleavage, a teasing vertical smile. She was extraordinary. Exotic. A goddess.

Seth replaced the photograph and went upstairs. He found their bedroom and began opening drawers until he found her pantie drawer. He pinched a pair of silky panties from the drawer and placed them on the bed. He knew what he was doing was wrong, but he was helpless to stop himself. He caressed the panties, feeling the crotch area, knowing that her genitals rubbed that area of the fabric. His mind filled with thoughts of Sabina's genitals—how they felt, how they tasted. He was so hard that his penis felt like a tree trunk. It was the first time he had let his sexuality rule him. He unzipped his jeans and took out his member. He placed the tip on the crotch of the panties. He pressed his body against the fabric. He told himself that it wasn't his rational mind, but rather, *it* was making him do this. Suddenly, his body convulsed, and he exploded onto the panties. His temples throbbed, and he struggled to catch his breath. His balls felt as though they had been squeezed in a vise. A flood of shame filled him. He balled up the ruined panties, stuffed them into his pocket, and raced down the stairs and out the back door.

Hazel had returned to the kitchen to refresh drinks just as Seth opened the back door.

"What were you doing outside?"

"G-g-getting some fr-fresh air."

She motioned toward two silver trays filled with meatballs, coconut shrimp, and small round toasts with smoked salmon. "Help me serve some of these hors d'oeuvres."

Seth followed her through the kitchen into the living room. Like a good son, he circulated through the crowd that evening serving hors d'oeuvres and refreshing drinks. While in the kitchen washing glasses, he overheard one of the wives tell his mother what a polite and helpful son she had. He smiled to himself as he dried the glasses and set them on a clean towel. None of them had any idea what was in his pocket. This thrilled him to the core. He knew he couldn't keep the panties. No matter where he hid them in the house, one or both of his nosey parents would find them.

The following morning on his way to school, Seth walked along the Chemung River. When he got to the South Walnut Street Bridge, he sidestepped down the steep riverbank to the edge of the water. He found a large rock, tied the soiled panties around it, and threw it into the river.

Chapter Fourteen

James had a younger brother named Ned who he had always referred to as a lazy good-for-nothing. The two brothers could not have been more different. James was tall and lean. Ned was short and had a body like a potato with legs. Where James attended SUNY Upstate Medical University in Syracuse, Ned became a plumber and ignored James's snobbery. According to Ned, both of them had studied pipes and both made good money.

Ned had moved back to Elmira after years of living and working in Buffalo. His first weekend back home, James invited Ned to Sunday dinner.

"Who are you working for now?" James asked, passing the green beans to his wife.

"I'm working for myself." Ned plopped mashed potatoes in the middle of his plate.

"Really?"

"Yes, really. I've been expanding my clientele south to the Twin Tiers for years. I now have enough business to go it alone."

Ned made a well in his potatoes with the back of his spoon. He licked the spoon clean, placed a slice of meatloaf in the well, and sprinkled green beans on top of the meat. James glared, eyebrows furrowed, as Ned poured gravy over the lot. Ned adjusted his thick glasses and nodded once at the food mound he had made. He rubbed his palms together and picked up his fork to dig in. Seeing his parents' horror at this dinnertime irreverence thrilled Seth to the marrow.

Ned purchased a hunting cabin in the middle of the woods in Groverton, New York. He began to pick up Seth after high school let out and take him to the cabin for a few hours several times a week. To Seth, the cabin represented freedom and independence.

"This is for you." Ned handed Seth a rifle. "It's a Timber Classic, a Marlin 336C, affectionately called the thuddy. It's the rifle I learned to hunt with."

Seth held the barrel in one hand and caressed the wooden stock.

Ned ruffled Seth's hair. "Let's take a walk."

They left Ned's hunting cabin and entered the woods.

"There are basically two ways to hunt deer," Ned said. "There's the stand-hunting method where you stand and wait for your prey to come by either on the ground or in a tree stand. Then there's the still-hunting method, the one I prefer. You stay on the ground and move quietly to sneak up on your quarry. It's also called stalk hunting or simply stalking."

As they walked further into the woods, Ned slowed his pace.

"Chances are really good we're not going to see anything today. For one thing, human stink is a dead giveaway to deer. You may have showered and think you're clean as a whistle, but trust me, to a deer, you stink to high heaven. Their noses are 1000 times more sensitive than our noses. When stalking on the ground, think of your scent in terms of a cone coming off your body. The farther away from you, the wider the concentration gets. There are products you can buy to reduce your scent, but I prefer to work with nature."

Ned bent down and picked up a handful of leaves. "You have to pay attention to the wind." He stood, and with his arm outstretched, crumpled the dry leaves in his fingers, and watched them float away with the wind. "Deer put their noses to the wind. If you spot a deer while he's looking into the wind, he'll walk away from you or take a wide berth, because he'll catch your scent. The best thing to do is to hunt crosswind so the wind is blowing side to side between you and your prey."

Seth picked up a handful of leaves and crumpled them into the wind just as his uncle had done.

"The reason I want to teach you to stalk is because this will teach you patience. And the patience you learn in the woods you'll carry with you into every aspect of your life."

They walked further into the woods ducking beneath branches.

"The best time to stalk is during a light rain. Listen to the way our feet make a ton of noise walking over the leaves and branches. During a light rain, the ground is less crunchy under your feet, and the soft patter of the rain against the leaves creates good background noise to cover any sounds you might make."

Ned stood still for a moment, then crouched a bit and moved forward.

"See what I'm doing here? I'm moving only using my legs. Deer are more easily spooked by motion rather than your shape."

Seth copied Ned.

"Try not to turn your head or arms. If you spot a deer, stand perfectly still. Chances are really good he's already spotted you and is checking you out. If he relaxes enough to start grazing again or turn away from you, you might be able to take a shot. He may suddenly snap his head up and look straight at you. He does that on purpose to get you to flinch. Don't fall for it."

Ned stopped walking, stood upright, and faced Seth.

"This is important," Ned said. "Don't ever take the shot unless you can make a clean shot to the heart. Even then, they'll run. I've seen it. You can shoot a deer straight through the heart, and he'll keep running 100 yards before he drops. He's already dead, but he doesn't know it."

Seth became an excellent hunter. He learned the patience Ned taught him in order to wait for his prey. He stalked them, read their habits. He was never squeamish about blood. Killing never bothered him. In fact, he was very comfortable with the dead. After graduation, Seth was accepted at the American Academy McAllister Institute of Funeral Services in Manhattan. He bought himself a beat-up Chevy and headed for the city. He found a roommate on Craigslist to share an apartment in a four-story walk-up on 10th Avenue and West 57th Street above Roosevelt Gourmet Deli.

While living in New York City, Seth sought out the help of a speech therapist to reduce his stutter. He successfully learned to slow his speech and avoid words that were his triggers. He also met up with Ned in the Catskills any chance he could. They bought 10 acres of wooded land in rural Neversink. They cleared part of the land and built themselves another U-shaped cabin—an exact replica of the cabin in Groverton. On weekends, they stayed in the cabin and went fly fishing in the local streams, or sometimes met up in the city when the Yankees were in town.

Seth excelled in his studies. In his free time, he started lifting weights. Within a few months, he developed a great body to compensate for his scarred face. He made a few close friends, and his confidence soared. For the first time in his life, Seth felt happy. He was about to graduate with honors with offers to apprentice as an embalmer in seven different funeral homes. His career was on track, and his promising future was opening before him.

Ned was driving home from his visit with Seth in the city three weeks before graduation. About two miles outside of Hancock traveling west on Rt. 17, a kid on a motorcycle sped past Ned's car. Just as he pulled back into the right-hand lane in front of Ned, he hit a large rock in the road and lost control. To keep from running the kid over, Ned jerked the wheel to the right, lost control, and crashed head-on into a tree. He was killed instantly.

Without Ned in his life, Seth's despair spiraled out of control. He became withdrawn and depressed. He went to a Yankee game for old time's sake. He thought he'd enjoy the memories he shared with his uncle, but not enough time had passed. To pour salt into the wound, the Red Sox blanked the struggling Yankees 8-0. Seth trudged to a nearby bar to drown his sorrows. He sat down at the bar and ordered a drink.

"Who is she?"

Seth heard a female voice and turned to find a pretty woman sitting a few feet away from him. She was smiling at him. Seth turned around to see if she was talking to someone behind him. He turned back to her.

"Did you say something to me?"

"Yeah. Who is she? You look like someone who was tossed out of the house by the missus."

"No. Just came from the game."

She fiddled with the ice in her glass with her straw for a moment, then lowered her chin and gave him a Princess Diana doe-eyed look. Seth studied his glass and swallowed hard. He took a deep breath, picked up his beer, and sat down next to her.

"Hello. I'm Seth."

"Carol Portman."

"Can I get you another drink?"

"That would be nice. Thank you, Seth."

They spent a few hours talking, laughing, and drinking. For the first time, Seth felt at ease in the presence of a woman.

"It's getting late," Carol said. She slid off her barstool. "I really should be getting home."

Seth stood and slipped the cardigan sweater from the back of her chair and draped it across her shoulders.

"Can I take you to dinner sometime or to a movie?"

"I don't think so," Carol said. "But thanks for the drinks."

"I don't understand. We had a good time tonight. I did anyway. Did I say something to offend you?"

"No, Seth. Not at all. This was fun, but I'm not interested in dating right now. I like to keep things light. Maybe I'll see you here again sometime? Good night, Seth."

Seth watched Carol weave through the crowd and slip out the door. He sat back down and looked up to see the bartender shake his head and chuckle.

"What's so funny?"

"That's Carol for you. She comes in here to use men to drink for free. I watch her come in once or twice a week. She sits at the bar and smiles at a guy sitting by himself. And a sucker is born every single time. Sorry, pal. It was your turn, I guess."

That bitch used me, he thought. He slapped the jacket from the back of his chair and left.

He came back to the bar the following night. He parked his car about half a block away from the entrance and waited. Just as the bartender said, Carol walked in around 9:00 p.m. At 11:00 p.m., he watched Carol leave by herself. He got out of his car and followed her seven blocks to her apartment. He stalked her for a week, getting to know her habits—where she worked, where she ate lunch, where she got her hair and nails done. He knew when she left for work in the morning and when she got home at night. He knew there was one dark block she had to walk through to get to her building.

One day, he rented a car and waited for her to come home from work. He sat in the car on the dark block and waited. He watched, unseen, as she walked toward his car. When she was close, he rolled down his passenger window.

"Hey, Carol, is that you?"

She peered into the car. "Seth?"

"Yeah, it's Seth." He got out of the car and joined her on the sidewalk. "What a coincidence. I'm waiting for a friend. You live near here?"

"Yes. This is my building here. It's a nice surprise to see you. And nice car!"

"You think so? Have a look."

He opened the passenger door. As she leaned in, he brought a leather flat sap down hard onto her temple. She crumpled head-first into the car. He moved her into the back seat where he injected her with ketamine. He gagged her with a wadded cloth, flipped her on her stomach, then bound her hands and feet. He hopped in the driver's seat and headed south on Bronx River Parkway to Southview Park. He drove into the park along the Bronx River and pulled the car off the narrow road in the park into a thicket of trees. Carol was still unconscious when he removed the rope from her hands and feet and pulled her from the back seat. He carried her into the thicket, sat her in the grass against the truck of a tree. He crouched down in front of her. He brushed the hair from her forehead and studied her face. He kept his hand on her forehead as he brought his knife across her throat. He pulled the cloth from her mouth and wiped the blade clean. He tossed the cloth on Carol's lap and stood. He walked back to the car and drove away.

As he pulled back up onto the highway, Seth let the fact that he had just killed another human being sink in. He was quite familiar with death associated with hunting and his profession, but this was altogether different. A human being died at my hand, he thought. There's no coming back from this.

He ruminated over what had just happened, and the strangest thing occurred to him. He thought he would feel sad, fearful, regretful, or guilt-ridden. Instead, he felt no remorse. Relief washed over him as though a tightly wound coil had released its pent-up energy. He had stepped into a whole new world. Like losing your virginity. Like being baptized. Washed clean in the blood.

"Well, so this was how others like me felt."

Seth rolled down the window and let the cool breeze caress his face. He felt calm and in complete control of himself and his world for the very first time in his life. He realized that he had the power to control the outcome. It was intoxicating.

Chapter Fifteen

Seth inherited both hunting cabins in Neversink and in Groverton from Ned. After graduation, he accepted a funeral director apprenticeship at Bannister's Funeral Home in Clivesville. He was happy to be a short drive away from his mother in Elmira. He enjoyed his work, and he was good at it. He moved into the Groverton cabin and bought himself a brand new Dodge Ram truck, black as ink. He loved the drive to and from work through the winding country roads. It gave him time to mentally prepare for his day in the morning and time to decompress during the drive home after work.

Seth visited his mother when he knew his father wasn't home. Without James there, his mother was relaxed and carefree. She laughed without covering her mouth. When he was there, however, Hazel quelled her nervousness in Little Debbie cakes. The Swiss Rolls were her favorite. She would take a break from her housework and go to their bedroom. She would retrieve a package of Little Debbie Swiss Rolls from the back of her underwear drawer. Hazel found herself nervous quite often. By the time Seth had moved back to the area, she tipped the scales at 220 pounds. This disappointed James a great deal, which made the Swiss Rolls taste even better.

Seth dropped by his parent's house one afternoon for tea and met his mother in the kitchen. He fixed the two of them a cup and brought them to the table.

"I'm sorry you weren't here last weekend." Hazel poured half and half into her cup. "How was the fishing?" She spooned in sugar and stirred.

"They were really biting."

"I don't understand why you drive two and a half hours to fish in the Catskills when you can fish right here."

"There's something about those hills I love. It's the best place for fly fishing. They've got 50 miles of trout tributaries and about 89 miles of warm-water rivers and streams. Besides, being out in the cabin reminds me of my time there with Uncle Ned, and that makes me happy. Sometimes, you just have to get out of Dodge to really relax."

Hazel nodded as she spread ginger jam on a slice of bread. A fly landed on the table near her plate, and she raised her hand to swat it.

"Wait. Don't kill it."

Seth rushed to the cupboard and fingered a glass from the shelf and pulled Hazel's shopping list from the refrigerator door. He lowered the glass over the fly and slid the list under its feet. He lifted the fly in the glass and headed toward the living room.

"Be right back."

He opened the front door and released the fly. He replaced the shopping list and placed the glass in the sink.

"Really?" Hazel shook her head. "It was just a fly."

"That doesn't mean you have to kill it."

Hazel shrugged her shoulders and spread jam on a second slice of bread.

After their cups were empty, Seth stood and brought his cup and plate to the sink.

"I should get going. Busy day." He kissed his mother on the forehead. "Call you later."

"You're a good son. I don't know what I'd do without you."

Seth drove to the Bannister Funeral Home and pulled into the parking lot. He entered through the back door and put on a suit. It was Friday afternoon, time for Betty Wilson's funeral. His eyes scanned the guests as they wandered in from the parking lot. He was on the hunt. The minute she walked in the door, he knew he had found his next victim. He could tell just by the way she carried herself that she was the popular, stuck-up type. She was tall with long black hair and green eyes. Her black knit dress hugged her every curve. The woman slid her sunglasses up onto the top of her head pushing her hair away from her tanned and flawless face.

Seth guessed she was in her early 30s. He walked over and stood beside the podium where the book sat illuminated under a small gold lamp. He watched her write her name in loopy letters. He made a mental note of her address. The guest book said she was a friend of Betty's. Seth watched the woman pick up a prayer card and slip it into her purse. She pulled a tube of lip gloss from her purse and traced her perfect lips in pink. Seth could feel beads of sweat form along his upper lip as he motioned for her to join the family in the chapel.

Seth watched the woman inch her way forward in the reception line then greet Harry and his family. She walked to the front of the chapel and knelt in front of Betty's casket to say a prayer. After she left the casket, she sat in the back of the chapel. Father Brown motioned for the family that he was about to begin and went to the podium beside the casket.

"Can I have everyone take a seat, please? We're ready to get started."

Father said a few prayers. Harry came up and read *The Dash* by Linda Ellis.

After the service, Seth stood in the parking lot directing traffic. He watched the woman get in her navy Honda Civic and mentally noted the plate number. That night, he drove to her address, parked half a block from her house, and waited. All that week, he shadowed her, still-hunting, waiting for the right opportunity to close in on his prey.

Chapter Sixteen

"Where are you?" Moon sat on her back porch in a rocking chair with her bare feet on the railing. A warm breeze lifted the hair around her face. Her phone felt hot against her cheek.

"I'm driving … thinking," Matthew said. "I'm not sure where I am to tell you the truth. I'm on a highway somewhere outside Boston. Turns out, I was right about Julie. When I confronted her about having an affair, she confessed. She's been seeing a dermatologist in Brighton. Apparently, it's been going on for a year."

"Oh, Matthew," Moon said.

"Here's the cherry on top—she's pregnant. She said she planned to leave me at the end of the month. She was waiting for Donald's divorce to be finalized before she moved into his house. He's 50 years old and bald. I've been cuckold by a bald Donald. I find it's a full-time job, feeling betrayed."

Moon waited for Matthew to speak again. She stared up at the Milky Way as she listened to the *thump*, *thump*, *thump* of the Boston highway as it beat backward underneath him, and Matthew's heavy sighs, and the tiny tin voice of the sports talk radio show through the telephone. He finally cleared his throat.

"I've always wanted kids. Julie told me she never wanted them. When I reminded her that she had told me from the start that she wanted a family she said, 'I realized that I just didn't want to have them with you.' So, there's that."

"Matthew. I'm so sorry. For you. For us."

There was silence again on the other end of the line. The vast space between them, inhabited by the echoes of the people they once were. Now, they were two should-have-beens.

Matthew finally spoke. "It's okay. I understand, and I've always respected your decision."

"I knew you desperately wanted to be a father. It was the hardest decision I've ever had to make. And I know it broke your heart, but I wasn't ready to be a mom. In truth, I don't think you were ready to be a father then either. We were kids, in our first year of college."

"Of course, you're right. I agree, we were kids, totally unprepared, and I have never once blamed you. Things happen for a reason. I don't think I ever told you this, but every May—"

"Me, too. Not just every May, but I think about it often. I might see a group of teenagers and try to imagine what our child would have been like. He or she would have been 14."

More silence.

"There's still time for you, Matthew. You could meet someone wonderful and start a family with her. I'm afraid the door is rapidly closing for me. I often wonder if that was my one chance at having a baby. Sure, I graduated, traveled, and pursued a career I love. Still, I live with the nagging feeling that I could have done that and still have been a mom. It would have been very difficult, but I could have done it I think. So many successful people have done it. Would that have meant that we would have been together? Or would the pressures have ruined our relationship forever? Who knows. I often think … what if."

"What. If. Two innocent words on their own, but put them together, and they have the power to haunt you for the rest of your life."

"Yeah. It's late, Matthew. You should head home."

"There is no home for me to go home to. I can't go back there with Julie still there. I'll be back in Clivesville in a few days. I have to deal with some legal stuff with my mother's estate. Maybe I can see you then?"

"Yes, please. I'd like that very much. Call me when you get to town, and we'll have dinner. Get some sleep."

"You, too."

"I haven't been able to sleep much lately. I have a sinking feeling everything is about to turn to crap."

"Hang in there. Thanks for letting me rant. Good night, Moon."

Maisie stepped out onto the porch and handed Moon a beer. She sat down in the rocking chair beside her.

"I couldn't help but overhear."

Moon took a long pull on the bottle. "Aunt Maisie, do you ever wish you had gotten married?"

Maisie smiled. "That came from left field. Does this have anything to do with Matthew?"

"Yes and no."

"There was someone I was close to at one time, but it didn't work out. Timing, I guess. Then after a while, I liked being alone. The thought of doing someone else's laundry didn't appeal to me. And I never wanted to have kids."

"I'm sorry I was forced on you when Mom and Dad died."

"Don't be silly. I wanted to be your guardian. Libby, Hugh, and I discussed that at length when you were born. Besides, you're such an old soul, it was always as though we were on equal ground. No, I meant that I never had that maternal gene—I never felt the need to be pregnant or physically bear a child."

"I suppose I could still find someone to start a family with. I spend most of my time thinking about the victims in my photos. I could step back and take time for myself. But I love my job. And I'm good at it. What I do helps people, and that makes me feel good. It fulfills me. Besides, the thought of dating again holds as much appeal to me as having a root canal. It's the same old thing. I meet someone for a drink and fall into the same tired conversations—where did you go to school? Do you have kids? What do you do? It somehow always ends up feeling like a job interview, with alcohol. No thanks."

"How do you expect to get that husband and family without dating?"

"Conundrum. The truth is, I feel a bit rudderless. I'm good at my job, but my personal life is a void."

"Can I make an observation? You've made it your mission in life to find justice for victims, and that's very noble. I wonder if you don't use that as an excuse to get close to someone."

"What do you mean?"

"I wonder if you are afraid of getting close to someone because you're afraid to lose them, the way you lost your mother and father. You look at life through a camera lens. It's safe. It is literally a barrier between you and the world."

"I don't think that's true."

"Isn't it? Maybe I'm wrong. I just want to remind you that you can't live life to the fullest and be safe. You have to risk getting hurt again. And you will get hurt again, and you will lose the people you love. That's life." Maisie smiled at Moon. "Okay, the lecture is over."

Moon smiled. "Thank you for the lecture."

They clicked bottle necks and drank. As they rocked, somewhere on the edge of the woods, a pack of coyotes began to howl. Moon pointed toward the woods.

"That's more intelligent than anything any human has ever said." Her phone buzzed. She smiled and flashed her phone at Maisie.

"Speak of the devil," Moon said. She picked up after a few rings. "Hello."

"Moon, it's Stuart. Can you drive out to the Catskills with me this weekend? I'd like for you to take a look at the victims' houses. See if you can get anything."

"Get anything?"

"You know what I mean."

"Yes. I was just teasing."

"Pack for overnight in case it gets late. I'll pick you up Sunday morning."

"See you then." Moon hung up and took another drink. "I can feel your look."

Maisie stood and tousled Moon's hair. "Come in and set the table. Supper's ready."

Chapter Seventeen

The following morning, Moon drove a few miles out of town to a diner named Mama's Place to meet Holly for breakfast. She walked inside and spotted her in a booth toward the back. Moon slid into the booth, and the waitress poured her a cup of coffee.

"The usual Eggs Benedict for you?" The waitress asked Moon.

"Yes, thank you."

"Western Omelet for you, Holly?" she asked, refilling her cup.

"Yes, please."

As the waitress walked away, Moon poured cream into her coffee. "It seems we're too predictable. We should ask for menus next time and order something new." Moon stared at her coffee as it swirled in her cup.

"What's up?" Holly asked.

"I spoke with Matthew. Turns out his wife's been having an affair. And she's pregnant. He's pretty shaken up about it, and I don't blame him. Talking to him brought up a lot of memories. Life choices I've made."

"Memories are fine, but it does you no good to dwell on decisions you did or didn't make. Keep in mind, we all make the choices we make with the information we have at the time. Don't get bogged down with regrets."

"Thank you. I needed to hear that."

The waitress placed their breakfast plates down and refilled their coffees.

Holly shook the Tabasco sauce bottle then unscrewed it and splashed the top of her omelet. "As for memories, regardless of whether they're good or bad, don't let them cloud your judgment. That's a great way to sabotage the present. There's no point in trying to live your life backwards." She handed the bottle to Moon.

"Point taken." Moon splashed Tabasco on her eggs.

Holly stabbed her omelet. "So, tell me about that detective you're working with."

"Stuart Bauer."

"What's he like?"

"Rude and full of himself. He's sullen. A brooder. A loner. He seems to be more comfortable being by himself than with other people."

"You both have that in common."

Moon smiled and shook her head.

Holly took a sip of coffee. "What?"

"Despite the brooding, he is hot."

"Oh, really?" Holly put down her cup. "Spill. I want all the details."

"Okay, he has a great body and big brown eyes. And a cleft chin—my weakness. He's so gorgeous. Oh, my God listen to me. What am I, Marcia Brady?"

Holly smiled as she stabbed at her eggs. "So, you like him."

"Yes, despite the brooding, I like him." Moon shook her head. "I don't have time for any of that now. I need to put all thoughts of romance out of my mind and focus on solving this case."

Holly gave her a side-eye. "Let's forget about the case for a minute. How do you feel?"

"When I'm with Stuart, I feel excited and alive. With Matthew, I feel calm and at home. Is it wrong for me to like the attention?"

"Not at all. And Moon, don't feel guilty about this or try to over-think things like you usually do or second-guess yourself. It's been such a long time since you felt this way about anyone. Listen to me, this is good, Moon. I think you shouldn't worry about it at all. Just have fun and enjoy it."

Chapter Eighteen

Moon and Matthew stood face to face under the soft branches of a large hemlock tree. A chilly rain fell softly against the forest canopy, but the two of them remained dry. Moon leaned her back against the trunk of the tree. Matthew smiled and took a step closer to her. He placed his hands on the tree trunk on either side of her head and leaned toward her. He was so close to her that she felt the heat of his body through their clothes. His face was less than an inch from hers—teasing. He kissed her, tenderly at first, but then his kisses grew more forceful, more passionate. He slowly kissed her neck. He nuzzled the collar of her shirt open with his nose to kiss her collarbone. He continued down, kissing between her breasts. She tilted her head back in complete surrender as he—

"Good morning," Maisie said from the edge of Moon's bed.

Moon moaned, still lost in her dream. Maisie stood up and sat-bounced back onto her bed. Moon blinked awake.

"Good morning." Maisie handed Moon a mug of coffee.

Moon rubbed her face and laughed. "Oh, my God. I'm sorry."

"Don't be. So, I take it you slept well. Don't tell me. I don't want to know. I'd have to poke my mind's eye out."

Moon sat up and took a sip of coffee. "Thank you for this. You're up early."

"Not really. You slept in."

"What time is it?"

"9:30."

"What?" Moon picked up her phone and read the time. "I forgot to hit save on the alarm."

"Stuart is downstairs waiting for you."

Moon threw off the covers and raced to the bathroom. She turned on the shower, stripped, and stepped in. "Tell him I'll be down in two minutes."

At 9:45 a.m., Moon met Stuart in the driveway. He held two Dunkin cups.

"Sorry I'm late," she said.

"No worries. I wasn't sure how you take your coffee."

"What have you got?" Moon dropped her camera bag and overnight duffel in his back seat.

"I have a caramel macchiato and a black coffee. Creamers and sugar are in a bag."

She took the macchiato and got in the front seat. "Thank you."

They headed east on Route 17. Moon leaned back and watched the morning fog roll across the green fields that ambled toward the steep hills surrounding the valley. Waterfalls poured over layers of shale rock. She let her mind wander. Almost 500 million years ago, all of upstate New York had been submerged under an ancient shallow ocean. After that, over the last two million years, the state experienced several Ice Ages burying the area in mile-thick ice.

They had been in the car for two hours without saying anything. A comfortable silence. She thought he'd be the perfect person to go to a museum with or watch a movie.

They pulled over to have lunch at Ramona's Diner. As soon as they entered the dining area, she touched Stuart's arm.

"What is it?" he asked.

"This way, please," the hostess interrupted.

They followed her through the dining area. College pennant flags were thumb-tacked along the top of all the walls. Random squares of pink neon lights dangled from the drop ceiling. Four-top tables in the center of the restaurant were filled with older ladies, families, and construction workers. Couples sat in the two-seated booths along the windows. The hostess led them to the far end of the restaurant, past the sit-down counter cluttered with empty plates and coffee mugs yet to be bussed, stacks of dollar tips, Heinz ketchup bottles, and silver cake stands piled high with plastic-wrapped muffins. She placed the menus on a table near the window.

"Can we sit in that window booth?" Moon asked.

"No. There's no one at that station."

"It's literally two feet away from this table."

Stuart picked up the menus and handed them to Moon. "The lady said she wanted to sit at the window booth."

"I said—"

"That wasn't a question."

The hostess stared at him like a pale goldfish behind thick glasses. She blinked. Stuart nodded for Moon to take a seat. She slid into the booth facing the front parking lot. Stuart did a double take at the hostess, and she blinked again.

"Oh, my goodness," he said, "I have to tell you, you have the most beautiful eyes I have ever seen."

The hostess's scowl immediately melted into a smile. Stuart smiled back, and the woman blushed.

"I'm Stuart. What's your name?"

"Rhonda."

Stuart placed a hand against his heart. "Oh, help me, Rhonda!"

Stuart and Rhonda both giggled.

"Your waitress will be right with you." Rhonda fanned herself and floated away.

Stuart slid into the booth with a smile. Moon shook her head.

"What?"

"Did you find any polyps up there?"

Stuart cocked his head. "How do you like your booth?"

"Touché."

"What's so important about this particular booth?"

Moon studied the parking lot. "The killer eats dinner here whenever he's in town. He sits right here, in this seat in this booth."

"So, he doesn't live here."

"No." She pulled a notepad and pen from her purse. "This isn't where he lives full time. He often comes here for dinner and waits for a young woman traveling alone to stop in at the diner."

She began to write something in the notepad.

"That sounds pretty random," Stuart said. "I can't imagine there would be too many women who fit that description."

"I didn't say this was the only place he hunts, but it's definitely one place."

"What are you writing?"

She looked down at the notepad. "Never."

"Never. Never what?"

"I don't know. Never something. It means something."

"That could mean anything, or nothing in this case."

Moon shrugged. "It definitely means something." She flipped the notepad shut and dropped it into her purse as the waitress approached the booth.

"I'll have a turkey burger and an iced tea, please," Moon said.

"A grilled Reuben and iced tea." Stuart collected both menus and handed them back. "Thank you."

When they were alone, Moon asked. "Did your sister live in the Catskills?"

"After her divorce, she began a serious relationship with a man who wanted to move out of the city. He found a place in Callicoon. She was happy until she found out that he was cheating on her. After they broke up, he moved to California with his new girlfriend. She thought about moving back to the city but loved the peace and quiet out here. She thought it was safer than living in the city. Ironic."

After lunch, Stuart followed Moon out into the parking lot. She stood still a moment and watched the traffic.

"People pulling in off the highway would slow down to park in the lot in front of the diner," she said. "Obviously, the front lot would be busy. The western lot wouldn't be good either, because there's an ice cream stand over there. Too many people." Stuart followed her as she walked to the east side of the building.

As soon as she rounded the corner, a sensation hit her with an almost physical violence. She took a deep breath in through her nose and blew out a hiss. She put her hand to her side as though she had a cramp.

"Are you okay?" Stuart asked.

"Yeah." She straightened up. "On this side of the building, there are only three windows. None toward the back of the building. If someone were to park on this side, chances are few people would see them. There are a few Tesla charging stations along this side, but people charging their cars would probably go into the diner and have a coffee or a bite to eat while they waited." Moon pointed to the street. "Anyone on that eastbound ramp would accelerate back onto the highway and look away from this parking lot toward the oncoming traffic." She walked to the end of the east lot. "The killer parks right here, toward the back of the lot."

She stood still and stared at the empty east lot.

"Are you okay?" Stuart repeated.

"Yeah." She rubbed her arms. "Do you remember when I told you that I can sometimes feel the energy of an event long after it has passed?"

"Yes."

"I can feel a strong energy right here. It's so powerful, the evil is thick—almost choking."

"Come on. Let's hit the road."

They got back onto Route 17 and headed east. Moon relaxed back into the seat and let her eyes scan the countryside. They drove about 10 minutes when Stuart flipped on his turn signal. Moon bolted upright.

"What is it?" Stuart asked.

Moon scanned the road. "Don't take this exit. I need you to keep going. Get off at exit 98."

"Okay."

A few minutes later, Stuart pulled off Route 17 at exit 98.

"Are you seeing something?" he asked.

"I'm getting a feeling, almost like déjà vu, as though I've been here before. Take a left onto Short Avenue under the highway."

Stuart glanced over at her but did as he was told.

"Short Avenue will turn into Cooley Road. It's just up here."

Beyond a thin line of trees along the road, there was an open field.

"Stop right here."

Stuart pulled off the road and parked beside the trees. Moon got out of the car and walked straight toward the field. Cicadas vibrated in the crowns of the hawthorn trees. As soon as she pushed through the line of trees and stepped into the field, the shrill cry of the cicadas suddenly stopped as though a phonograph needle had been lifted from a record. The field was preternaturally silent. Moon felt the air go still as she circled the field, then she stood motionless.

"Right here," she called over her shoulder. She crouched down and ran her fingers along the rough grass. Stuart joined her in the field.

"This is where Christine's body was found," she said. "This is where he dumped her."

"Yes. Moon, you're exactly right."

"But this isn't anywhere near where she lived."

"Right again."

"Take me to her house."

Chapter Nineteen

They got back in the car and drove west to Livingston Manor, then got off at exit 96 and headed into town. Stuart pulled onto Church Street and into the driveway of a small white cottage-style house with maroon shutters. The lawn was still neatly mowed, and bundles of pink coneflowers and golden Black-eyed Susans tumbled over the rock walls that lined either side of the driveway.

Stuart grabbed his duffel bag from the back seat. Moon looped her camera bag across her body and clipped the tripod to her belt loop. She followed Stuart along the brick walkway that led to the narrow porch. They both slipped on gloves and booties over their shoes. He removed the crime scene seal on the door, and they went inside.

In the entryway, a Tiffany-style lamp graced a three-legged half-moon table. Under the lamp was a silver-framed photo of Christine in a cap and gown and what Moon assumed were her proud parents.

Stuart headed toward the living room.

"Wait." Moon circled the entryway with her arms extended to her side. She glanced back at the door. There were two narrow windows on either side of the front door.

"The report said—"

"Don't say anything. Hang on a minute." Moon blinked and took a step toward the front door. "Come with me. Take out your dusting powder and brush."

Stuart followed her outside. He dug a jar of fine black dusting powder and a soft-haired brush from his duffel bag. Moon removed a flashlight from her camera bag and shone the light at an angle against the window to the left of the front door. Stuart dipped the brush into the powder and moved it back and forth over the surface. Something appeared on the glass. He looked at the print and followed the loop pattern with his brush. The image of a latent palm print appeared.

"Hold this scale for me, please," Moon said. She handed him a ruler. "While you hold it, could you point up to indicate the orientation of the print?"

Stuart held the ruler against the glass beside the print and pointed to the porch ceiling. Moon kept her flashlight at an angle and snapped several pictures of the palm print at 90 degrees to the glass to prevent any distortion to the print. Stuart then took lifting tape from his bag and smoothed it across the entire print.

"How did you know this would be there?"

"Fluke. If the killer is a hunter, he would have stalked his game. I guessed that he would come here when she wasn't home to learn more about her. Get to know her tastes, her habits. He might have tried to pick the lock or pry open a window."

Moon dug through Stuart's bag and pulled out a sheet of acetate. She went inside and removed the picture frame from the entryway table. She placed the sheet on the table. Stuart peeled the tape from the window outside and transferred the palm print to the acetate sheet. Moon snapped more pictures of the print on the sheet before Stuart slid it into an evidence bag.

"Nice catch," he said.

They entered the living room. Blond wood floors, white cotton curtains, and sky-blue walls gave the room a fresh, nautical feel. A Christmas cactus stood on a plant stand in front of a window. The numerous areoles of the cactus held withered blossoms at the ends of each segment.

"Christine was a nurse practitioner at the Livingston Manor Health Center," Stuart said.

While Stuart stayed in the living room, Moon went to Christine's bedroom. She opened dresser drawers and thumbed through the clothes in her closet. In her bathroom, Moon peeked in her shower and rifled through her hamper. She came back out and sat on Christine's bed. Stuart popped his head in the door.

"Anything?"

"Nothing. Sorry."

Moon laid down on the bed. As she stared up at the ceiling, out of the corner of her eye she saw a shadow drift across the window. Moon sat straight up and turned her head toward the window.

"What is it?" Stuart came toward her.

Moon sprang to her feet and rushed to the window. She parted the laced curtains and looked at Christine's small backyard. There were a few dark purple lilac trees and an apple tree. The yard was surrounded by a wooden fence. A clothesline ran the length of the right side of the yard along the fence.

"A fenced-in yard would have afforded him privacy if, let's say, he was trying to open the window during the day or peer through it at night," Moon said. "He could take his time. Observe her without having to worry about anyone seeing him. Check this window for fingerprints and the ground underneath it for shoeprints. The killer stood right outside this window and watched her through the lace curtains as she slept."

They walked around to the back of the house and through the

fence door. Moon took pictures of the yard and the ground around Christine's bedroom window.

"Bingo," she said. "A boot print."

"It looks like some sort of a rain boot or hiking boot by the deep treads."

Moon backed up and took several photos of the boot print in relation to the window. Stuart dusted the area for fingerprints. While Moon took pictures of the window, Stuart placed an L-shaped scale beside the boot print. She then set up the tripod directly over the print and snapped close-up photos while he prepared to create the cast. He pulled a bottle of hardening spray from his duffel bag and sprayed the print at an angle. He opened a Ziploc bag of premixed casting compound and added bottled water to the bag. He massaged the bag for a moment to make sure the compound was thoroughly mixed. He then removed the scale and poured the mixture back and forth, starting at one end of the print and letting it flow over the entire area plus a few inches more. He smoothed the surface with a tongue depressor.

"That should do it." Stuart stood and brushed his hands. "We'll let it set and finish up inside."

They walked around to the front of the house.

"One of the many things I don't understand about what you do is why you hear and see some of the dead but not others."

Moon shrugged. "Like I said, I don't have any control over what I see. When souls leave the human body, some choose to communicate to humans cross-dimensionally, but other souls may not be ready, willing, or able to reach out. There are many who believe that the manner in which we die determines our soul's transition from this life to the next. There are some who have lived through near-death experiences and have observed their own dead bodies as they float above the hospital room or the crash site. They might try desperately to communicate but no one hears them. Still others don't want to communicate. They silently try to process what has happened to them. For some unknown reason, they reenter their bodies and resume their lives."

Moon sighed, then continued. "There have been cases where someone commits suicide while deeply depressed only to become intensely remorseful in the afterlife. Sometimes, they regret not having the chance to live out their lives in order to learn the lessons they needed to learn. Other times, their regret is in knowing they caused their loved one's pain. Those souls try to reach out to their loved ones for their forgiveness. The souls of some victims of violent murders refuse to leave until they have been avenged. Once the murderer has been captured and justice served, the soul can then move on to the astral plane to ready itself to be born again."

They stepped up onto the front porch. Stuart asked, "Do you actually believe in all that—the astral plane and born-again stuff?"

"This kind of thinking isn't new. People throughout time and across many different cultures believe that some part of their mind, soul, or spirit lives on after death. The great philosopher, Plato, believed that there are higher planes and dimensions of reality. The First Nations peoples traditionally accept and understand that they are spirits having a human experience. For the Haudenosaunee or the Five Nations of the Iroquois, the four stages in the journey of the human spirit—birth, life, death, and the afterlife. They believe the souls of the dead have the power to affect the living, and it is dangerous to neglect the spiritual needs of the dead. At the time of death, their breath is taken away by the Faceless One. The spirit takes a number of days to get used to the death of the body and to prepare for its journey. Ceremonies and practices assist the spirit on the path, said to be the Milky Way. They also believe that there is another sky path that exists for evil souls. It leads to a place halfway between the earth and the Sky World."

"I'll never look at the night sky the same way again," Stuart said.

"All I can say for certain is that this life isn't it. Here's the weird thing."

"You can't possibly say that with a straight face."

"Christine might not know she's dead."

"Okay, now you have officially left the planet. What are you talking about?"

"For some people who die suddenly and violently, their soul leaves the body so fast that they don't realize they're dead. They go through their daily routines as if nothing happened. They wander around the earth wondering why everything feels so weird."

"Yeah, but wouldn't she get it after a while? Wouldn't she sense that she was dead once she understood that nobody could hear her or see her?"

Moon shrugged. "Not necessarily. What if she encountered someone who could see her?"

"Another medium?"

"This might come as a surprise, but I might not be the only medium in town."

"Why isn't Christine here?"

"It's daytime. She lives here, but I assume she works during the day. She might have been back home during the night."

"You think she comes home at night," Stuart asked.

"Yes, but it's not as if she gets in a car and drives. Without her physical body, there are no limitations to time and space. Movement from one place to another is instantaneous. You said that Christine was a nurse practitioner at the Livingston Manor Health Center. They may have Saturday hours. Let's go see if she's there."

Chapter Twenty

They pulled into the parking lot of the Livingston Manor Health Center and went inside. Stuart stood by the door while Moon looked around the waiting room. She leaned through the window into the reception area and looked both ways. A nurse came to the front desk from one of the offices in the back.

"May I help you?" the nurse asked.

"No, that's okay. Thank you."

Moon met Stuart at the door and they went outside.

"Nothing?" he asked.

"Not yet, but I have an idea."

Stuart followed Moon as she walked around to the back of the building. She spotted Christine sitting by herself at a picnic table under a blue tent. It was the break area for employees. Moon nodded to Stuart and walked over to her.

"Can I help you?" Christine asked. A haunted look occupied her face.

"I hope you can. And I think I can help you. You're Christine, right?"

Christine looked at her almost in a daze. She seemed confused. "Do I know you?"

"No. My name is Moon McFadden."

"What time is it? I have to get back inside. I have a busy day ahead, I think. I don't remember the day's schedule. I don't remember taking a break."

Moon sat down beside her. "I think I can help you. You feel that you keep losing track of time as though you've been daydreaming, and you can't remember how you got from one place to another. But for some reason, you find yourself here most of the time."

"I have no idea what you're talking about. I've got a busy schedule, as I told you. Now if you'll excuse me." Christine stood.

"Wait. Christine, haven't you wondered why you keep losing time? What is the last thing you remember?"

Christine sat back down. "I don't know. Going to work."

"Before that?"

Her eyebrows furrowed. "Someone was pulling my hair."

Moon looked over at Stuart.

"No," Christine continued, "I had gone for a hike in the woods and my hair became tangled in a branch. I was just out for a hike. It was raining. Yeah, I remember it was raining hard."

"Then what happened?"

"Nothing. I was in the woods and it was dark and raining. Nothing happened."

"Are you sure? Do you remember a man chased through the woods?"

"I don't remember that."

"Yes, you do. He shot you in the back as you were running away. Do you remember hitting the ground?"

Christine looked confused, then hurt. She swallowed hard as tears flooded her eyes.

"Yes. I hit the ground hard. He walked up behind me slowly."

Her hands went to her throat. "He looped a rope around my neck. I couldn't breathe. I couldn't reach up to my neck to loosen the rope because my hands were tied behind my back. The sticks along the ground pierced my back as he dragged me through the woods. He was whistling." She let go of her throat. A look of anguish washed over her face. "Oh, my God. He was whistling!" She looked at Moon. "I don't remember anything after that."

"After that, it doesn't matter. Did you happen to see his face? Hear his name? Anything?"

"No. I never saw his face. I only heard his voice. That voice. I'll never forget that voice. What's going on? You can see me."

"Yes."

"Does that mean that you are … "

Moon shook her head.

"So, I'm dead."

Moon nodded.

Christine let out a big sigh. "I wish things could have been different. I was getting engaged. His name is Justin Eldridge. I see now that he bought me a beautiful ring. I can see it all now. Everything. My birthday would have been next week. Justin planned to rent a boat on Seneca Lake. We were going to have drinks at sunset. He planned to propose then. From the day we met, I wanted to marry him. Have his children. Grow old together, sit side by side on our back porch in the evening, surrounded by our grandchildren and looking out over our dairy farm."

"That all sounds lovely."

Christine shook her head. "He won't marry, you know. After this. Justin will remain single for the rest of his life. I so wanted to marry that man. Maybe in the next life?"

"Yeah."

"So, how does this work? Should I be afraid? What do I do?"

"You don't have anything to fear. This next place is incredible. It's better than you could possibly imagine, and all you have to do is close your eyes and relax."

Just then, someone opened the back door. A woman wearing the clinic's uniform pulled a pack of cigarettes from her purse.

"Can I help you?" the woman asked.

"I was just—" Moon turned back. Christine was gone. "No, I'm fine. Thank you."

Moon stood. She nodded to the woman, then she and Stuart headed back to the car. They drove back to Christine's house to collect the cast of the boot print, then drove 30 minutes to Callicoon. Stuart pulled in front of a yellow cottage on Eggler Road and turned off the car. He handed the keys to Moon.

"If you don't mind, I'm going to stay in the car."

"I understand."

Moon took the keys and walked up the pathway to the porch, which extended the entire length of the front of the house. Four white pillars along the front of the porch gave the small cottage a grander feel. A gentle breeze sighed through the old pine trees that surrounded the cottage. The breeze and the deep gong of the wind chimes that hung on the porch were the only sounds Moon heard.

A wreath made from blue silk forget-me-nots hung on the front door. She stepped onto the porch, slipped on booties and gloves, removed the crime scene seal, and went inside. The cozy living room contained a sofa and two chairs that huddled around a fieldstone fireplace. They were upholstered in a soft pink peony fabric. Family photos graced the mantel beneath an antique mirror. Moon ran her fingers over a photograph of Stuart and Sandra as children. They were standing on a dock. Stuart looked to be about nine years old. He was holding a fishing pole with a bluegill on the end of the line. His younger sister, beaming with pride, clung to his T-shirt.

"I never saw him coming."

Moon turned and saw Sandra standing behind her.

"It was a beautiful day. I decided to go hiking at the Neversink Gorge Trails."

"Neversink."

Sandra nodded. "I hiked that afternoon along the walking trail that led to the waterfalls and the river. I stood near the bank and watched a few men fly fishing for a while. Fly fishing is so graceful—almost poetic, don't you think? The way the line floats in the air in long unhurried loops."

Sandra swept her arm out in a big arc. She sat down on the arm of her sofa. Her fingers traced the petals of the peonies.

"I walked back to where I had parked my car. I never knew he was behind me. I felt a sharp pain on the side of my head, then woke up in a dark room. I begged him not to hurt me—pleaded. I told him I was pregnant. None of it mattered, in the end."

"Did you see his face? Can you describe him? Anything you remember would be helpful."

"I was on my stomach on a bed. The room was very dark, so I never saw his face. All I remember about him was his voice. He spoke slowly, almost conversationally, as though the two of us had known each other for ages. As for a description, I'd say he was evil incarnate."

Sandra walked over to the window and parted the curtains. "He's not coming in."

"No."

"I don't blame him. He's been through a lot lately."

Sandra kept her eyes on Stuart. "He doesn't know this. I wanted it to be a surprise. Did you know that you can have a prenatal blood test and find out the baby's sex as early as 11 weeks?"

"I didn't know that."

"Of course, the ultrasound is considered fully accurate at 18 weeks. I had the blood test." She looked at Moon. "It said I was having a boy."

Sandra looked back out the window. "I was going to name him Stuart. He would have loved his uncle."

"I have no doubt. I'm so sorry. We will get this guy. I promise you."

Sandra let the curtains flutter back into place. "Thank you."

Moon took the photos she needed from inside the cottage, locked the front door, and got back in the car. Stuart stared through the steering wheel at the dashboard not seeing anything.

"Don't tell me anything. I can't handle it. Not with her."

"I understand."

He gripped the steering wheel so hard his knuckles were white. "I feel guilty."

"How could you when this wasn't your fault?"

"It's irrational, I know, but that doesn't change the way I feel. She was my last surviving relative. Both my parents were only children. As her older brother, I needed to protect her. I wish I could have protected her. Losing the ones you love is a lesson in humility. I can't stop wondering why. I mean, why her of all people?"

"Why and why not are two powerful questions."

A wave of emotions flashed across his face. The muscles in his jaw rippled. He furrowed his eyebrows in anger then relaxed them as the tears puddled his eyes.

"The point of all this killing is that it is pointless," Stuart said. "After all these years, I still try to make sense of death, fend it off by outsmarting it, but it just keeps rolling along, picking us off one by one."

"You can't control this, Stuart. Death takes care of itself. In so many ways, it's harder to become old. We have a job to do right now, and we need to find who did this."

He nodded. "Let's get out of here."

As he started the car and pulled away, Moon turned to look through the rear windshield at the cottage. Sandra was standing on the porch, waving goodbye.

Chapter Twenty-One

They drove out of town and pulled onto the highway. Stuart shifted in his seat, staring straight ahead.

"Where are we going?" Moon asked.

"I booked two rooms at the Days Inn in Liberty." He rolled down the window and honked at the driver in front of them. "Get off the road grandpa." His nostrils flared. "I swear to God they should take everybody's licenses away once they reach sixty."

Stuart looked at Moon. "What?"

"I didn't say anything."

"I just want to get out of this town, all right?"

"Understood."

Stuart honked again, then rolled up his window. Moon sat silently for a moment, then pushed her lower lip down and stuck her tongue out across her upper lip. She crossed her eyes and faced Stuart.

"What are you doing?"

"Just trying to lighten the mood a little." She wiped her mouth.

"I'm edgy. I know. I'm sorry."

"I want to get this guy as much as you do. Let's go over what we know or think we know. He's white and educated. He works with or is skilled at using knives. He abducts these women and tortures them. On rainy nights, he hunts them down, kills them, and disposes of their bodies in the rain to wash away the evidence and DNA. All of his victims that we know of have been beautiful, confident women in their late 20s or early 30s located in the Catskills and near Clivesville."

Stuart pounded the wheel. "We know all this. We have all these stats, but for some reason, I'm just not getting a picture of this guy."

Moon turned on the radio.

"What are you doing?"

"The Law of Reverse Effect states that the greater the conscious effort, the less subconscious response. In other words, if you think too much about something, your subconscious is just going to fight you and shut down. When I find myself stuck, I walk away from a problem and give my brain a break. I take a walk, go for a run, go shopping, watch a movie. Usually, something surfaces."

She found a clear station playing the Bee Gees' "How Deep Is Your Love?"

"I'm good at this," Stuart continued. "Usually. I'm so frustrated right now. Mendoza is breathing down my neck."

Moon looked at Stuart and turned up the volume.

"Something always comes to me," he continued. "Not this time. I'm furious. You know, I remember this one time—"

Moon shifted in the seat to face Stuart. Pretending to hold a microphone, she sang, "I see your arse in the morning sun. I'm feeling touchy in the foreign rain."

Stuart did a double take. "Foreign rain?"

She turned up the volume. "And you come to me on this submarine, keep me warm in your glove, then you softly pee—"

"Pee?"

"Be quiet, I'm singing." Moon pressed a palm to her heart. "It's me you need to shove. How deep is your glove?"

He burst out laughing. "Thanks. I needed that."

She turned down the volume. "You're welcome. Listen, I know you don't want to hear any details about Sandra, but you must. It might be important to the case. She was out hiking and was attacked while going back to her car. After her hike, she stood on the bank of a river and watched some guys fly fishing. As she left to go to her car, she was struck on the temple from behind. When she woke up, the killer had her."

"Where was she hiking?" Stuart asked.

"Neversink."

"Neversink. There's the 'never' you wrote."

"Yeah."

They pulled into the hotel parking lot and headed to the front desk. Stuart secured the rooms and handed Moon a key.

"We're on the second floor. Let's circle back in about an hour for dinner."

Moon took her key. "Meet you in the lobby at seven."

After a quick nap and a shower, Moon dressed in jeans and a T-shirt and went to the lobby. Stuart stood beside a display case reading local trip brochures. As soon as he saw her, he replaced the brochure and came toward her.

"You look great."

She smiled. "So do you."

"There's isn't a big culinary selection around here. BK is across the street. There's a Mexican place and a diner. I was thinking pizza."

Moon smiled. "Pizza. Good thinkin' Lincoln."

"I aim to please, Louise. Eat there or here?"

"Here. We can eat in my room or yours."

"I was hoping you'd say that, too. It's been a long day."

Stuart looked up the number on his phone and dialed. He held a hand over the phone. "What do you want on it?"

"Whatever. No anchovies."

"Yes, I'd like to order a medium pizza to be picked up. Half green pepper and mushrooms and the other half meat. Whatever meat you've got. Sure. Twenty minutes? Thanks." Stuart hung up. "Twenty minutes. I looked up the address of a local liquor store. Let's pick up some wine while we wait for the pizza."

They got in the car and drove to the liquor store just around the corner on NY-52. After, Stuart drove to the pizza place and parked.

"Be right out."

Moon watched him enter the pizza place. She smiled and shook her head. She pulled her phone from her purse and dialed a number. Stuart came out balancing a pizza box on his palm. He got in the car and handed Moon the box. She juggled the phone back into her purse and took the box.

"Who were you calling? Sorry, that's none of my business."

"No, it's okay. I was calling a friend of mine. Holly. I wanted to share some thoughts on life with her." Moon smiled at Stuart.

"What did she have to say?"

"Nothing. She didn't answer. The call went to her voice mail."

He pulled out of the parking lot and headed back to the hotel. Moon slowly lifted the lid of the box and inhaled.

"This smells amazing," she said. "I'm so hungry, I could eat my own head."

Stuart glanced out his window and up toward the sky. "Oh, man. Look at that moon." He pulled into the Days Inn lot and parked the car. The parking lot lights glinted off the windshield. They got out and stared up at the full moon.

"Let's go to the side of the building for a minute away from the lights," Moon said.

As soon as they rounded the corner, they were enveloped in darkness. The dome of the sky, glutted with stars, opened before them like an enormous umbrella.

"Look at that sky. You never see anything like this in the city," he said. "Too many tall buildings. Too much light. And look at that ring around the moon."

"I miss the city," she said. "All the restaurants, my friends, the museums, and the park. But not on a night like this."

Stuart looked at her and smiled.

"What?"

"Nothing. I'm just enjoying the moon."

At that same moment, about ten miles away off Schumway Road in Neversink, Seth was enjoying the moon, too. He was especially pleased to see the lunar halo that surrounded the moon. The 22-degree halo got its name because the radius of the circle around the moon is approximately 22 degrees. The ring is caused by the refraction and reflection of light from ice crystals that are suspended in the thin, wispy, cirrus clouds at that high altitude.

Black branches stretched their lacy arms across the sky, quivering against the full moon's glow. Silver light reflected off the Fat Tire beer bottle as Seth raised it to toast.

"What's that old wives' tale? A ring around the moon means rain is coming soon."

He had settled into an Adirondack chair at the end of the courtyard of his Catskills cabin. The moon's bulging eye cast the light of her fullness onto the grass. A long blue shadow bled across the yard as he lifted the bottle to take another drink. He often gazed at the face of the moon. He understood her. For over 4.5 billion years, her face had been pockmarked by countless asteroids and meteorites colliding with her surface. What may have originated as a medieval Serbian tale about a fox tricking a wolf into thinking the moon's reflection in a pond was actually cheese, or a 1546 document titled *The Proverbs of John Heywood* where the author jokingly writes that "the moon is made of greene cheese"—not the color green, but because it was old, or even a cat and mouse wisecracking about the cheesy moon in the cartoon *Tom and Jerry*—for a thousand years, people have mischaracterized the moon. Made fun of her. Never fully understood her. He knew what that was like.

They also underestimated her power. For over four billion years, her gravitational pull has been responsible for Earth's length of days, its stable seasons, and its tides. People have long underestimated her strength. He knew what that was like, too.

"The moon's an arrant thief."

He raised his beer bottle again to her. He had had a successful evening's hunt. A few hours after Moon and Stuart left Ramona's Diner, Seth stopped in for a light supper. He sat in his usual window booth and ordered a Caesar salad with chicken and an unsweetened iced tea. Whenever Seth had a weekend free, he liked to unwind by doing a little fly fishing in the Catskills. Most evenings, he had dinner at the diner. And most nights, he ordered an entrée and followed that up with a piece of lemon meringue pie and a coffee refill. He read his book but also kept an eye on the parking lot. He was hunting for his next beautiful woman. He studied the parking lot as cars came in and out. Most weekends were a bust, but every now and then, a beautiful woman who was traveling alone pulled into the east lot and parked. He was only interested in those women who parked along the east side of the building.

Earlier that evening, just as he stabbed a piece of chicken, he watched her pull in and drive around to the east side. Seth could feel his pulse quicken. After a few minutes, the attractive blond woman followed the hostess into the dining room. Once she was seated, Seth timed his meal accordingly. If he had already eaten, he might order his pie. Or just a refill on his coffee. He read his book and watched the waitress serve her meal. That's when he'd close out his tab and go to his truck at the end of the east lot. He located her car, and if possible, reparked his truck closer to her car. That night, he found an open spot three down from hers. He got out of his truck and stood next to the tailgate and waited. Finally, he spotted her out of the corner of his eye. She had come around the corner of the building heading toward her car. Her car keys jangled in her hand.

"Oh man," Seth said to himself, but loud enough for her to hear. He bent over scanning the ground.

"Can I help you?" She walked toward him.

"I dropped my key, and I can't seem to find it. It must have bounced on the ground somewhere."

Like clockwork. She came near him and bent over to scan the ground to help him find his key. He struck her on the temple with a leather flat sap. He scooped her into his arms, lowered the tailgate with a remote on the keychain hidden in his palm, and rolled her inside. He quickly injected her with ketamine and closed the tailgate. He drove 28 minutes to his cabin and into the driveway around the back. He lowered the tailgate and made sure she was still out. He gagged her, zip-tied her hands, and bound her feet. He carried her down the hall to the windowless bedroom. Depending on the weather and how much work he had to do the following week at the funeral home, he would either play with her for a few days or hunt her immediately.

Those decisions could wait. He sank further down into the Adirondack chair, crossed his legs, took another long languorous drink of beer, and gazed up at the lovely ringed moon.

Chapter Twenty-Two

A few days later, Moon's phone went off shortly after the sun had risen. The ringtone was the *Star Wars* "The Imperial March." Chief Quinn. She slid her sleep mask up onto her forehead. Her hand fumbled across her nightstand in the dark, knocking over a book and a bottle of water. She finally located the phone.

"Moon, a farmer found the body of a woman outside of Hammondsport."

"Okay." She sat up in bed and dragged her fingers through her hair.

"Moon, it's Holly Sherman."

Moon's breath caught in her throat. She felt cold and nauseous, as though someone had punched her in the stomach.

"Moon."

"I'm here."

"We can get someone else—"

"No. I want to be there. I'm on my way."

"Meet us on Cold Spring Road off Fish Hatchery Road between Bath and Hammondsport near the Crooked Line Farm."

Moon sat in bed for a moment rubbing her forehead. She took a deep breath to try and steady herself, but she couldn't hold back the tears. She let go and sobbed into her hands. The wave of sorrow soon turned to anger, then to determination. She threw the covers off and got out of bed. She quickly dressed and went to the garage. She double-checked that she had everything in her camera bag in the van and got in. She pulled onto Route 86 and headed west to Hammondsport. The sky was smoke-gray, the color of a faded dream. She thought of the first time she had met Holly. Her parent's cottage on the lake was next door to Matthew's parent's cottage. They clicked right away. Ever since, they had shared all of their greatest joys, saddest heartbreaks, and their deepest secrets. Holly knew Moon better than anyone.

Moon pulled onto Route 54, a two-lane road that cut through a U-shaped valley that had been carved by glaciers more than 2 million years ago. The glaciers crept south, pushing earth and rocks with them. Gradually, the ice melted and the glacier receded, leaving behind shale valleys of water that make up the eleven Finger Lakes. She drove through miles of cornfields that filled the flat valley surrounded the deeply grooved glacial hills.

Moon turned onto a dirt road that curled across miles of blooming alfalfa fields. Their purple blossoms stretched across the valley like a violet sea. She soon spotted a line of official cars and parked. Stuart hopped across a ditch and met her at the back of the van.

"Moon, I'm sorry to hear about your friend."

"Thank you."

She grabbed her gear and followed him across the ditch into the field. Mendoza and Chief Quinn stood on the edge of the field shoulder to shoulder whispering to one another. As soon as they spotted Moon, they separated. Mendoza punched his fists against his hips and walked off without looking at her. Chief Quinn headed toward her.

"I'm sorry, Moon," Chief Quinn whispered.

"Thank you. I appreciate that."

"It looks like the same M.O. as the others," Chief Quinn said. He motioned with his head. "The farmer over there, Larry Gorton, found her. It's his field."

They both looked back over at the farmer. He was a tall man who wore faded jeans, a T-shirt, and a blue University of Buffalo baseball hat. He stared at the ground and stroked his gray beard. Just then, a car sped up the dirt road and skidded to a stop. A man jumped out and ran toward the field.

"Where's my daughter?" the man screamed. He stumbled into the field. "Where's my Holly?"

Chief Quinn waved to the officers nearest the man. "Grab that guy." The officers ran to intercept the man and restrain him.

"Sir, you can't go into the field," Officer Patterson said. "You'll contaminate the crime scene."

The officers held him, but he fought back like a wild animal. "I don't care. I have to see my daughter. Larry, tell them!"

Moon walked over to the man and stood before him.

"Mr. Sherman," Moon said. "John." She placed her hands on his shoulders.

"Moon?"

She looked him straight in the eye. "Yes. I'm here, and we're going to catch the man who did this, I promise you. But the only way you can help Holly now is to let me and the police officers do our jobs. Trust me."

All energy drained from John. It was as if a light had gone out inside him, and he stopped fighting the police. As Moon ran her hand along his arm, John's mouth silently opened and closed like a fish's. Then as he began to sob, Moon nodded to Larry who stepped in and held him in his arms. When the storm of grief had passed, Larry and

John walked away from the field without looking back. They both got in John's car and drove off.

Moon walked back over to Chief Quinn. Mendoza muttered something unintelligible under his breath, then spat on the ground.

Chief Quinn sighed. "Whenever you're ready."

Moon nodded and pulled out her camera. She let out a deep sigh and began shooting. She paced the perimeter of the field working her way through the three-foot alfalfa shoots. When she reached Holly's body, Moon crouched down beside her.

"Oh, Holly." Moon pushed a tear from her cheek with her palm. "My dearest Holly. I am so sorry." She took a deep breath and took a picture of her ear. She reached out and brushed a lock of Holly's long dark hair away from her face. As soon as she touched her hair, Moon saw a vision of a man pulling Holly's hair, jerking her head back violently. Moon lowered her camera, leaned in close to Holly, and whispered. "You know I can hear you. Come on, Holly. Help me find him. Please, talk to me."

The alfalfa sprouts shook their heads in the wind. Moon closed her eyes and listened. She could hear the flapping of the crime scene tape and a jumble of voices coming from the edge of the field. She heard the piercing cry of a red-tailed hawk as it circled above. Nothing from Holly. Moon stood and scanned the field hoping Holly would appear, but she saw no sign of her.

"Okay," Moon said.

As soon as Moon was finished taking her photos, she motioned for Lloyd Babbitt to start his examination. She walked to the edge of the field and joined Stuart, Chief Quinn, and Mendoza.

"The condition of Holly's body is different from the others," Moon said. "Her neck shows signs of injury. It might even be broken. It's as though her head had been thrown backward."

"Whiplash?" Stuart asked.

Moon shrugged. "I saw the killer's hand yank her hair. We'll see what Lloyd says."

"Did you pick up anything else?" Mendoza asked.

"Not yet, sir. I'll take a look at the photos for any clues. Since we're near Holly's house, I thought Stuart and I could go over there and take a look."

"The police are still there," Mendoza said. "As soon as you're done, I want the two of you to meet me back at the Chief's office." He turned and walked to his car.

Chief Quinn sucked air through his teeth, gave them a look, and followed Mendoza out of the field. Dread settled into Moon's chest like a stone.

Chapter Twenty-Three

Stuart lifted Moon's camera bag from her shoulder and carried it for her on the way to their cars. They pulled back out on Route 54 and drove west to Hammondsport. The sleepy village curved itself around the heel of Keuka Lake. The fire station was located near the shore with a large lawn that ran up from the beach to its hydraulic doors. A large banner on the lawn advertised the upcoming county fair. In front of the town hall, a giant cannon commemorating some ancient war slept within a flower bed.

Stuart and Moon pulled onto Main Street. She averted her eyes as she passed Elmwood Cemetery on the right side of the road. She followed Stuart's car as it turned onto Myrtle Avenue. They parked behind the line of police cars in front of Holly's house. It was a snug cottage with gray siding and white trim. White wicker chairs huddled together on the front porch.

Three ceramic pots with sunflowers painted on them had been placed on the left side of the three steps leading to the porch. Each one overflowed with orange and yellow marigolds. The front door was open as police streamed in and out of the cottage.

Moon and Stuart stood on the sidewalk in front of the house.

"I've always liked this house," Moon said. "I was with her at a farmer's market when she bought those ceramic pots." A lump suddenly caught in Moon's.

"You okay?"

Moon nodded. They climbed the steps to the porch, slipped on booties and gloves, and went inside. The living room, dining room, and kitchen were one great room with blond wood floors and warm gray walls. A wooden beam ran the length of the cathedral ceiling. Police officers huddled over furniture and next to windows, searching for clues and dusting for prints.

"You want to look around?" Stuart asked.

Moon took in the room. One month earlier, she had helped Holly paint those walls. She remembered Holly had special ordered the paint from Farrow and Ball. The color was called Elephant's Breath. Moon closed her eyes. She could still smell the fresh paint.

"Moon?"

Moon opened her eyes and shook her head. "There's no need to look around. Nothing happened in here. We need to go outside around the back."

They left the house, and Stuart followed her to the backyard.

"Here." She pointed to the stamped concrete porch just outside the back door. "He watched Holly come out this door." She pointed to a corner of the backyard that was shaded by a large black cherry tree. "He stood in the shadow, in the corner of the fence behind that tree and watched her."

They made their way over to the tree and searched the ground.

"There!" Moon pointed at the base of the wooden fence. "A boot print."

While Moon set up her tripod over the print and took photos, Stuart mixed the casting compound. He poured the mixture back and forth over the print, then stood and stretched his back.

Moon studied the camera display. "These look like the same boot print treads that we lifted from the Christine Krohmalney's house. That one was a size 11. Do we dare celebrate?"

"Not until we compare it to the other boot print and get an exact match from the lab."

Moon pulled out her phone. "Chief, we might have something. A boot print. We'll head back as soon as it sets. Okay. See you soon."

Back at police headquarters, Moon and Stuart entered Chief Quinn's office. The Chief was seated behind his desk while Mendoza paced the floor. Neither Chief Quinn nor Mendoza acknowledged them as they took a seat. Both the men held cocktail glasses of an amber liquid in their hands. An opened bottle of Johnny Walker Blue was on the desk. It was 10:30 a.m. Mendoza's face was flushed. He frowned, and the wrinkles around his mouth gathered into a bow of smoldering fury. He stopped pacing and threw back what was left of his drink, then placed the empty glass on the desk. Chief Quinn poured more scotch into the glass, keeping his silence.

"First, let me say how sorry I am, Moon," Mendoza said.

"Thank you."

"Now, let me recap recent events for both of you." Mendoza scooped up the fresh drink, his bean-shaped nostrils flared. "There has been another grisly murder—another beautiful woman with her entire life ahead of her. Instead of getting to live that promising life, her body was found in a field making this the fifth victim that we know of."

Mendoza took a long drink and studied his glass. He cleared his throat.

"What you might not know is that I got a call from Madelaine Spencer about an hour before we learned about Holly's murder to tell me that the unidentified body of another beautiful young woman was found in a field just outside the town of Aden, New York near the Neversink Reservoir. Another beautiful young woman with the same body parts removed. Another life brutally cut short." Mendoza stopped pacing and stared at the floor. "That makes six victims, again, that we know of."

Mendoza took a step toward Stuart's chair and stood in front of him.

"This monster may already have his next victim held captive somewhere." His body shook as he shouted. "Yet, we have no idea who he is or where that somewhere may be. We have no idea how to find him or how to make him stop killing innocent women. How am I doing so far?"

Stuart and Moon remained motionless, studying the floor.

"People are terrified. The press, feeding into their fears, have now dubbed this guy *The Rainy Night Stalker*."

"They gave him a name?" Moon asked.

Mendoza ignored her. He was just getting started. "Now, every beautiful young woman within a 200-mile radius who spots a man simply glancing in their direction or hears the wind blowing in the trees thinks the killer may be following them, and that she'll be this monster's next victim. Mayor Verdier is demanding an update from me on all we know so far. The public deserves answers. They have the right to get those answers from us."

Mendoza pointed at Stuart.

"I hired you—for quite a large sum of money, I might add—because you are the best. I'm paying you to get this guy, sooner rather than later. We've spent thousands of dollars, of the taxpayer's money. What have you come up with so far? Nothing!"

"We found a boot print behind a tree in Holly's backyard," Stuart said. "The lab will compare it to the boot print we recovered at Christine's house. It's something."

Mendoza's only response was to raise one eyebrow. He took a step to the right and stood in front of Moon.

"Moon, you're supposed to be able to communicate with the victims. According to you, they tell you things—things they know from wherever they are now. I don't understand why they're not giving you more clues."

"You know it doesn't work that way," Moon said. "Death doesn't always grant omniscience. For some reason, this time the victims who have been communicating with me have said that none of them saw the killer. They only heard his voice. He was a stranger to them, but he knew everything about them. The women didn't know each other, and they don't know what their connection is to one another. The killer attacked them from behind. They were unconscious before they knew what hit them. When they woke up, they were blindfolded. They were so focused on getting away, that's all they remember. That's all they're showing me."

"Something's got to give. I've scheduled a press conference for 4:30 tomorrow afternoon. You all have until then to come up with something I can give the public."

"We're grasping at straws here," Stuart said. "He's winning so far. We've got no evidence, and we have very few clues as to who this guy is. The one thing we're sure of is what he likes to do in the rain. I'm left scratching my head."

"Scratching? I'm clawing at my head. I'm getting my ass handed to me by the governor. We have to do better. We have to reassure the public that we're close to catching this guy."

"So, we're going to lie."

"Do not test me, Bauer."

Mendoza downed the rest of his drink, spun his glass on Chief Quinn's desk, and stormed out. Chief Quinn remained in his chair, tight-lipped, with his eyes on the scotch bottle as he screwed the top back on and stashed it in his bottom desk drawer.

Chapter Twenty-Four

Stuart and Moon slunk from Chief Quinn's office and rode the elevator wordlessly to the basement. Moon set her camera gear on her desk and walked down the hall to Stuart's office. She found the door ajar. The room was dark except for a cone of light from his desk lamp. Shadows seemed to pour into every crease and wrinkle in Stuart's face. He held his head in his hands. She knocked on the door frame and walked in.

"Can I come in?"

"You're a little in to be asking." Stuart rubbed his temples. "Sorry."

"We've all been chewed by Mendoza."

"I deserve it. If I was in his position, I would have reacted the same way."

Moon stood in front of his desk. "What are you reading?"

"*Diagnostic Statistical Manual of Mental Disorders.*" He closed the book. "This is what I do. I gather information and let it stew in my brain for a while. Stir the pot. Most of the time, something floats to the top. With this guy? Nothing yet."

Stuart stood, walked around his desk, and turned on the overhead lights. Moon noticed the large magnetic whiteboard across from the front of Stuart's desk. It covered the entire wall and contained a large map of New York State and Post-Its with the names of the victims and the locations where their bodies were found. Moon stood in front of the whiteboard, studying the Post-Its.

"It's very frustrating," he said. He took a magnet and placed a Post-It representing Holly Sherman on the map. "I can list the stats on a typical serial killer, but that's all they are. Stats." He stepped back and took in the map. "Here's a statistic you might not know. Most sexual deviants have a fetish that often involves footwear."

Moon smiled. "Really?"

"Really. Ted Bundy owned 30 pairs of socks. I'm filled with useless knowledge."

"You'd be great on *Jeopardy*."

"Yes. I'll take sexual deviants for $200."

"In tracking all these serial killers, do you ever worry that they'll find out who you are and come after you?" Moon asked.

"Every minute of every day. What about you?"

"Never. I'm in the background. No one knows who I am or what I do. I give the information I get to the police, and then they do their job to capture the killer."

Moon ran her fingers over the map. "I keep wondering, what is his want? It can't just be the thrill of the hunt for this guy. What's the emotional thrill for him? And why is he removing the areolae? We assume that includes the nipples. It's got to mean something. Is he keeping them or destroying them?"

Stuart paced the room. "My guess is that he's keeping them, most likely as souvenirs. Again, that's what the stats tell me. Serial killers, by nature, are peacocks. They almost never disguise their crimes. They want their activities written about. They want their personas speculated. There's always evidence. We just have to find it."

Stuart stopped in front of the whiteboard. "The stalking is part of the thrill for him just as the hunt thrills him. Speaking of thrills, one thing that many serial killers thirst for is to create and sustain an almost mythical status. How do you do that? Give them a name. The press has played right into his fantasies by labeling him *The Rainy Night Stalker*."

"What makes someone into a serial killer?" Moon asked.

"No one knows for sure. Some think that it's all about genetics—that the person is born broken or missing some crucial element that allows them to learn appropriate social behaviors. Others think it's environmental—that the individual suffered an abusive childhood at the hands of a parent. I think it's a combination of both."

Stuart sat on top of his desk facing the whiteboard. "In 1888, the German psychiatrist Julius Koch coined the term *psychopastiche*, or psychopath. It literally means 'suffering soul.' This was at a time when Jack the Ripper was terrorizing London's impoverished areas in and around Whitechapel in the East End of London. Koch believed that psychopaths were flawed or evil from birth. More than evil, I consider these people truly as suffering souls. Parents have a limited ability to shape their children's behavior, except for the worse. I think much of a child's perception of their world is a result of their experiences. If someone was mean to them and didn't show them empathy, they learned that that was how the world worked. The Rainy Night Stalker was once a little boy. I think that poor boy was in a terribly abusive environment and was shown meanness and cruelty. In his case, he literally became a suffering soul."

"Many children experience abuse but don't turn into serial killers."

"True," Stuart said. "Children are pretty malleable. It doesn't take much to allow them to see that the world can be a kind place—a loving grandparent, a caring teacher, a trusted sibling. Someone to show them love and kindness can do wonders for their perception of the world. I have a feeling our killer didn't have anyone in his life like that as a small child. The pain he felt was internalized. The man he grew into harbors incredible pain. There's something about these women that triggered his pain."

Stuart slid down off the desk and began pacing again. "The most terrifying thing about a true psychopath? They seem completely normal. That's what's most chilling. These monsters walk unseen among us. Ted Bundy brutally murdered countless women, yet he was intelligent and charming. Two traits are almost always associated with psychopathic killers: sexual abnormality and an all-consuming need for power. Killing satisfies them sexually, and it gives them ultimate power over someone. Think about it. They choose whether the person lives or dies. The Rainy Night Stalker is a psychopathic killer. What he does to these women gives him such heightened satisfaction that he cannot achieve from anyone or anything else in his life. He won't get bored, and he won't stop."

Moon motioned to the map. "Take a look at the places the killer has struck that we know of. It's rural, hilly, with lots of lakes and streams. He chose this area because it's in his wheelhouse—his comfort zone."

She stepped back to look at the whole map. "Take a look at these Post-Its. Don't the locations look clustered a little to you?"

"I guess."

"These Post-Its represent where each of the bodies were located. So, regardless of where he immobilized his victims, they were all held in his cabin and killed in the woods there. I'm guessing he found a field about 20 miles from his cabin to dump the body. This whole area is remote. He wouldn't need to drive farther than that."

Moon snatched a pen from Stuart's desk. She slipped off her pendant necklace and stretched the chain across the mileage scale on the map. She held the pendant chain at 20 miles with her thumb and index finger. She removed the first victim's Post-It and placed the chain on the exact location she was found on the map. She extended the chain out and, with the tip of the pen, drew a circle on the map around the location the victim was found. She replaced the Post-It and traced the same circles around the rest of the victims' locations on the map.

Moon gestured to the map. "If I'm right, both of his cabins will be found where these circles intersect in both Groverton and Neversink."

Stuart nodded. "Good. It's something. I'll get a list of all the residents who live within these circle intersections and get a few officers to take a drive out there. Sniff around. Typically, organized offenders kill in one location and dispose of the body at another. They're very careful with DNA. They don't leave any evidence behind. Except our killer made a mistake."

Moon turned to him and smiled. "The skin cells under Rachel Mariner's toenail. He didn't expect any of his victims to fight back. That must have really pissed him off. For that brief moment, he was no longer in control. That's why he lunged at Rachel and cut her throat. Allegedly. Do you think our killer will be watching the press conference?"

"If I was a gambling man, I'd put a lot of money on him watching. I can't imagine he'd pass up a chance to feel superior. I'm not certain of much, but I'd take that bet."

"During the press conference, I'll stand behind you and take pictures of the crowd." Moon held up her index finger. "I just had a thought. Can we come up with something, a story or a false description of the killer that only he would know was untrue? Say something that might upset him?"

"Piss him off?"

"The last time that happened, he made a mistake underestimating Rachel." Moon shrugged. "Maybe he'll make another mistake."

"It's worth a try."

Chapter Twenty-Five

The street in front of the police station was lined with television broadcast vans from the five major local affiliates. Cameramen established their positions and planted their tripods. The sun beat down on the on-camera reporters who tested mics, straightened skirts and suits, and refreshed makeup.

A small stage and podium had been erected in front of the police station. Chief Quinn and Mendoza huddled in conversation a few feet away from the podium. Stuart stood on the other side of the podium with Moon. He fiddled with his necktie.

"What did they say?" Moon took over straightening his tie.

Stuart wiped the sweat from his brow. "They're not crazy about the idea. Frankly, they shouldn't be. No self-respecting officer would give a statement like this, and no decent reporter would print it. At this point, they're willing to give it a try. The good news is that Chief Quinn has assigned a few officers to check out all the residents who live within the intersecting circles on the map in Groverton. Mendoza made a call to District Attorney Spencer in the Catskills for their officers to do the same there. It's something."

"Hey stranger," Matthew said from the grass along the side of the stage.

"Hello. What are you doing here?" Moon asked.

Stuart nodded at Matthew and gave him a strained smile. He turned and joined Chief Quinn and Mendoza.

"I read about the press conference online in the Clivesville newspaper. I drove out to support you and take a chance you might be free for dinner."

"Thank you. That sounds nice."

"Okay, then. See you afterwards. Break a leg."

Chief Quinn glanced at his watch and motioned for Moon and Stuart to join them. The press gathered around the podium as Chief Quinn and Mendoza stood before the microphone. Moon took a few steps back, focused her camera on the crowd, and started shooting.

"I'd like to thank you all for being here," Mendoza said. "As you know, we've been tracking The Rainy Night Stalker for several weeks, and we feel we're close to capturing him. I'd like to ask Detective Stuart Bauer to give you all the latest information we have and an updated description. In the meantime, we're asking all of you to keep your eyes and ears open. If anyone sees anything suspicious, please contact us immediately. Detective Bauer."

Stuart stepped up to the microphone. "As the district attorney said, we're close to catching the killer. We believe he is a white male in his late 20s or early 30s. This man is intelligent, strong, skilled with knives, and more than likely lives alone. There's a good chance he suffered at the hands of an abusive parent."

Moon stepped forward and handed Stuart a piece of paper. He unfolded it and read it.

"Another detail about the killer we know is this…"

Seth was in Clivesville at his cabin. He sat on his couch watching the press conference. He spotted the beautiful woman as she stepped from behind the detective at the podium and handed him a piece of paper. Seth sat straight up and rewound the broadcast. He hit play and watched her step in front of the camera again. He rewound once more, then hit pause just as she filled the TV screen.

"Well, hello gorgeous."

He hit play.

"Another detail about the killer we know is this. The victims' wounds have all been consistent with an attacker who suffers from very small or ambiguous genitalia. It's possible that he may have an undescended testicle. Much like Adolf Hitler, the killer may have a slew of below-the-belt issues. Low testosterone levels during the critical stages of development can result in a condition called micropenis. We will provide more information in the coming days. And as District Attorney Mendoza asked, if anyone sees or hears anything unusual, please reach out to him or Police Chief Quinn. Thank you."

Reporters raised their hands and shouted questions. Seth muted the TV and laughed.

"You don't know jack shit, asshole."

He rewound and paused again on the woman's face.

"I have a feeling we'll be meeting very soon. Yes. Very soon. In fact, I think I need to take a drive into town right now and check you out in person."

Within 15 minutes, Seth had parked his truck near the police station employee parking lot. He got out, walked around to the front of the police station, and melted into the crowd of reporters. And there she was. In the flesh. As the smug detective fielded post-conference questions, the lovely woman took photos of the crowd. He was captivated by the way she moved back and forth across the stage. He watched her hands deftly reach into a camera bag and switch lenses.

He imagined how those hands would look tied behind her back.

After fielding dozens of questions, Stuart glanced over at Mendoza who circled his index finger signaling he needed to wrap it up.

"That's all for now, everyone," Stuart said. "We'll keep you updated as more information becomes available."

He walked to the back of the stage toward Moon and loosened his tie.

"How do you think it went?" Moon asked.

"We'll sink or swim together."

Matthew met Moon as she stepped off the back of the stage. His eyebrows were furrowed, and he stood with his hands on his hips.

"What is it?" Moon asked.

"I was watching one of the TV crew's monitors. You were on TV."

"That's the point of a press conference."

"No, you specifically were on TV. You stepped forward, and the cameras captured you handing a piece of paper to that detective. Everyone watching the broadcast saw you, including the killer."

"We're doing everything we can to identify and capture this guy."

They headed toward her car in the employee parking lot.

"You don't understand. You just put yourself in danger," Matthew said.

Moon stopped walking. "We have to try. I have to try to stop this guy."

"Why you?"

"Because it's my job." She got in her car and slammed the door shut. Just then, Matthew got in on the passenger side.

"What do you think you're doing?" Moon asked.

"I want to know why you're taking such unnecessary risks.

There's got to be a reason."

"Many years ago, I made the conscious decision to allow this kind of evil to enter my mind. You know that I can see things, hear things, feel things—terrible things. I didn't ask to be this way, but I knew if I was to live with this gift, I wanted to dedicate my life to listening to victims. They describe their deaths to me, sometimes in gruesome detail. I see things that no one would willfully want to see. And it is never pleasant. And it has changed me. But it was still my choice to try and help these victims in any way I can. I have an edge, an advantage. How can I not use it to help the police capture these monsters? This is who I am and what I do."

"That's not the only reason."

"What are you talking about?"

"There's something else. Something you've never really talked about."

"I don't understand what you're trying to get at."

"You never talked to me about your parent's murders," Matthew said. "I just knew you were twelve when it happened."

"There's not much to say. A man broke into our house and shot them. That's it." Moon turned the key in the ignition. "Are we going to dinner, or what?"

Matthew reached over and turned the car off.

"Hey!"

"I want to hear everything."

"Why?"

"Were you in the house when it happened?"

Moon sighed. "Yes. It was the middle of the night. I woke up when I heard what I thought was glass breaking. I ran to my parent's bedroom to wake them. We heard a creak in the steps leading to the second floor. Mom told me to quickly get in the closet."

"So you hid there."

"Yes. I closed the closet doors and climbed into the wicker hamper. When the bedroom lights came on, I could see through the wicker weaving. I could see a man with a gun through the closet door slats."

Moon paused and studied the dashboard. Matthew waited for her to continue.

"I watched the man shoot my father in the head, then shoot my mother in the stomach. She didn't die right away. I watched the man cross over to my mother's side of the bed. She tried to move but couldn't. She fought him off as best she could, but he quickly overpowered her. When he was finished with her, he shot her in the head, turned the lights off, and left the house."

"He never knew you were in the closet."

Moon shook her head. "No. If I had made the slightest sound, he would have known I was there. He would have found me and shot me, too. I stayed in the hamper until the police came."

"Did they ever catch the man?"

"Yes. My father was the district attorney for the Eastern District of Virginia. The last case he worked on was prosecuting a man who was convicted of murdering his wife. The jury took an hour to deliver a verdict of guilty of murder in the first degree. He was given a life sentence. The man who killed my parents was that man's brother. 'Payback' he said at his trial."

Moon stared out the windshield. "There are certain moments in your life that become a part of you—details that you never forget. I went to my grandparents that night and cried into my pillow. I can still smell the pillowcase."

"And you still dream about that night."

"Yes."

"You know that there was no way for you to save your parents."

"Yes. I do know that."

"But you still feel guilty."

She studied Matthew's face. "Yes. I do."

"And you think if you can stop this killer from killing another woman the guilt will finally go away."

"I don't know." Her gaze drifted back through the windshield. "I don't know."

Chapter Twenty-Six

Seth climbed back into his truck and watched the blond man leave the woman's car and drive off in his own car. He then followed the woman as she pulled out of the parking lot, drove behind her for three blocks, and parked a few spaces behind her car on Beechwood Row. He turned off his ignition and rolled down the window. He watched as she entered a restaurant and was greeted by the blond man from the parking lot. They took a seat at a table beside the front window.

Seth gazed up at the night sky. It was one of those perfect summertime evenings. There wasn't a cloud in the sky, and it was 62 degrees—just this side of sweater weather. He pulled out his phone and checked the city hall and local police websites, but found no mention of the woman. He'd have to do some more digging. He watched the couple talk. Their faces glowed in the flame of the candle on their table. The woman placed her elbows on the table and rested her face in her hands as she listened to the man. She snatched a fresh flower from a vase on the table and held it to her nose. The soft light from the candle on the table made her exquisite face simply luminous. The erratic rhythm of the wavering flame sent the shadow across her face in perpetual motion. A noiseless flighty dance. She laughed at something the man said. Seth couldn't hear her laughter, but he longed to hear it in person.

After the couple finished dinner, Seth watched the man and woman leave the restaurant. They got in their respective cars and drove off. Seth started his engine, pulled out onto Beechwood Row, and followed them. He doused his lights as he followed them up the hill six blocks through the Southside Historic District. The residential area had been developed in the mid-1800s, and the large original high-frame houses in the Federal, Greek Revival, and Victorian style still stood. Even the trees were younger than the houses.

Seth watched them pause at a stop sign at the top of the hill. He saw that the road continued up another 20 yards before it curved into a private driveway. Seth parked his truck on Sixth Street and walked up the road, past the stop sign. He crept into the woods, slowly cat-walking his way along the side of the driveway that led to a large Victorian house.

The blond man had parked in the driveway, and his headlights spotlighted the garage door. Seth watched, unseen, about three feet from the couple as they lingered in her driveway. The man's car was still running, and both the drivers' doors were open. The couple stood in front of his car, illuminated by the headlights. With the garage door as a backdrop, the two looked as though they were on stage. "Harvest Moon" by Neil Young floated out from the man's car speakers.

"Can I have this dance?" the man asked.

The woman cocked her head, not sure if he was joking. The man held out his hands. The corners of her mouth edged up into a smile, and she stepped forward into his arms like a warm spoon into mint chip. As they danced, their faces spun from shadow to light. The man nuzzled her hair and softly sang into her ear about going dancing in the light and because I'm still in love with you. Seth shook his head. *What a sap. She can't possibly fall for this drivel.*

The man extended his left arm, and the woman twirled under it then turned to face him. They stopped dancing and stood still in front of one another. Seth felt the need to clear his throat but instead swallowed hard. The man hugged the woman, stroking her hair.

"I forgot how nice it is to be held by you," she said.

Seth watched the man cup the woman's face in his hands. They gazed into each other's eyes as if for the first time. The man's eyes scanned her face and settled on her lips. As the man kissed her, rage burned in Seth's stomach and rose like bile up the back of his throat.

"I should go, shouldn't I?" he said. "Or maybe stay?"

"Not yet, and not with Maisie here. Besides, you still have a lot to deal with."

"Understood. Hey, can I ask you a favor?"

"You can ask."

"Would you please postpone your morning runs, just until this guy is caught?"

"I already park under streetlights near entrances. Because I'm a woman, I have to clench keys between my knuckles when I take a walk, or carry sprays, or be escorted. I lock my car door when filling my gas tank."

"It's unfair, I know. And it's unfair of me to ask. But the truth is, women are being targeted. I care about you. I worry."

"Thank you for caring. I will think about it. Thank you for dinner. I had a lovely time."

"Me, too."

"Are you staying at the Hilton again?"

"Yeah. I'll head back tomorrow morning."

Seth watched, nostrils flaring. As the man and woman stood in the headlights cocooned in each other's arms, Seth turned abruptly and headed down the hill to the road. He ran 20 yards to the stop sign at the top of the hill, then backed into the woods beside the road. Seth watched as the man pulled out of the woman's driveway. As soon as the man's car paused at the stop sign, Seth pulled out his Ruger Mark IV with its suppressor. His left index finger whitened on the trigger. His face showed no emotion as he pumped several rounds into the car. He watched the man slump forward against the wheel. The car rolled through the stop sign and picked up considerable speed as it hurled down the steep hill until it crashed into a tree.

Seth raced back up the hill to the woman's house. He darted up the driveway, tiptoed across the small front yard, and melted back into the woods in front of her house. From there, he was visible only in silhouette. He could see past the yard and the wraparound porch into her windows without being seen. He watched the woman disappear into another section of the house. She reappeared with a mug in her hand, the teabag string spun and fluttered. She was in what appeared to be the living room. He loved the way she moved. She lit a fire in the fireplace and sat on a sofa. An older woman entered the room with a mug of tea and sat on a second sofa opposite her. He watched the women talk and laugh. That laugh. The woman had a thousand-watt smile. She was incandescent. *Yes. I will have her.*

Seth made a note of the address: *340 Heliotrope Lane.* He typed it into Google Maps and clicked on Street View. An image of a grand purple Victorian home appeared on the screen. He tapped the screen and tried to get the image to appear on all sides of the house, but it stayed on the front of the house. *No worries. I'll be back here again very soon.*

Seth rambled down the driveway and back down the road to the stop sign. He looked down the hill and saw that a police car had blocked the street and an ambulance was already beside the crashed car. Seth made his way down the hill. A crowd of onlookers swarmed like blackflies on the sidewalk a block away. A policeman stood in the street keeping those who had gathered at a distance. Seth joined the crowd.

"What happened?" Seth asked a man in the crowd.

"A guy crashed into the tree. He had to have been going pretty fast judging by what's left of the front of his car. Apparently, someone shot him."

"Shot him?"

"Yeah." He shook his head. "You expect that kind of thing in a big city, but not here."

"Yeah," Seth agreed. "What a shame. So, he's dead."

"I dunno. First a serial killer and now this. What's the world coming to?

Seth watched the EMTs extract the man from the crumpled car using the Jaws of Life. They strapped him to a gurney and loaded him in the back of the ambulance. Seth could see one of the EMTs hang an IV just before the doors closed. For the time being at least, the man was still alive. Seth walked back up the hill. He kicked a stone in frustration, then climbed into his truck and drove home.

Chapter Twenty-Seven

Stuart and Chief Quinn stood near the door of the hospital room. The only sound in the room was the deep, rhythmic gasps of the ventilator. Matthew lay unconscious in the hospital bed, leached of color. Stuart watched Moon stroke Matthew's arm as she sat beside his bed. Her eyes were red and swollen.

"Who would do such a thing?" Moon asked without looking away from Matthew.

Just then, Matthew opened his eyes, and with a weightless expression, cupped Moon's hand in his. Chief Quinn eyed Stuart and jerked his head toward the door.

"Nothing was stolen," Chief Quinn said to Stuart as soon as they were in the hallway. "It seems completely random."

"When was the last time you had a drive-by shooting in Clivesville?"

"Never."

"And a serial killer?"

"Never."

"Maybe it's not so random. Maybe Matthew was collateral damage."

"Could be. Maybe Matthew pissed him off somehow. Maybe the

killer wanted to send a message."

Moon came out into the hall. She punched her hands into the pockets of her oversized cardigan. "I'm going to get some coffee. You guys want some?"

"No, thanks," Chief Quinn said. "I've got to get back. You should get some rest. You've been here all night. You look like hell."

Moon massaged her neck. "I'm all right. I just want to be here to make sure he gets through the worst. The doctor said he got lucky—the bullets missed every major organ and his spine, and it's a miracle he wasn't killed when his car hit the tree. I'll see you guys tomorrow."

Stuart watched Moon walk down the hall. At one point, it looked as though she suddenly struck up a conversation with someone, but no one was there. He shook his head and blinked.

"Chief, can I ask you something?"

"Shoot."

"What's going on between Moon and Matthew? Are they an item? She doesn't really talk about him at all."

"They were together for a long time. High school romance and such. They were pretty crazy—always up to something. I'm 20 years older and went to school with her father. When you live in a small town where generations of families have lived, you get to know each other very well. Moon and Matthew at one time were the 'it' couple in town. Most likely to do anything. They encouraged each other to live life to the fullest, to swing for the fences. I remember we went gliding one time—"

"Gliding, as in the airplane?"

"Yeah," Chief Quinn said. "We were up in the glider doing loops."

"I didn't know you had your pilot's license."

"I don't. Moon was flying. She got all those licenses—hunting, boating, fishing, motorcycle, pilot's license. She was, she is, pretty fearless. You could say she has iron in her spine."

Stuart looked down the hall at Moon. "Really? So, what happened?"

"To the two of them? They graduated from high school and went to different universities. Life paths separated. I think they kept in touch for a while, but he met someone else and married her."

"Did she ever marry?"

"Nope." Chief Quinn smiled at Stuart. "I don't think it was because of Matthew, though. I just think she never found the right guy."

"Hmm."

Chief Quinn and Stuart headed out the door and into the hospital parking lot.

"What's with the twenty questions?" Chief Quinn asked.

"How do you mean?"

Chief Quinn gave him a side glance.

"I don't know what you're talking about." He folded a stick of Big Red gum into his mouth.

"I have eyes."

"It looks as though there's still something there—between the two of them. If what you say is true, that's a lot of history with someone to ignore."

"So she has a past with this guy. BFD. A past doesn't make a present or a future. Just saying. Besides, you've got an advantage over Matthew."

"What's that?"

"You're walking upright."

Stuart smiled. "Thanks, Chief."

At that moment, Seth was setting up a hunter's lean-to deep in the woods in the back of the Victorian house that belonged to the woman at the press conference. That evening, his belly hugged the damp ground as he watched her and the old woman through binoculars as they relaxed on the back porch. Seth had followed the woman from the day he first laid eyes on her at that press conference—as she took her morning runs, as she walked to the diner in the morning, as she ran errands around town.

The next morning, Seth sat in his truck on Sixth Street sipping a cup of coffee, waiting for Moon to leave her house. Finally, he spotted her car at the stop sign and watched her descend the hill into town. He drove up the hill and parked at the end of her driveway. He walked up to her front porch and peeked into the window. He watched the old woman enter the living room, climb the stairs, and walk down a hallway out of sight. He picked the front door lock and slipped inside the house. He spotted several sets of keys on a key holder on the wall just inside the door. He tried a few until he found the one that opened the front door. He closed the door and stepped back outside on the porch. He held a cigarette lighter under the key's teeth until the metal was covered in black char. He placed the key on a small wooden table on the porch. He snapped off a piece of Scotch tape and laid it over the key. He lifted the tape from the key. The charring left behind a perfect shadow image of the key's teeth. He pulled the lid of a tin can from his pocket and pressed the tape onto the middle of the lid. With sharp scissors, he carefully cut around the charred pattern on the tape making a spare key in less than two minutes. He opened the front door and tried the tin key. *Works like a charm.* He smiled at his own ingenuity. He wiped the charring from the original key and replaced it on the key holder. He closed and locked the door, then slipped the spare tin key into his pocket.

He walked back down the driveway and got in his truck. It was a sunny Friday morning. He decided to take a trip out to the Catskills and spend the weekend. He drove out of town and pulled onto Route 17 east. In just under two and a half hours, he parked near the Willowemoc Creek's lower section where it spills into Beaver Kill. This section of the stream was much wider than the rest of the stream measuring up to eighty feet in some parts. He found a large pool interrupted by fat riffles and runs. He lowered the tailgate and stepped into his waders. He pulled out his Orvis fishing rod, tied on a Panther Martin fly, and headed toward the stream. As soon as he stepped into the water, he could feel his shoulders lower and his stress levels decrease. He teased a few arm lengths of string from his spool and brought his left arm back above his head. With the flick of his wrist, he snapped the tip of the rod forward, and the string arced over his head.

Seth took great pleasure in casting his line. He believed that fly fishing was an act of meditation. Standing in the middle of the stream, he felt the power of the water surround him. The hypnotic loops of the line overhead relaxed his brain. Sunlight glinted off the fairy-like fly as it lit on the water's surface. With another flick of the wrist, the fly was launched overhead once again.

Spending a few days in the Catskills gave him time to ponder all the things he could do with the woman from the press conference. He could take her anytime he wanted, of course, but the sweetness of the anticipation was intoxicating. *I will have her eventually. But for now, I want to savor the thought of what she will look like naked. What will her screams sound like? What will her blood taste like?*

Seth smiled as he pulled the tip of the rod back and flicked it forward once more.

Chapter Twenty-Eight

oon heard a knock on the doorframe of her office door. She spun around in her chair to see Stuart leaning in the doorway.

"Come in. I thought everyone had gone home."

"Everyone has except the two of us. I was just heading home and thought I'd check in on you." Stuart walked toward Moon and leaned on her desk. "How long have you been doing this type of work—helping the police by communicating with the dead?"

"Several years. I feel like I'm doing good when I can give the police the clues they need to capture a killer."

"It seems you're working particularly hard on this case. Why? What makes this one different?"

Moon turned off her computer and stood. "When he killed Holly and nearly killed Matthew, it became personal."

"How is Matthew?"

"Much better. They released him over the weekend. He's back in Boston." She opened the bottom drawer of her desk and pulled out her purse.

Stuart walked with her to the elevator. "No leads came in after the press conference, not that I expected them to come pouring in."

They stepped into the elevator, rode up to the first floor, and out the back door into the employee parking lot.

"Can I interest you in some dinner or a drink?" Stuart asked.

"I'd love to, but I think I'll head home, take a bath, and turn in early. See you in the morning."

When she pulled into her driveway a few minutes later, she noticed the house was dark. It wasn't like Maisie to stay out late without letting her know where she was going. Moon entered the house and clicked on a few lamps in the living room. She headed toward the kitchen and saw that the back door was open. Moon turned on the kitchen light and stood in the doorway. She listened to the nonstop harmonica chord the wind played through the screen door. She leaned against the doorframe and watched Maisie. The rails of the rocking chair thumped out a lazy rhythm as they moved back and forth over the wooden floorboards. The flame from the citronella candle on the small wooden table beside her elbow gave the shawl around her shoulders an amber glow. Her gaze was focused on a point somewhere in the night sky.

"I'm home," Moon said.

Maisie turned in her chair. "I didn't hear you come in."

"I'm getting some tea. Want some?"

"That sounds nice."

Moon lit the burner under the kettle and got down two mugs. She lowered tea bags into the mugs and went upstairs to change into yoga pants and a T-shirt. She returned to the kitchen just as the kettle began to whistle. She poured water into the mugs and bumped the screen door open with her hip. As soon as she stepped onto the porch, she saw the ghost of her father sitting on the railing.

"What are you doing here?"

"Hello to you, too."

"I'm sorry. I didn't expect to see you."

"Hugh and I were just talking," Aunt Maisie said.

"What's going on? What's wrong?" Moon said as she handed Maisie her mug.

"Thank you." Maisie cupped her hands around the mug and cast her gaze back up at the sky where the trillions of stars and planets created a milk-splattered dome. And the Milky Way—a 45-degree splash smack in the middle of it all.

"I've lived in this house all my life," Maisie said. "I've always been happy here."

Moon sat down in the rocker beside her. She regarded her beloved aunt, her one remaining living relative, and her heart swelled. Certainty unfolded inside her the way morning light pours into an eastern room. "How long have you got?"

"She always was a smarty pants," Hugh said.

Maisie shook her head. "Never could pull one over on you. How long have you known?"

"Just now. You're pensive. Dad's here. It made sense."

"I went to the doctor last week. A routine checkup. I had been having, well let's just say I've been having bathroom issues. They ran some tests. I got those results back yesterday. They called me in for more tests. I knew before they said the words. The cancer is back."

Moon took a deep steadying breath and placed her hand on Maisie's arm. "Okay, what's the game plan?"

"To behold these lovely stars and appreciate every last minute I have here."

"What did the doctor say?"

Maisie's eyes left the sky and found Moon's face. "Stage four colon cancer. The PET scan confirmed that the cancer has metastasized to nearby organs and my bones. Chemo would only prolong things. And I've done the chemo-radiation dance before. No more. Besides, the doctor said the amount of radiation I had the last time may have weakened my heart. Chances are, I might not even survive the treatments this time around. I've decided to let the cancer run its course."

"How long?" Moon asked.

"The doctor said the timing is very unpredictable. It could be a few weeks. A month at the most. I'm sorry you lost Holly, and soon, me. It's not fair that you have to deal with all this all at once, but that's how things work out sometimes." Her eyes returned to the sky.

Moon wiped a tear from her cheek. "Okay. Do you have any last-minute bucket list items we need to check off? A trip to Hawaii? A Latin lover?"

"You always want to do more," Hugh said. "I know I did."

"Are you in pain?" Moon asked.

"No. The doctor gave me plenty of pain meds."

Moon turned to her father. "Does it hurt?"

"What?"

"Dying."

Maisie and Hugh laughed.

"It's as easy as falling asleep."

"What's it like?"

"I'll try to put it this way," Hugh said. "Have you ever seen a snow-capped mountain chain reflected in a clear glacial lake? Or the sunrise over the ocean, or maybe the purple heather-covered hills of Wicklow, Ireland—something so beautiful it literally takes your breath away? It's like that. The beauty you experience is breathtaking. The purpose of death is release. A return to our essence. A homecoming of sorts. When the soul abandons the body, it's freeing. It's as though you can breathe for the first time. And the love you feel is profound. It's all about love."

"I'm happy with my life, Moon," Maisie said, "and I'll be happy with my death. The fact is, we're all born with an expiration date. None of us are getting out of here alive."

"There's a positive side to death," Hugh said. "Nothing puts things into perspective quite like facing your own mortality."

Maisie nodded. "I've lived a very happy life. Now I want to accept and embrace this last stage of my life."

"You don't have to fear death, Moon," Hugh said. "I should know. The fact is, you aren't ever going to lose us, because we're soul mates. We're a part of a soul group—you, me, Maisie, Mom, Grandma, and Grandpa, as well as others you've been with in past lives and those you've yet to meet in your future lives. We'll always be together. We help each other. We're all like the leaves on a particular branch of a tree. We die then we all return in new bodies. We're all works in progress waiting for our next revision to hopefully complete the lessons we need to learn on our way."

"On our way to where?" Moon asked.

"Perfection. Enlightenment. I've progressed since my murder. I've pondered the lessons I needed to learn in that life. This time around, I came back as a girl named Mallory Broderick. I'm 22 years old and live in Galway, Ireland."

"Wait, I don't understand. You're here."

"My soul is here on this porch, but my body is asleep in my new flat over there."

"How is that possible?"

"Funny thing about time and space, Einstein had it right. It doesn't exist. Get this, your mother is my best mate, Grace."

Moon shook her head.

"It's a lot to take in, I know," Hugh said. "Life seems so fragile, and death so final, but it's not. And there's one thing that's stronger than death. It's love. Love is never lost. Not even in death."

Hugh turned to Maisie. "I know I was a real rock in your under-wear. I apologize for that. We'll be right here to help you through your passing. You don't always see us, but we're around. Now, I've got to go. Big day tomorrow. I get my acceptance letter for the NUI Galway Law School."

"Law school again?" Moon said, laughing.

"What can I say? I adore the law. Love you, baby. Take care, Maisie. See you soon."

"Not if I see you first," Maisie said with a wink.

Hugh shot Maisie a finger pistol and a wink then vanished.

Moon sat back in the rocking chair and sipped her tea, trying to take it all in. When her cup was empty, she stood and headed toward the door. "I'm making dinner. What would you like? How about breaking the rules and having dessert for dinner?"

"Anything you make would be fine."

That night, Moon made fettuccine alfredo, diet be damned. She went over to the record player in the living room. The needle dropped on an album, and John Denver's sensitive and earthy voice flooded the room like a tonic. They opened a bottle of red wine and savored every mouthful. They talked about the old days and laughed until their sides were sore. While Maisie headed upstairs, Moon put the leftovers in the refrigerator and did the dishes. She plucked a book from the bookcase in the living room, turned off the lights, locked the doors, and went upstairs. She poked her head into Maisie's room.

"Just checking to see if you were asleep."

"Not yet. Come in."

Moon entered and pulled a chair from the corner of the room and positioned it beside the bed. She sat down and opened the book. She sat back, crossed her legs, and began to read. She brushed her hands over the soft finger-worn pages as she read.

"When I wrote the following pages, or rather the bulk of them, I lived alone, in the woods, a mile away from any neighbor, in a house which I had built myself, on the shore of Walden Pond, in Concord, Massachusetts—"

"This house suits you," Maisie said.

"It does. I've always been happy here. I imagine I will always live here."

"I've spoken to my attorney. Sometime this week, he'll meet with us so I can transfer the deed to the house to you. It's just less to worry about afterward. I also want to go to the bank and add you to my bank account. My will states that you get everything I own, so that makes things easy."

Moon studied her lap. "I'm going to miss you so much—your cast-iron concoctions, watching you sit in the dirt in the middle of your garden, Glen Campbell or Johnny Cash on your record player—"

"Now your record player."

"I don't know what I'm going to do by myself in this big house. I have my friends and my job. But sometimes… I am just so lonely."

"You'll be all right. If anyone can take care of herself, it's you."

Maisie closed her eyes. Moon continued to read into the night. She paused every now and then to watch Maisie sleep. It was soothing to see her chest rise and fall, her long gray braid in a soft coil on her chest. The Tiffany-style lamp on her nightstand cast muted colors of red, yellow, blue, and green onto her white nightshirt sleeves. Moon wanted to capture that moment in time, to fix it in her mind forever, but she watched as the future encroached and the present slipped away.

The window was open, and the cool breeze sucked the curtains against the screen then billowed them into the room perfuming the air with the clean scents of Tide and Downy. The cacophonous chorus of buzzes, chirps, and trills made by the male katydids, crickets, and grass-hoppers all trying to serenade females until the first frost of autumn vibrated the air. Every now and then, a screech owl sounded her even-pitched trill often referred to as a "bounce song." It sounded like the whinny of a tiny horse. In 1845, Henry David Thoreau described their call as "the most solemn graveyard ditty, the mutual consolation of suicide lovers remembering the pangs and delights of the supernal love in the infernal groves … Oh-o-o-o, had I never been bor-r-r-n."

Time, Moon thought. It is priceless, though it costs nothing. You can spend it, but you can never own it. And you can't keep it. Once it's lost, there's no getting it back. It's gone forever.

She remembered a time when Maisie sat beside her bed. Moon had had a bad flu one winter as a child. To check for a fever, Maisie would press the back of her finger against her forehead—a sensation Moon loved. Maisie read her bedtime stories every night until she fell asleep in her chair.

Moon stood and stretched her back. She closed the book and placed it on the chair. Then she leaned over and kissed Maisie's forehead. She turned off the lamp and went down the hall to her room. Before she entered, she glanced back down the hall at Maisie's door. She walked across her bedroom to the dresser, took out her PJs, and headed to the bathroom. Moon stepped into the shower and let the hot water pound her back as she wept.

Chapter Twenty-Nine

Moon hated the summer. Never mind the fact that summer is the most dangerous season in terms of violent crime. She hated the heat. It made her edgy, grumpy. She longed for the cooler days of fall.

She decided to visit a few of the fields where the victims had been found. It was a long shot, but she thought that maybe she would pick up something. She drove to the field off Whiskey Hollow Road where Margaret Bender had been found. She parked her car along the road and looped her camera bag over her shoulder. She paced back and forth across the field. The grass was brown and dry and the air was thick and still. For a second, she longed for rain to cool things down, but immediately realized what that meant. Finding nothing, she uttered a few swear words and headed back to the car. While buckling in her seatbelt, the metal scorched her thigh. More swearing ensued. She drove back out onto the highway, and twenty minutes later pulled onto Hardscrabble Road, where they had found the body of Rachel Mariner.

She parked her car and hitched up the hill. At the top, she took a moment to catch her breath in the shade of a tree. Heat slithered into the shade as her eyes scanned the landscape of dead grass. The once verdant field dotted with daisies that had reminded her of a Van Gogh painting was now brown and lifeless. Sunlight shivered in the haze. As she paced a grid pattern across the field, the sun pressed down onto her shoulders and the top of her head. Her cheeks and the bridge of her nose tingled. She cursed herself for forgetting to wear a hat. The wind kicked up sending dust into her eyes and her hair. She felt grit between her teeth.

Moon squatted next to the ground and picked at the grass. She looked up and saw Rachel Mariner standing in front of her about fifteen feet away. The last time Moon saw her in that field beside the hay bale, she was naked. This time, Rachel appeared to her wearing jeans and a white T-shirt. Moon stood and took a step toward her.

"Rachel. My name is Moon McFadden."

Rachel held up her hand as if to stop traffic. "I know who you are and what you want. I wish I could help you, but I can't. I didn't know who he was." Rachel studied the ground. "You saw what he did to my body."

"Yes. I also know that you kicked him. You scratched him. Did you see his face?"

"No. He wore a mask that covered his head and neck. If I had to guess, I'd say he was a white man, about 30. I saw that he had a tattoo in the middle of his chest."

"A tattoo?"

"Yeah. Right over his heart. I've never seen that image anywhere, so I don't know what it means. It looked like an upside down cow's udder. It was orange."

Moon got out her phone and Googled images using several different keywords.

"It had the shape of a delicious apple," Rachel said, "or an upside down pear, only it was orange. And there were nubs along the top."

As soon as Moon typed "orange upside down cow's udder," an image popped up on the screen.

"Oh, my God." Moon showed Rachel her phone. "Is this the image of his tattoo?"

"Yes. That's it exactly. What is that?"

"It's called a nipple fruit."

At that, Rachel shook her head and looked up toward the sky. "I'm sorry I couldn't be more help. As soon as he came toward me, I kicked him as hard as I could. I don't remember anything after that."

"You've been a big help, Rachel."

"You'll get this guy?"

"Yes. I promise."

Rachel nodded once then vanished. Moon stood alone in the trampled field. She glanced up at the clear blue sky and wondered where Rachel's soul had gone—the ether of some unseen distant world. Moon dialed Stuart's number to tell him about the tattoo, but the call didn't go through. She raised her phone and spun around hoping to get a signal, but there were no bars.

"Great. I just had service."

As she turned to walk toward the road, she noticed that a man had stepped into the field. He looked to be about her age. He wore denim overalls without a shirt.

"Hello," she said.

"Hello, yourself."

He cocked his head and observed her. She realized she was alone in the middle of the country with no way to call anyone for help. The man took a few steps toward her along the path down to the road blocking her way.

"What's a good-looking girl like you doing out here in this field?"

"I work for the police and the district attorney," she said, hoping that would be enough to make him back away. That was not the case.

She put her hand in her left pocket and found her car keys. She pinched them firmly between her thumb and index finger. She could open the car door faster than if her keys were in her right hand, but she could still use them as a weapon.

"Is this your field?" she asked. "I didn't mean to trespass. We're following up on the murder investigation."

She walked in the direction of the road taking a wide berth through the field. He stepped in front of her. He looked around, then looked back at her and smiled.

"Where are you off to in such a hurry?" he said, moving toward her.

"Stop right there."

"I'm just being friendly." He closed the gap between them.

She tried to run past him, but he blocked her way. He took another step toward her. They stood a few feet apart, face to face. He unbuckled the straps of his overalls one by one and let them slip off his shoulders. He looked her up and down, then licked his lips.

"Don't bother hollering, cause no one's going to hear you." The man took another step forward, closing the gap between them. "This will go a lot quicker if you don't put up a fuss."

"Don't come any closer."

The man chuckled and swallowed as though his mouth watered. He was so close, Moon could smell his rancid breath. She flipped her camera gear from her hip to her back. She dropped into a fighting stance with her hands in imaginary boxing gloves shielding her face. Her legs were wide with her left leg forward and her right leg back. With her knees bent, shoulders up, and her chin tucked, she faced the man. As he took another step closer, she rotated and drove her body forward forcing the heel of her palm up into his nose. The sound of the man's nose breaking was like the sound of punching Styrofoam. His head snapped back, and she delivered another quick jab to his throat. He staggered backward with his hands covering his bloody face. He lost his footing and stumbled to the ground.

Moon ran as fast as she could down the hill. She jumped in her car, locked the door, and started the engine. She slammed her foot on the accelerator and spun away from the ditch. She was going away from the direction of the highway, but that didn't matter. She wanted to put as much distance between her and the field as possible. She shivered, not from being cold, because the inside of the car was like an oven, but because of the adrenaline coursing through her veins. As soon as she stopped shaking and could breathe normally, she pulled off to the side of the road. She plugged the GPS into the cigarette lighter and punched in her address. Once on the highway, she dialed Stuart.

"Hey, Moon."

"Stuart, I think we got a break. The killer had a tattoo in the middle of his chest. A very unique tattoo. It was an image of a nipple fruit."

"You've got to be kidding me."

"I am not. I'm not familiar with tattoo parlor protocol, but I imagine there aren't that many from here to the Catskills. Something that unique would be custom-made. Assuming he had it done locally, the artist would definitely remember it and hopefully have their client's contact information."

"I'll get a list of all the tattoo parlors here and in the Catskills and start making phone calls. Well done, Moon."

"Thanks."

She leaned back in her car seat, turned the A/C on full blast, and let out a sigh. As soon as she returned home, she headed straight upstairs and into the shower. Afterward, she came back down and poured herself half a tumbler of whiskey. She sank onto the sofa and took a long drink. Her phone rang.

"Moon," Stuart said, "I found the tattoo parlor. The Inka Dink in Liberty. The guy who did the tattoo wasn't there, but the manager looked at the record books and found that tattoo. They got the guy's New York

State driver's license. The name on the license is Bruce Altman."

"Yes! That's our killer. We got him!"

"Not so fast. Although any good tattoo parlor would ask for identification, the man gave the artist a fake. I checked with the New York State DMV for a Bruce Altman. There are only three records of a Bruce Altman having a driver's license in New York—none fitting our killer's description. One is a 16-year-old kid in Saugerties who just got his license. The second is a 78-year-old man living on Long Island in Dix Hills. The third Bruce was 56 years old and died this year from pancreatic cancer."

"Crap." Moon took another long drink of her whiskey. "Hey, call the parlor back. If they have a record of that tattoo, they should have a day and the approximate time it was done. See if they have a surveillance camera in the parking lot. If not, see if there are other stores in that area that have cameras. Maybe we can see if someone pulled up and went inside around that day and time."

"Good thinking. You're firing on all cylinders today."

"Blind squirrel and acorn come to mind. Let me know what you find out."

She hung up, finished her drink, and laid down on the sofa.

Chapter Thirty

As soon as her head hit the sofa pillow, Moon was asleep. It was like a warm pool she dove into. Her phone startled her awake, and she answered it in a daze.

"Moon, it's Stuart. A few Liberty officers went to The Inka Dink to take a look at the surveillance footage of their parking lot."

"And?" She sat up.

"One man pulled up in a black Dodge Ram and went inside around the time the artist made that specific tattoo. Get this—whoever the driver was didn't want us to read the license plate. It was covered in mud, but the rest of the truck was clean."

"Interesting."

"The officers said he was a white man in our killer's age range," Stuart said.

"Assuming the driver has a license in New York State, we should be able to see all the black Dodge Rams currently registered. That will give us a name and address."

"That list shouldn't be too long. We'll compare it with the intersecting circles on our map. I'll keep you posted."

Moon stood and went upstairs to her bedroom. She splashed water on her face in the bathroom, then sat down at her desk in the bedroom and opened her laptop. She scanned the deed to the house that had been transferred to her and saved the document in Dropbox. She pulled open the top drawer of the desk, pulled out a wooden cigar box, and flipped it open. Inside were items that were most important to her. A stash of treasured things. She fingered through her birth certificate and Social Security card and photos of her parents, and a few black and white photos of her grandparents with the wavy edges. She picked up a skeleton key that had belonged to her mother. The bow was twisted into a Celtic knot. Whatever the key had opened was long gone, but Moon kept the key anyway.

Moon picked up Daniel's class ring and slipped it on her middle finger. It was from Yale, class of 2012. The insignia on the top of the ring was an open book with Hebrew characters. Yale's motto is "Urim and Thummim," which is Hebrew for "Lux et Veritas." Above the open book were the Latin words, "Lux et Veritas," meaning "Light and Truth."

With a heavy sigh, she slipped the ring from her finger, kissed it, and placed it back in the cigar box along with the folded deed. She came downstairs, poured herself an after-dinner coffee, and joined Maisie on the back porch. Moon balanced on the wooden railing with her back against the column. She caught the setting sun through the trees, and the light was so golden she wanted to cry. Sitting there on that porch with Maisie sipping coffee, Moon fervently wished that nothing would change, that they could spend every evening like that. The sunlight bathed the back porch crimson. She watched the gray shadow of her aunt's chair advance and retreat across the porch floor in the warm light as she rocked. Maisie's skin was as translucent as onion peel. It looked so thin and papery that you could push a knitting needle straight through it and not draw blood.

"You can feel that summer's almost over." Maisie hugged her warm mug to her chest with one hand and leaned back. Her free hand ran across the arm of the rocker—the wood was worn velvety from generations of palm rubbing. "There's a sharpness to the air. The sound of the wind in the trees is different, too. The leaves sound crisper like they're drying up, getting ready for the change." She closed her eyes and recited:

"That time of year thou mayst in me behold,
When yellow leaves, or none, or few, do hang
Upon those boughs which shake against the cold,
Bare ruined choirs, where late the sweet birds sang … "

"I know that one." Moon sat in the rocker next to her. "Sonnet 73. It's not just about the change of season but the coming of old age."

Maisie nodded. "I'm looking forward to meeting Shakespeare."

"I think I'd like to meet Amelia Earhart. Now there's a woman with a story to tell."

Maisie shivered and brought her wrap closer around her shoulders.

"Are you ready to go in?" Moon asked.

"Yeah. I feel the change in my body. Death seems to be coming on fast."

Maisie shifted forward in the chair but didn't stand.

"Do you need me to help you get up?"

"It appears so."

Moon stood and put both their mugs on the railing, then pulled Maisie to her feet.

"Thank you. I'm good for now. Catch me if I start listing."

"I'll get you to bed then lock up."

As Maisie shuffled toward the screen door, Moon gathered the mugs from the railing. She stopped suddenly and looked across the backyard into the woods. She could have sworn she saw something move. She put the mugs back down, leaned over the railing, and looked closer. She walked down the steps off the porch and across the yard toward the woods. She stood on the edge of the woods and squinted, studying the forest floor. The setting sunlight reflected off something. She took a step forward.

"You coming in?" Maisie called through the screen door.

"Yeah." She backpedaled away from the woods. She hurried across the yard and up onto the porch. She picked up the mugs and opened the screen door, but just before she went inside, she glanced back at the woods once more.

Moon placed the mugs in the sink and guided Maisie up the stairs. By the time they got to the top, it was all Maisie could do to totter down the hall and into bed. Moon pulled a thick quilt from the cedar chest at the foot of the bed and spread it over her blanket.

"I'll call Chief Quinn tomorrow and let him know I'll be working from home the next few days."

"You don't have to do that."

"I want to. Be right back."

Moon went downstairs and locked the doors. That night, she double-checked that every door and window was locked and secured. She snatched a book from the bookcase in the living room and flicked the lights off on her way back upstairs. As she entered Maisie's room, the odor of sickness hung thick in the air as the cancer consumed her aunt. Moon pulled up the chair and opened the book. The house seemed to hunch quietly around them.

"I'm getting used to these bedtime stories." Maisie settled back against the pillows, smoothing wrinkles from the quilt. "It's nice when you can let go and lean into the dying process. Parents take care of the children who eventually take care of the parents. This reverting to babyhood is really a beautiful life cycle. You'll see. Now, what have we got tonight? More Thoreau?"

"Robert Frost."

"I'm looking forward to meeting him, too. Did you know he received so many honorary degrees in his lifetime that he had his academic hoods made into a quilt?"

"I didn't know that."

"He often said that he heard everything he wrote—that poetry was first a matter of sound. You know, he wasn't a New Englander. He was from San Francisco."

"A fish out of water. We have that in common."

"A fish out of water can learn how to run. He moved to New England as a boy and made it a point to listen to the sounds, the cadences, and rhythms of the New Englanders' daily speech. Taking the time to observe what was right in front of him served him well."

Maisie winced.

"Can I get you something?" Moon asked. "Are you in pain?"

"No. I'm okay." She closed her eyes, took a deep breath, and sighed. "Which one will you read me?"

Moon sat back in the chair, crossed her legs, and opened the book. Maisie tucked the quilt under her chin.

"The first one I'll read tonight is titled 'Now close the windows.'

Now close the windows and hush all the fields:
If the trees must, let them silently toss;
No bird is singing now, and if there is,
Be my loss.
It will be long ere the marshes resume,
It will be long ere the earliest bird;
So close the windows and not hear the wind,
But see all wind-stirred."

Moon closed the book and paused for a moment. The bedroom walls were bleached pale in the twilight. She slid forward on her chair with her elbows on her knees and watched Maisie sleep. Her frail body was cocooned in cotton, her feet pigeon-toed under the quilt. Moon observed Maisie's chest rise and fall, rise and fall. Watching her sleep was fascinating. Like watching a baby sleep.

Moon blinked. She had no idea how long she had been watching Maisie. Outside, the wind had picked up, howling them into the night. She squinted her eyes. Did Maisie's chest rise or had it remained still? Her breath had become so shallow, she doubted her aunt could blow out the candles on a baby's cake. Moon hadn't noticed before how skinny Maisie had become. She looked so peaceful. Moon gasped. Amazingly, it appeared as though Maisie's wrinkled face had transformed into smooth, almost glowing skin in the soft lamplight. Moon shook her head, sat back, and opened the book again.

"Okay, this one is called 'Reluctance.'

Out through the fields and the woods
And over the walls I have wended;
I have climbed the hills of view
And looked at the world, and descended;
I have come by the highway home,
And lo, it is ended."

Moon felt a hand on her shoulder.
"Moon."
She turned and saw Maisie standing beside her. She turned back and saw Maisie's body on the bed.
"Oh, no."
"It's okay. No, it's much better than okay. I feel no pain at all. In fact, the only thing I feel is a profound sense of love. I need you to do

something for me. I need you to go to bed now. You'll need your rest. You have an emotional day ahead of you. Go on now."

Moon closed the book and placed it on the chair. She stood and turned to say something to her aunt, but she was gone. She leaned down and kissed Maisie's forehead, turned the lamp off, closed the window, and went to bed. As she lay in bed, her breath vibrated, fighting back tears. She stared at the ceiling and listened to the wind shriek so loudly it drowned out even the coyotes' howls.

In the book of Ecclesiastes, King Solomon said, "Greater is the day of death than the day of birth." That sounded strange to Moon at first, but the Chassidic masters explained that the soul's departure from the physical body like this: "At the time of a person's passing, it is the culmination of his or her mission in this life—the sum-total of his or her achievements in this life come to fruition. The physical body may have broken down, but spiritually, the moment of passing is when we're at our highest potential."

Moon wiped the tears from her cheeks. She smiled at the thought of Maisie meeting Robert Frost and Shakespeare. And Walt Whitman. And for Maisie, repurposing a verse from *Leaves of Grass* for her …

There was never any more inception than there is now,
Nor any more youth or age than there is now,
And will never be any more perfection than there is now,
Nor any more heaven or hell than there is now.

In between the gusts, Moon could hear the trees creaking as they swayed. She smiled and thought about Maisie's freed soul as her eyelids fluttered and closed.

Chapter Thirty-One

oon woke, and in that false awakening, where she was awake but still dreaming, she heard Maisie downstairs humming and brewing fresh coffee. Moon blinked twice, and the lucid dream drifted away, leaving behind a silent house. She lay in bed, fingers meshed behind her head. Moted sunlight spilled into the room. It was like any other day, but it wasn't. From that day forward, her life would never be the same. Not that she thought it would necessarily be good or bad—just different.

Moon knew that Maisie was right. This would be a very emotional day. Of course, she knew this day would come. Thinking of her last days with Maisie, Moon realized that regardless of whether she had a day or a month or a year to spend with her and say all the things she wanted to say before she passed, there was never be enough time. There were never enough words.

Moon dressed and went down the hall to Maisie's room. She half expected to see her sitting up in bed, but her body lay as it had the night before. She pulled the lightbulb chain in her closet and found a note that Maisie had written clothespinned to the hanger of a lavender dress.

This is the dress I'd like to be buried in. It should look good with the funeral makeup. Don't bother with shoes. You wear them if you like. If not, donate them or give them a toss.

Moon took the dress from the closet and laid it on the bed. She crossed the room to the dresser. She opened Maisie's jewelry box and found another note.

Don't even think about burying me with jewelry. Most of this I got from my mother. I want you to have it all. I mean it!

Moon looked over her shoulder at Maisie's body and shook her head. She closed the jewelry box and went downstairs. She put the kettle on to boil and dialed David Bannister. She had just enough time to finish a cup of tea before she heard a knock on the door.

"I'm very sorry, Moon," David said, wiping his feet on the welcome mat.

"Thank you, David. She's upstairs. Her dress is on the bed."

David stepped aside while a young man pulled a gurney through the door.

"Moon, I don't think you've met my apprentice, Seth Woodman. Seth, this is Moon McFadden."

"Moon McFadden," Seth repeated slowly.

"Pleased to meet you, Seth."

"Have we met before? You look so familiar."

"I don't think so."

She extended her hand to shake his. As soon as she touched him, her knees buckled. She brought her hand to her mouth as though she might get sick. David caught her by the arm and brought her over to the sofa.

"Are you okay," Seth asked.

"Yeah. I'm so sorry. I don't know what happened. I think I've been trying to keep a stiff upper lip for Maisie's sake, but maybe this is finally getting to me."

"That's to be expected." David sat beside her. "Can I get you some water?"

"No. I'm fine. I'm going to head outside and get some fresh air. I'll make a few phone calls from my car. When you're through, I'll lock up and follow you over to the funeral home."

Moon got in her car, started the engine, and turned the A/C on full blast. She called Matthew and Stuart and left them both messages. She watched as Seth and David guided the gurney out the front door and into the back of the hearse. Moon locked the front door and drove slowly behind them. She pulled into the funeral parking lot and spotted Stuart leaning against his car. She got out and walked over to him.

"What are you doing here?" she asked. "You didn't have to come."

"I got your message. I thought you might like some company. If not, I'll take off and check in on you later."

"No, come in with me. That's very thoughtful."

They entered the funeral home, and David showed them to the conference room.

"Let me get Maisie's file, and I'll be right back," David said.

As soon as David left the room, Stuart reached under the table and took her hand. She laced her fingers in his but kept her eyes on the table. She could feel her cheeks flush. As soon as David came back, she released Stuart's hand and clasped hers together on top of the table. David took a seat and pulled a plastic cigarette from his shirt pocket. He pinched it between his lips.

"David, is everything okay?" Moon asked. "You look stressed."

David plucked the cigarette from his lips. "I'm on my fifth day without smoking. Believe it or not, it helps to have this." He flashed the burnt tip. "I can't tell you how many times I tried to light this stupid thing. The truth is, I'm having one of those days and it's not even 10 o'clock. We've just embalmed a six-year-old boy who found his father's gun last night. These cases, working with children, really affect me. I call these awful days my 'Rum-a-Dumb' days. I go home and make myself a rum and Coke so strong, it makes me dumb. My wife can tell I've had a Rum-a-Dumb day as soon as I get out of the car and walk across the driveway. As soon as I step inside the front door, she's there with my rum and Coke. I take it to my La-Z-Boy and try to forget."

"I'm so sorry," Moon said.

"It's part of the job. Anyway, we're here for Maisie. She had already made her funeral arrangements and paid for everything in full." David handed her a pen. "You just need to sign these papers."

Moon signed wherever David pointed on the pages, then handed back the pen. She and Stuart stood and headed toward the door.

Moon shook his hand. "Thank you for all your help, David."

"It's my pleasure, Moon. See you at the wake."

Stuart walked her to her car, and they stood beside her door. They looked at each other for an awkward moment. She thought he might kiss her. She wanted to kiss him, too, but then realized where they were and what she was doing. He seemed to read her mind, and the seriousness of the moment was defused with laughter.

"Hey, listen, I know you've got a lot on your mind, but I'd love to treat you to dinner tonight. If you're not up to it, I'll completely understand."

"Dinner would be nice."

"Great. At the risk of sounding old-fashioned, I'll pick you up at seven."

Moon stood beside her open car door and watched him walk across the parking lot to his car. She breathed in the spicy scent of his cologne as it lingered in the air for a moment before a gust of wind picked it up and carried it away.

As soon as she got in her car, her phone rang.

"Moon, it's Matthew. I got your message. Where did I find you?"

She watched Stuart pull out of the parking lot. "I'm at the funeral home." A sudden wave of guilt washed over her.

"I booked a flight into Ithaca that lands at around 3:00 p.m. I should get to the hotel in Clivesville around four. I'd like to take you to dinner if you're up to it. If not, I completely understand."

"I'm sorry, Matthew, I have plans tonight."

"That's okay. I'll see you at the wake."

"Have a safe trip."

She stared at her phone. She was startled by the sound of a sharp knocking on her window and rolled it down a little.

"Are you okay?" Seth asked. "I saw you sitting in your car and wondered if you needed anything."

"No, Seth, I'm fine. Thank you. Just taking a phone call."

"Okay, then."

She rolled up her window, turned the key in the ignition, and left the parking lot. Instead of going home, she left town and headed for the countryside. She needed to think. She spent hours crisscrossing country roads. In the late afternoon haze, the rolling hills appeared to her as though she was steering a ship along a calm sea. Farmland was divided into fields of varying crops like the patches of a huge quilt. Regarding the fields, she thought of the victims and wondered where the killer was at that moment. As she drove up a hill and rounded a curve, she suddenly faced a menacing wall of clouds like full-rigged galleons that rose high above the western horizon with the promise of rain.

Chapter Thirty-Two

oon waited for the doorbell chime to fade before she opened the door. Stuart stood in the doorway, smiling.

"You look beautiful," he said.

"Thank you."

Moon glanced at herself in the entryway mirror. She wore a V-neck charcoal gray dress that hugged her body. A black pearl pendant necklace swayed as she moved. She snatched the keys from the keyholder and locked the door behind her. Stuart opened his car door, took Moon's hand, and guided her into the passenger seat. He drove through town and out onto the highway.

"Where are we going?"

"I thought we'd take a little drive. I found this restaurant about 30 minutes outside of town. It always helps me to get out of Dodge for a little while whenever things get emotional."

"Good idea."

Moon relaxed into the seat. She rolled down the window and let the wind flow through her hair. They pulled into the gravel parking lot of a wooden Alpine-style restaurant. Red geraniums tumbled from each of the window boxes. Stuart parked by the front door, and they went inside. Large wooden beams ran the length of the dining room ceiling. Soft candlelight cast a warm glow and gave the room a romantic feel. The hostess led them to a table beside a large fieldstone fireplace that cupped a crackling fire.

"Is this okay?" Stuart asked.

"More than okay. I never knew this place existed."

The waitress handed them menus and filled their water glasses. Stuart snapped his menu shut. "Shall I order wine?"

"Sure."

He turned to the waitress. "A bottle of Blaufränkisch, please."

"Very good sir." The waitress nodded and walked away.

"I don't think I know that wine."

"It's a pretty popular wine in Austria."

Moon wiped imaginary crumbs from the tablecloth and cleared her throat. "I don't know why I'm so nervous. We see each other every day."

Stuart leaned forward to say something, but the waitress returned with the bottle. He leaned back and smiled at Moon while the waitress uncorked the wine and poured them both a glass. Moon handed her the menu.

"I'll have the Wiener Schnitzel," she said.

"The same," Stuart said.

As soon as the waitress walked away, Stuart laughed. "I'm nervous, too." He leaned forward again, and with his elbow on the table, he rested his chin in his hand.

"What's your favorite color?" he asked.

"Light blue, the color of a cloudless sky. Why do you ask?"

He smiled. "I like you, Moon. I think you're beautiful and sexy and funny. I've never met anyone like you. I thought I'd take you to dinner, not only to take your mind off things but to get to know you a little better outside the office."

"Well, you covered a lot of ground in a few short sentences."

"So, what do you think about my sentences?"

Moon smiled and took a sip of wine. "I think you're handsome and sexy and very intelligent."

"Sexy was second."

"Many times, it comes in first. I know almost nothing about you."

"Okay, you know what I do. You know I was married. No kids. I grew up in an Austrian family. My ancestors fled from there in 1933 a year and a half after Hitler came to power. Unfortunately, many of our family stayed behind, thinking things would get better. They ignored the signs until it was too late. Most of them were murdered in the Holocaust. I grew up in Manhattan on the Upper East Side in a brownstone my great-grandparents bought. Three generations of our family lived there together. After high school, I went to college and got my master's degree. After I married, I got a job as a cop in D.C. You pretty much know the rest."

He leaned in close to her face and kissed her neck. She could feel the warmth of his skin. He leaned back and took a sip of wine.

"I want to be truthful," he said. "Once we catch this guy, I'm not sure where I'll be—if I'll be back in D.C. or sent to work with the team in New York City. I don't know what my future holds. All I know is how I feel about you."

"I understand. And I'm okay with not knowing. It's sort of fun not knowing."

They raised their glasses to one another.

After dinner, Stuart drove Moon home. She held Stuart's hand and thought about what it was going to be like when he walked her to her door. Standing face to face as she fumbled for her keys. Waiting for the first kiss. She glanced at him and sensed he was thinking the same thing. As soon as they pulled into the driveway, Stuart's headlights flashed against another car.

"Someone is here," she said. "I don't recognize the car."

"Stay here."

Stuart parked the car, got out, and approached the stranger's car. The door opened and Matthew stepped out.

"You again," Matthew said. He stood with his legs apart. His eyes, two warnings. Moon got out of the car.

"Matthew, what are you doing here?"

"I texted and called you several times, but there was no answer. Given the fact that you have a serial killer on the loose, I got nervous and came here to see if you were okay."

"I'm so sorry. My phone was off."

"I didn't know your evening plans involved him."

Stuart took a step forward. "Who died and left you in charge of her social calendar?"

"Great choice of words on a day like today, asshole." Matthew snickered. "It's amazing the stuff you can find on Google. You're the cop who killed that unarmed kid. This would be a last-chance assignment for you, am I right?"

Moon stepped in front of Stuart. "Matthew."

Stuart chuckled and stepped from behind Moon. "Right, I know you, too. You're the almost divorcé who's sniffing around your hometown trying to recapture your high school glory days, including the high school sweetheart, am I right?"

"Suck my dick willingly."

Stuart lunged at Matthew and punch-shoved him in the chest sending him back a few steps. Matthew charged toward Stuart and returned the shove with one of his own. In a flash, the two men locked their arms around each other and tumbled onto the front lawn.

"This is ridiculous!" Moon screamed at the men as they rolled back and forth across the lawn. "Stop it. I said stop it!"

Matthew and Stuart continued to roll, slapping and growling, until a cold spray of water snapped them out of their fury. They looked up to see Moon standing in front of them with a garden hose in her hands.

"That's enough," Moon said. "I'll give you both the hose again if you don't stop right now and grow up." She pointed the nozzle at them.

Stuart pushed Matthew away and stumbled to his feet. Matthew stood and brushed the grass from his wet shirt. He walked toward Moon, and she placed the hose on the ground.

"I just wanted to make sure you were all right." Matthew stood beside her but kept his eyes on the ground.

"As you can see, she is fine," Stuart said, adjusting his grass-stained tie.

Moon raised her palm to Stuart. She turned to Matthew. "Thank you, Matthew. It was very thoughtful of you to check in on me. I'll call you in the morning?"

"Sure."

Matthew got in his rental car and shut the door with more force than was necessary. He maneuvered around Stuart's car and backed out of the driveway. Stuart took a step toward Moon and let out a whistle.

"That was awkward. He was kind of a jackass."

"So were you."

"Oh, right." He backpedaled toward his car. "I'll see you tomorrow."

Moon took a step toward Stuart. "Wait. I'm sorry."

Stuart shook his head and opened his car door. "No problem."

"Thank you for dinner. I had a nice time tonight, despite the ending."

Stuart backed out of the driveway and sped off into the night. Moon unlocked the front door and turned on the light. She hung the keys on the keyholder and closed the door with a heavy sigh.

Chapter Thirty-Three

The following evening, Moon stood beside Maisie's coffin in the flower-crowded chapel at the funeral home and greeted guests. She spotted Matthew as he inched his way toward her. When he finally got to her, he wrapped his arms around her and held her.

"I'm so sorry," he whispered into her ear.

"Thank you," she whispered back.

She closed her eyes and let him hold her. She clung to him as though he was saving her from a sinking ship. A few moments later, Chief Quinn and Stuart made their way to her and hugged her, too.

After the wake was over and the guests had gone, Moon spotted Matthew sitting alone in the back row of the chapel. She leaned over the casket and kissed Maisie's forehead one last time. As David entered the side door of the chapel, Moon walked over to him and reached out her hand to shake his.

"David, thank you. Everything was perfect."

"I'd like to think Maisie would have been pleased."

"She would have been thrilled."

"How are you holding up?"

"I'm okay."

"Good. Try to get some sleep. I'll see you at the church in the morning."

David held the chapel door open for Moon and Matthew, then saw them out of the funeral home. Matthew walked Moon to her car.

"Can I buy you dinner and/or a stiff drink?" he asked.

"Both, please."

"I know just the place. Follow me."

Just before she got in her car, Moon turned her head back toward the funeral home. She could have sworn she saw Seth's face in the window looking at her just before the lights inside went out and his face dissolved into the darkness.

Moon followed Matthew to Gallagher's Steakhouse five miles outside of town. They were seated at a table that overlooked the valley. It was a warm night, and the sun had long set behind the hills. The fixed oculus of the moon as it rose above the hills cast its blue-white radiance over the valley. The fireflies were putting on a light show—the males flashing to the females who then responded with a glow of their own. In the dark, their dating ritual appeared like small fireworks rhythmically shining in soft waves, first here then over there. It was as if the valley was breathing.

"Can I start you off with a drink?" the waiter asked.

"May I have a Manhattan, please?" Moon asked.

Matthew smiled and nodded.

"Would you like that with bourbon or rye?"

"Bourbon. Woodford Reserve if you've got it."

"Very good. And you, sir?"

"The same."

After the waiter left the table, Matthew turned to Moon and whistled. "Nicely done."

"It's been a long day with an even longer day tomorrow. Wine just won't cut it."

"Listen, I want to apologize for last night. I let my temper get the better of me. I had no right to be jealous."

"I'm sorry I wasn't more upfront with you. And I do appreciate you looking out for me. That means a lot to me."

"Maybe I'm just more emotional than normal these days. Coming toe to toe with death will do that to you."

Moon reached across the table and took his hand. "You gave me such a scare."

He kissed her hand. "I'm okay. The wake was nice."

"Yeah. It was a good turnout," Moon said. "I had no idea Maisie knew that many people."

"Everyone loved her, as they love you."

Matthew gave her the look, and Moon immediately felt her face blush. The waiter came to the table with their drinks.

"Thank you," Matthew said. "We'll need a minute."

He raised his glass. "To Maisie."

Moon raised her glass and took a sip. She studied her cocktail glass for a moment. The amber liquid glowed in the table's candlelight. She had no idea what the future would hold, but at that moment, Matthew's presence was safe and comforting. And that was just what she needed.

"How are things going back in Boston?" she asked.

"Julie is gone. The house has only been on the market for three days, and I already have an offer. They accepted my counteroffer this morning. I can't bring myself to stay there. She brought almost nothing with her, declaring that Donald has 'quite an antique collection.' I'll put a few pieces in storage then have an estate sale next weekend for the rest. What doesn't sell, I'll donate. I'll close on the house, and that will be that."

"What then?"

"I'm still deciding. How are you doing?"

"I'm okay. I don't look forward to rattling around in that big house by myself."

"Something tells me you'll feel better about that in no time."

After they enjoyed their meal and lingered over dessert and an after-dinner drink, Matthew walked her to her car. They stood face to face. Moon looked up at the dome of stars that bowled over them as though they were inside the sky.

Matthew reached over and opened her car door for her. He noticed a stack of autopsy files in a cardboard box on her front seat.

"I don't know how you can look at those gruesome photos. The killer is somewhere out there, and you stare at his handiwork."

"I don't stare. I study. The evidence is there. I just have to let it in."

Matthew nodded. He rested his hands on his hips and shifted his weight to his right leg. "How are you feeling? Are you okay to drive home? I can still produce a breathalyzer."

He pulled out a pocket-sized breathalyzer attached to his keychain.

"You weren't kidding. Why do you have one of those? How much do you drink?"

"Not much at all. After a number of my father's DUIs, he lost his license for a while. Right then and there, I made it a point to never go down that road. Besides, I have way too much at stake with my business to ever jeopardize it by having one too many drinks. Whenever I go out, I double-check that it's safe for me to get behind the wheel."

"Okay, let's have it."

"Wait, I have to turn it on." While he fiddled with the device, he straightened his back and stuck out his chest, movie-sheriff style. He hoisted his pants up above an imaginary pot belly. "Now, Miss, I'm going to have to see your license and registration."

"Oh, officer, I only had one drink." Blink, blink. "I swear."

He sucked air through his teeth. "We'll see about that, Miss."

He handed her the breathalyzer.

"I've never blown anything before. Well, that's not entirely true." She winked at him, blew into the device, and handed it back.

"Looks good, .03."

He blew into it and read the BAC level. "Same. We'll have to do better next time."

He tucked the keychain in his pocket and held her car door open. He kissed her and closed her door once she was behind the wheel.

"Look out for deer and get home safely. Text me when you get home."

"Okay."

"I'll pick you up in the morning."

As she sat behind the wheel, she suddenly felt smothered. *Seriously, did he really think I couldn't get home safely on my own or that I wasn't going to look out for deer?*

Moon watched Matthew get in his rental car, feeling more confused than ever.

Chapter Thirty-Four

A chilly fog had descended during the night. By the following morning, the town was still blanketed by the tiny water droplets and suspended ice crystals that formed the billowy clouds. Fog forms under stable conditions and clear skies. Moon gazed out her bedroom window and smiled, remembering how much Maisie loved foggy mornings. They always led to the promise of a perfect sunny day.

Moon dressed and lingered on the back porch, feeling bereft, fishing for solace and a sense of a new belonging. There were no bites that morning. She rocked slowly, sipped her coffee, and let her mind wander for a while. A waiting stillness hovered over everything. She half expected Maisie to materialize and sit down next to her. Just then, a monarch butterfly fluttered up onto the porch and settled on the arm of Maisie's rocking chair.

Moon's mouth dropped open, and she gasped. Fall was right around the corner. Monarch butterflies spent April through September in New York, then flew back down to Mexico for the winter. They are native to tropical environments and prefer hot temperatures and high humidity. Butterflies aren't active at all on cold, foggy mornings. Its presence was impossible. She knew it had to be Maisie.

Everything in the universe is made up of energy. Earth is at a much lower vibrational frequency relative to what untethered souls experience. Those souls can learn to move objects in our world by lowering the vibrational frequency of their "hands" to move a solid object. They can materialize objects in our world such as coins or feathers or a book by focusing the energy of that thing and bringing it into being.

One of the many ways untethered souls make their presence known is through children and animals. They remind us that the three-dimensional world we live in is only the tip of the iceberg, and that our true existence is so vast and meaningful.

Moon glanced at her phone for the time.

"No more procrastinating," she said to the butterfly. "It's time I get going. You know I'll do your funeral right."

The butterfly slowly lowered her wings then brought them up again. A graceful nod.

"Okay, then. I'll see you later."

Moon stood and went inside and rinsed her cup in the sink. She heard a knock on the front door. She walked through the dining room and opened the door.

"Are you ready?" Matthew asked.

"As ready as I'll ever be."

"You look beautiful. Is that too weird to say on a day like today?"

"No. It's never a bad time for a compliment."

He opened his car door for her, then got behind the wheel. He drove to Saint Catherine of Bologna Parish and parked in the lot on the side of the church.

"I'm going to head around to the front," Moon said. "See you inside."

Moon stood at the top of the front steps of the old stone church and greeted guests as they entered. A parade of loss. She could hear the choir as they sang Gregorio Allegri's "Miserere" as the congregants took their seats. Moon spotted the hearse as it drove past the front door on its way to the side entrance, so she followed the last of the guests inside. She made her way down the center aisle and spotted Matthew. She extended her hand out to him. He stood and walked hand in hand with her to the front of the church. They sat together in the first pew. Moon admired the flowers on the altar that had been brought over from the funeral home. She closed her eyes and let the music wash over her.

Weak sunlight trickled through the stained glass with what little consolation it could give. David and Seth wheeled the casket in through the side door at the front of the church to the left of the altar. The priest came from the sanctuary behind the altar carrying a silver holy water bucket and aspergillum.

"Please stand," the priest said to the congregation.

A white folded pall was draped over his arm. He walked over to the casket and sprinkled it with holy water. He placed the bucket on a small table beside the casket and draped the pall over the casket. After the priest finished his blessing, David and Seth positioned the casket in the center aisle just before the altar. The priest walked up onto the altar and began the funeral mass.

Moon took in the familiar church—the church she had known since she had moved to Clivesville. Maisie enrolled Moon in the Catholic school across the street from the church for 7th and 8th grade before she was transferred to the city's high school on the Northside across the river. That church had been the cornerstone of that neighborhood for generations. As an adult, Moon rarely went to mass anymore, only going with Maisie on Christmas and Easter. It was the music and the ritual and not necessarily the dogma that she appreciated.

From the first pew, Moon glanced back at the large columns

planted throughout the church that seemed to stand sentinel over the congregation. A few of them showed signs of wear, their cracked paint looking like veins. The columns rose up to meet the arched ceiling, ornately decorated with gold leaf ivy branches. The walls were painted in a soothing buttery yellow, and when the sun warmed the stained glass windows, the inside of the church glowed.

She turned back to face the altar and watched as the priest lifted the lid of the brass thurible and sprinkled in incense. He lowered the lid and lifted the thurible by its long chains, stepped down from the altar, and stood in front of the casket. Smoke poured through the thurible's holes as it swung over the casket and then toward the congregation. The sweet-spicy scent of frankincense, an ancient gift from the Magi, lingered in the air.

After the mass, Moon and Matthew walked behind the casket through the side door. They got in the car and followed the hearse to the cemetery. As Moon and Matthew walked toward the tent that had been erected over the open grave, she thought about when she had walked with Matthew to his mother's grave. They joined the rest of the mourners who stood beside the priest as he read scripture passages and spoke kind words. After the priest had finished, he closed his Bible and shook Moon's hand.

Moon and Matthew got back into his car and followed the procession of the other cars slowly along the narrow dirt pathway through the cemetery toward the exit. She looked out over the 200-year-old cemetery and spotted Maisie. She was leaning against an angel tombstone. She smiled and waved at her, and Moon waved back.

They were back at the house in less than twenty minutes.

"Can I help do anything for the luncheon?" Matthew asked, pulling into the driveway next to the catering truck.

"No. The caterer is doing everything including cleaning up. I certainly wasn't going to cook. Maisie was the cook. I can make tea, boil pasta, and open a jar of sauce. That about covers it. Besides, that's what take-out is for. If it was up to me, I'd store my sweaters in the oven."

They stepped up onto the front porch.

"I just want to get through this afternoon," Moon said. "The truth is, as soon as the last guest and the catering crew leave, all I'll want to do is lock the door behind them, climb into bed, and pull the covers over my head."

They entered the house into a flurry of uniformed waiters. Moon had expected mourner's black, but the caterers had transformed the living and dining room into a serene space with white linen, vases of white roses, calla lilies, and gladiolas, and groupings of white pillar candles. It was beautiful. Magical. Even the waitstaff wore white. Along one wall, a buffet table had been set up with chafing dishes filled with hot food. The caterer, JoAnne Richland, checked her clipboard and nodded directions to her crew.

Moon crossed the room to JoAnne.

"Everything is stunning," Moon said. "Thank you."

"It's my pleasure. You wanted the feel of an appreciation and a celebration. And thank you for the playlist." She nodded to one of her crew standing beside the record player. He placed the needle on "Saturday Night Fever" by The Bee Gees. "Playing Maisie's favorite songs is a sweet touch. Relax. Eat something. Grab a drink. Leave everything to me."

As people arrived, waiters emerged from the kitchen carrying trays of hors d'oeuvres and drinks. Moon and Matthew stood off to the side with a glass of champagne.

"Maisie would have loved this," Matthew said.

"Yes. It's so strange that she's not here. The other day, I came home from work, and the house was dark. I promised myself I'd get one of those lamp timers, but I wouldn't know how to program it."

A voice from behind her said, "I could help you with that."

Moon turned and saw Seth standing beside her.

"I'm sorry, I couldn't help but overhear."

"Thank you, Seth. That would be great."

"I can pick up a nice one and install it this week sometime. Just let me know when."

"Okay. I appreciate that."

"It would be my pleasure. In fact, I think I have an extra one of those timers at home. I can stop by tomorrow morning before work and install it if that works for you. It won't take but a minute."

"That sounds good. I'll see you in the morning—around 7:30?"

"You can bet on it."

Chapter Thirty-Five

After the guests had given their condolences and said their goodbyes and the caterers had cleaned, packed up, and gone, Moon closed and locked the front door. Matthew leaned into the dining room from the kitchen.

"Can I get you a cold beer?"

"Love one. Meet me on the back porch. I'll be right out."

She grabbed the cat food bag and pitcher of water and shouldered her way through the screen door. It slapped shut behind her.

"Let me help you with that," Matthew said.

He put the beers on the railing and took the cat food bag from her. He followed her out to the cat shelter winding his way through the hungry cats. They filled bowls with food and water and walked back to the house. She brought the cat food and pitcher back inside, then joined Matthew on the porch. She leaned against the railing and scanned the backyard. The sun had set behind the horizon, and Jupiter and the stars blinked on. She picked up her beer bottle and ran her fingers across the white paint on the porch railing. It was now her railing. Her house.

"I love this time of day," she said. "Whether it was good or bad, the day is over and done. A brand new one isn't here yet, but it's about to begin. I'm standing in time's doorway, contemplating both."

They settled down into the rockers.

"How are you holding up?" Moon asked.

"Okay, I guess. I have to figure out my next move."

"Will you stay in Boston?"

"There's nothing holding me there."

"True. Where do you want to go?"

Matthew shrugs. "It depends. My life is a 52 pickup. Our fund has done well. I can afford to uproot and start a new life—even retire or start a new profession if I want to. What I do now depends on a few variables."

"Like what?"

Matthew took a long drink. He leaned forward on his elbows and looked up at the sky.

"When my parents divorced when I was in high school, I made a promise to myself that I would never get a divorce."

"Never say never."

"Yeah. It was tough. I knew my parents still loved each other very much. I could see that they both regretted the divorce, but neither one of them had the guts to do anything about it. Dad died loving Mom. While going through his house after the funeral, I found that he had taken out a sizable life insurance policy in her name six months before he died."

"He showed her that he loved her. Beyond the grave."

"See, the thing is, they could have been together. They could have grown old together. Mom said she would have reconciled, but Dad was too proud. Or stubborn, or stupid. Maybe his problem was that he could never find the words to tell her that he was sorry and that he loved her. In any case, he died never having found those words."

Matthew placed his beer bottle on the floor, leaned in close to Moon, and took her hand in his.

"I don't want to make that same mistake. I want to find the words. Moon, it's always been you. I have always loved you. We've shared so much together, and I still love you after all these years. So much time has passed, and I know neither one of us is the same person we were all those years ago. But I want to get to know the person you are now. I want to know if there's a chance for me—for us."

"Matthew—"

"Let me finish. I was thinking of moving back here."

"Moving back to Clivesville? Why?"

"You know why."

"Listen, Matthew, you know how I feel about you, but don't move here for me."

"I don't understand. I thought you'd be happy that I was closer."

"The truth is, you're 'in it' right now. You're technically still married. Even after your divorce is finalized, you have to let some time pass before you make any big decisions. You have to get on your own two feet emotionally before you can think about another relationship. This would be frying pan-fire stuff. You should move somewhere because it's advantageous for you. You should be somewhere that will help you move through this difficult time. If we get together again in the future, it will be because we're both in a good place and because it was meant to happen."

"I understand. And you're right, but it's not as though we just met. You've been in my life in some form or another since we were kids. I want to make a move that sets up my future. Sure, there's a chance things might not work out. After all this time, I doubt our friendship would be in jeopardy. That's why I'm willing to give romance a chance. I might just get everything I've wanted since I was 17. The question is, at some point do you think you might be willing to take that chance, too? We've always had shitty timing. Maybe we can get it right this time."

There was a knock on the front door. Moon stroked his hand, then let go and walked into the house. She passed through the dining room and opened the front door.

"I wanted to see how you were doing," Stuart said with his hands behind his back. "You've had a long day." He presented her with a bottle of bourbon.

"1792. Very nice."

"I thought it might help."

"You again," Matthew said, stepping into the living room. After an awkward moment of silence, he nodded resignation. "Well, I'll take off. I'll call you later."

Matthew hugged Moon a little longer than the average goodbye warranted. As soon as the front door had closed, Moon walked over to the curio bar.

"Can I offer some of this?"

"Absolutely. Listen, Moon, I want to apologize for the other night. I'm not normally the jealous type. I guess there's something about Matthew that gets under my skin. Maybe it's the fact that you guys have a history. That's no excuse for my behavior."

"Thank you."

She took two tumblers from the curio bar cabinet and poured each of them doubles. He followed her through the kitchen out onto the back porch. They stood side-by-side at the railing and gazed up at the stars.

"It's a beautiful place you have here. It's so quiet."

"It will be quieter now without Aunt Maisie. Gregory Peck was devastated over his son's suicide. He once said, 'I don't think of him every day. I think of him every hour of every day.' That's how I felt about my parents for many, many years. That's how I think I'll feel about Maisie for some time to come."

"There's no way around grief. You have to slog through it. Trust me, I know."

Moon nodded. "I already miss the sounds of the house—Maisie playing her Glen Campbell albums. She would belt out 'Wichita Lineman' at the top of her lungs. God, that woman was a terrible singer." Moon laughed thinking of her aunt. She took a sip of the bourbon and let it linger on her tongue a moment before she swallowed. "I miss her laugh and her stupid jokes. I miss her sticking her head in my bedroom nearly every night and saying in her sing-songy way, 'Good night, sweet girl.' Those are my four favorite words."

Moon held onto the railing and leaned back. "There's no one left in my family. Both my parents were only children, and Maisie never had kids. It's a strange feeling, like climbing the last rung of the ladder or stepping onto the front line in war. The buck stops with me. I'm 32 years old and certainly didn't need Aunt Maisie's help or support, but it was always nice to know it was there."

"I felt the same way when my parents passed. My mother died eight years ago. My father had been in an Alzheimer's home on Long Island. I'd take the train up from D.C. every week to visit him, but after a while, he didn't recognize me. Then when I came, it only confused him. When I reminded him of who I was, he felt guilty and got very upset that he had forgotten his own son. Twenty minutes later, he had forgotten our conversation and asked me who I was. I used to stop on the way to pick up his favorite ice cream—maple walnut. I began to tell him that I was Stuart the Ice Cream Man. He was so happy to see me, and that made me happy. He passed away a week before my sister was murdered."

"Oh, Stuart. I'm so sorry."

"Thanks. It's been a shitty year."

"Yeah." She studied the amber liquid in her glass. "The truth is, I feel lost. I don't know how to process this aloneness. Many times, I find it's easier to isolate." She took another sip of bourbon. "My life is like this quirky old house on the outside of town. I've always felt as though I was on the outside, never quite fitting in. I have a feeling I'm destined to spend the rest of my life alone."

"How can you say that?"

"I move my lips. I push out air."

Stuart set his glass down on the railing and moved in close to Moon.

"I've been meaning to tell you something. It's about your lips." Stuart leaned in and kissed her.

She let him kiss her, at first softly, then with more passion. She took a step back.

"I don't think this is a good idea," she said. "We're involved in this case, and I don't want to complicate things."

"You're probably right. This is a bad idea. We've already confessed how we feel about each other."

"True."

"So, it's already complicated." He nodded. "Listen, I know you've had a tough day, so I won't take advantage. I'll call you in the morning. I'll see myself out." He downed his drink and kissed her again. "Good night, sweet girl."

She watched him step through the screen door and listened to it wheeze as it fluttered shut behind him. She heard the front door close and Stuart's car engine turn over. She listened to the silence and waited for his car to make its way down the driveway and then accelerate above five miles an hour when he reached the road.

She looked back out over the backyard. The scream of a red fox echoed through the woods. A path of silver moonlight stretched across the grass. She followed the light up to the unnervingly large moon and to the immensity of the stars beyond and suddenly felt helpless—swallowed by something much larger than herself.

Chapter Thirty-Six

Seth rang Moon's doorbell. As he waited for her to come to the door, he fiddled with the tin key in his pocket, knowing he could enter her house whenever he pleased. Moon opened the door, and he smiled at her.

"Good morning," Seth said.

"You're perky. I take it you're a morning person. I just made coffee. Would you like some?"

"Sure. Black." He pointed to the floor lamp beside one of the sofas. "Is this the lamp?"

"Yes. Thank you for doing this. How much do I owe you?"

"Nothing. It's my pleasure, really."

Moon disappeared into the kitchen, and Seth got to work. He rotated the dial on the timer to p.m., unplugged the lamp from the wall socket, and plugged it back into the device.

"What time would you like this to come on?"

Moon joined him in the living room and handed him a cup of coffee. "I think maybe 5 o'clock. Once it's on, can I turn it off manually, or do we have to set a time for it to turn off?"

"Either. Whatever you like."

"I don't plan to be out too late. I'll just turn it off when I get home."

Seth plugged the device into the wall socket and stood. "You're all set."

"That was easy."

Seth sipped his coffee and looked around the room. "You have a beautiful home." He spotted a photograph on the fireplace mantel and walked over.

"Is this you?" He pointed to a picture of her at the wheel of a large sailboat.

"Yeah." Moon joined him. "It was taken in New York. I was on a 40-foot schooner sailing up the Hudson. I asked the captain so many questions about steering, he finally asked if I wanted to try. I think he just wanted to shut me up."

"Precocious."

"I'm afraid so."

When Moon's back was turned, Seth planted a small camera in the silk plant on the mantel.

"I should let you get to work," he said. He gestured to his cup. "I can drop this in the sink."

"No, I've got it."

She took the cup and walked toward the kitchen. Seth spotted her open purse on the dining room table. He dropped a tiny tracking device into her purse just before she turned and walked back into the dining room.

"I'm on my way out, too," she said. "Thank you, again."

"My pleasure, Moon. Have a nice day."

Seth exited out the front door and got in his truck. He drove down the hill and turned onto Sixth Street. He drove a few blocks and parked. He switched on the tracking device and watched the beep as

Moon made her way down the hill into town.

That afternoon, he watched Moon's movements on an app on his phone. The beep showed the device as Moon left work and spent time on Beechwood Row. It showed Seth that Moon had gone to the farmer's market behind the clock tower in the town's square, to the library, and then back to the police station.

Later that evening, Seth opened his laptop on his coffee table and poured himself a drink. He watched the beep that showed Moon was in her car on her way home from work. As soon as Moon entered her house, he activated the camera on the mantel. He watched her take off her blazer and drape it over the back of the sofa. She disappeared into the dining room. He had wanted to plant another in the kitchen, but one camera would have to do. He listened to her hum an unfamiliar tune off camera. After a while, she came back into the living room with a cup of tea. She plucked a book from the bookcase and went to the sofa. He watched her take a sip of tea and place the cup on the coffee table. She opened the book and laid down on the sofa with her feet toward the fireplace allowing him to see her face.

"What are you reading?" he muttered.

Seth zoomed in on the book cover. "*The Devil in the White City.* That's a good one. Of course, H.H. Holmes's technique was altogether different than mine, but I do admire his style. If he were alive today, I'm sure he'd think the same things I do—that he would enjoy looking at you and imagine what your screams sounded like."

After a few minutes, Moon tented the book across her chest and fell asleep. He zoomed the camera in on her face. He touched himself as he watched her sleep. He zoomed the camera in further on her face and watched her softly breathe.

The next day at work, Seth popped his head into David's office.

"I was just going to grab lunch," Seth said.

David waved him in. "Have you seen this?" He pointed at the

television on the wall across from his desk. "These protestors have been at it all morning."

Seth came into the office and faced the TV. A large group of protesters had gathered in front of the police station. Some people shook their fists and shouted that The Rainy Night Stalker was still at large. Others carried signs that demanded Chief Quinn's resignation. Still others took the opportunity to protest on behalf of schools, Planned Parenthood, and their religious freedoms. One held a sign that read "And saying, Repent ye, for the kingdom of heaven is at hand! Matthew 3:2." Several women held signs that read, "Rainy Night Stalker, take us!" Others were selling Rainy Night Stalker T-shirts and umbrellas. Hours passed, and the crowd grew bigger and louder. And the TV cameras captured it all.

Watching the crowds pumping their homemade signs and shouting his name—The Rainy Night Stalker—gave Seth a sudden shudder of pleasure. His heart raced, and he swallowed hard. All those people had gathered outside the police station because of him.

"It's crazy." Seth smiled. He dropped the smile as he turned to face David. "Like I said, I'm heading out for lunch. Can I bring you back something?"

"Yeah, thanks. Turkey and Swiss on wheat."

Seth had to see the crowd for himself. He got in his truck and drove to the police station. He parked across from the front of the station. The shouting made him feel giddy. He got out of the truck and walked across the street. He spotted the TV cameras and joined the protestors in calling for Chief Quinn's resignation. Seth watched as a beautiful blond reporter muscled her way into the crowd to ask some questions. He moved in close to her, and they locked eyes. She thrust a microphone toward his face.

"Tell me, sir, why are you here this morning?" the reporter asked.

"I'm a concerned citizen," Seth said. "I want to know what the police are doing to capture this monster."

She nodded at the cameraman to keep rolling.

"How does this chaos make you feel?" the reporter asked.

"It makes me feel unsafe. I have read that the killer only targets women, but knowing that a murderous lunatic is out there somewhere makes me feel nervous. God knows who he plans to target next. It might even be you."

The reporter's breath caught, and she cleared her throat. "Can I have your name, sir?"

"Seth Woodman."

"Thank you."

"No, thank you for covering this."

Seth meandered through the crowd. He stood next to his groupies and gave them a hearty thumbs up. He continued nonchalantly through the crowd until he stood in front of a folding table selling Rainy Night Stalker merchandise. A wild-eyed fat man with long hair sat behind the table beside a metal cash box. He could have easily passed for Meatloaf in his "Paradise by the Dashboard Light" days.

"How much for the black T-shirt?" Seth asked.

"Twelve dollars."

"And the umbrella?"

"Ten."

"I'll give you twenty for both."

"Done."

Young Meatloaf took Seth's money, dropped a shirt and umbrella in a plastic shopping bag, and turned his attention to the next buyer.

With merchandise in hand, Seth crossed the street and got back into his truck. He drove around to the back of the police station and spotted Moon's car in the employee parking lot. He drove to her house and parked in the driveway. He crossed the porch and took out his tin door key. According to an article he read in the New York Times, only

30% of households had a home security system. This house was one of the 70% without one. *Stupid.* He slipped his spare tin key into the lock and opened the door.

He studied the framed photographs on the wall. He went through the dining room to the kitchen. He opened the cupboards. He removed all the knives and hid them in another drawer under the dish towels. He spotted a white ceramic cookie jar on top of the refrigerator with the word "Cookies" written in black cursive on the jar. He tacked a tiny black camera on the i's dot and angled the jar toward the center of the room.

On the way back through the dining room, he pulled a grape off the vine from the fruit bowl on the dining room table and popped it into his mouth. He went upstairs and down the hall to Moon's bedroom. He ran his fingers across her pillow. He sat on her bed, then laid down. He got up and went over to the dresser, picked up a perfume bottle, and dabbed his wrist with perfume. He opened the drawers and caressed her underwear. His fingers found something hard and metal. It was a canister of Mace spray. He slipped it into his pocket with a grin. Before he closed the drawer, he picked up a pair of panties and examined it. White, silky. He rubbed it against his cheek then tucked them into his pocket as well.

He crossed the room into her bathroom. He peeked in drawers and in the medicine cabinet. He took the opportunity to use the toilet.

"Winston Churchill said, 'Never pass up the chance to sit down or go to the bathroom.' I might as well do both."

When he was finished, he washed his hands and dried the sink with the hand towel. He headed downstairs. *Time to go. I shouldn't overstay my welcome. Although I'd so love to stay and linger a bit longer, I'll be back soon enough.*

Chapter Thirty-Seven

efore taking the elevator to her office in the basement, Moon popped her head into Chief Quinn's office. He sat at his desk, nodding at the person on the other end of the telephone receiver.

"Yes, sir. I understand."

He hung up and held his head in his hands.

"Are you all right?" Moon asked.

"Peachy. I assume you saw the crowd out front." Chief Quinn massaged his temples which served as a megaphone to amplify his voice. "For the love of God and all that is holy, this guy has groupies. Groupies! Nutjobs are out there selling Rainy Night Stalker merchandise."

"Yeah, I saw that."

"The whole world has fallen off its fucking axis. Sorry."

Moon held a hand up and shook her head.

"The press has started a countdown to the next forecasted rainy night. Two days. Unlike the last time it was supposed to rain and didn't, this time promises to be stormy. Speaking of storms, that was the governor on the phone, tightening my balls in a vise. He wants me to, in his words, 'wrap this up.' Oh, hey! Thanks for the guidance way up there in Albany, Gov. I'm only a simple-minded country bumpkin down here, so what the hell do I know? Apparently, I don't have the brains God gave a donut to have a single thought about wrapping it up all on my very own. Now that you've enlightened me, I'll get right on that. Prick. Sorry."

Moon waved him off again.

"Have you ever noticed that when an investigation goes flat, and there's nothing to go on, everyone involved starts turning on each other? They've got no one to blame, so they turn their ire inward—like a snake eating its own tail."

"I'm going to take a look at the photos I took of the crowd during the press conference," Moon said. "Maybe something will surface."

Chief Quinn nodded. "I'll head down with you. I've asked Stuart to request copies of all of the autopsy reports from Lloyd. We'll review each one of them again to see if there's anything we missed."

As they rode the elevator to the basement, the drone of the crowd outside bled through the walls. They paused before her office door.

"I'll let you know if I see anything," Moon said.

"Ditto."

Moon spent an hour looking at the photos, but the crowd noise was too distracting. She closed her laptop and leaned back in her chair.

A voice from behind her said, "Can I buy you a late lunch? Or a stiff drink?"

She swiveled the chair around. Stuart leaned against her door. "Thanks, but no. I think I'll take this home where it's quieter. I'll see you in the morning."

"I'll be the one with the bagels and hot coffee in my office."

"Sounds good." She stood, tucked her laptop in her bag, and walked toward the door. "Make mine an everything."

Within 15 minutes, Moon was sitting at her dining room table.

She opened her laptop and brought the loupe up to the monitor. She stared intently at the photos. The phone rang and she jumped. She dropped the loupe and it rolled on the rug under the table.

The landline only rang when telemarketers phoned. Maisie insisted they keep a landline in case of emergencies. Moon waited for the ringing to stop and listened for the machine to come on. After the beep, Moon heard static. She turned to look at the phone. Suddenly, she heard a voice. It was faint, but she heard it.

"It's me. It's Maisie. It's Maisie."

Moon ran to the phone. She saw that the number read "unavailable." Before she could pick up, the call disconnected. She pressed the button to play back the message.

"You have no new messages," the computerized voice said.

The message count read zero, but she clearly heard Maisie's voice. She stared at the phone for a moment then went to the kitchen to light a fire under the kettle. She dropped a teabag into a mug and went back to the dining room table. She picked the loupe up off the floor and continued to study the photos. She scanned each of the photos she had taken of the crowd at the press conference, enlarging sections of every one of the photos from top to bottom and side to side. When the kettle began to whistle, she stood and headed for the kitchen. Moon poured water into the mug and sat back down at the table to study the photos again. She stopped on one of the photos and enlarged it further.

"Oh."

She saw a man in the crowd waving as if he was waving to her as she took the photo. She enlarged that section of the photo even more.

"That's strange. Is that Seth from the funeral home?" She brought the loupe over his image. "What were you doing there? Who in the world were you waving at?"

A voice behind her replied, "I was waving to you."

Moon's eyes grew wide. She spun around in her chair. Seth. Her throat suddenly tightened. She tried to scream but couldn't. He cocked his head and smiled at her reaction. She picked up her mug and threw the hot tea in Seth's face, but he batted the mug away. She started to run toward the back door, but in an instant, Seth grabbed her and slammed her against the dining room wall. He wrapped his hands around her throat. Moon clawed at his hands and could feel herself start to lose consciousness. She raised her arm, turned her body, and brought the arm down across both of his hands releasing his grip. She immediately brought her elbow up into his face knocking his head back.

"Son of a bitch," Seth said, pressing his palm against his eye.

She drove her foot down hard onto his instep and thrust her elbow into his solar plexus. She ran toward the back door, but again she wasn't fast enough. He grabbed her shirt, lifted her, and threw her against the kitchen floor. She landed hard, knocking the wind from her lungs. She felt a searing pain and couldn't catch her breath. She was sure she had broken a rib or two, and her head was bleeding badly.

She pushed her body along the floor in an army crawl, but Seth calmly walked over to her and stepped on her spine forcing her body onto the floor. He knelt on her neck.

"How did I get in you might be wondering? I've had a key to your front door for some time now. You are so lovely when you sleep. I'm fascinated by the things you can do and the things you can see. It's pretty unnatural if you ask me. Given all you can see, you never saw me coming. Imagine that."

He grabbed her right wrist and forced her hand up between her shoulder blades, then knelt on her arm with the other knee. She tried to move but was immobilized. Moon tried to kick him by bringing her feet up to her butt.

"That's enough," Seth said. "I didn't want to have to do this."

He struck her on the side of the head to momentarily daze her long enough for him to get off her neck and back without her trying to escape. He held a stun gun to her back for what seemed like an eternity. Moon felt as though she was being electrocuted. Her body involuntarily arched away from the shock. When he removed the stun gun, she fell back down hitting her cheek against the floor. Seth knelt on her neck once more, pressing her face into the floor.

"I've had a ball watching you," he said. Moon could hear Seth's voice, but his words sounded watery and very far away. He continued, "As you know, all good things must come to an end. The good news is, the next phase of our relationship is about to begin."

He extended her left arm out straight and pulled it back away from the floor. She felt a sting and burning followed by a falling sensation as though she had separated from her body and was plunging into a black hole. She tried to say something, to plead with him, to appeal to his better nature if he had one, but her mouth refused to work. She tried to move her arms or legs, but she was paralyzed. She lay perfectly still on the floor, panting. Her eyes locked onto the linoleum floor her grandfather had installed in the 1950s. The pattern was of repeated diamonds in black, aqua, teal, and cream. The diamonds floated and began to swirl like the current in a river just before darkness closed upon her.

Chapter Thirty-Eight

oon woke in the dark, bound and gagged. Her wrists had been zip-tied behind her back. Her legs were spread apart, her ankles bound to the bedposts. She was naked and lay on her stomach on what felt like a bare mattress that stank of blood, urine, vomit, and sweat. Her nostrils prickled. The room was weighted with the dark brown smell of death. Her nose and throat were sore. Seth had stuffed a cloth into her mouth. She turned her head from side to side. As best she could tell, there didn't seem to be any furniture in the room besides the bed. She had to think.

She heard footsteps from somewhere in the house. They seemed to be coming from behind her, which meant the bed's headboard was against the wall opposite the door. The footboard was closest to the door. The first thing the person walking in the room would see would be her exposed genitals.

From somewhere in the belly of the house, classical music played. How long had she been unconscious? Time had thickened like wet cement. She felt nauseous. She took a deep breath and let it out slowly. Although the room was dark, she could make out the corners of the room. She had double vision. The muscles in her left arm jerked uncontrollably. All side effects of the ketamine. The music stopped. She heard footsteps. They appeared to be coming toward the door. Keys jangled, then clicked against the doorknob. The door opened.

Seth.

Chapter Thirty-Nine

fficer Teddy Stevens had grabbed a cold-cut sandwich and a drink at the Riverside Subway before driving on Route 41 out to Groverton Road. Detective Bauer had given him a list of addresses to check out. He told Stevens that they may have a lead in the Rainy Night Stalker case, and that he was to knock on some doors and report anything he saw that was suspicious or out of the ordinary.

Stevens had visited about twenty houses in that general area the day before. That morning, he scanned the list of addresses he still needed to check off. After driving about fifteen minutes through the thick woods, he came to a clearing and pulled off to the side of the road. A farmer had plowed under the field and left it fallow in order to rebalance the soil nutrients, break any crop pest and disease cycles, and provide a haven for wildlife.

Stevens cut his engine and rolled down the window. He pulled out his sandwich, spread napkins across his lap, and snapped a healthy half-moon out of the bun. He took a sip of his orange soda and listened to the twits and twirls of a number of different bird species in the nearby trees. He watched two barn swallows swoop from treetop to treetop.

Stevens looked down at the list of addresses. When he had finished eating, he crumpled the sandwich wrapper and napkin, had a last sip of soda, and turned over the car's ignition. He pulled out onto the road, and a few minutes later, pulled onto the gravel driveway at 1550 Groverton Road. The driveway ran along the side of a U-shaped cabin and ended at the back of the house. He got out, stepped into a courtyard, and stood beside an old oak tree. He stared up at the sturdy hoist that was fastened to the tree. *The guy must be an avid hunter.*

He made his way into the courtyard. He glanced over at the table under the awning beside the sliding glass doors. He cupped his hands against the glass and peered in. He saw a living room to the left with a fireplace and a dining room to the right. There seemed to be a towel draped across the back of one of the dining room chairs. The dining room table appeared to be empty, although he could only see half of the table. As far as he could tell, nothing seemed out of the ordinary.

Chapter Forty

Chief Quinn closed the last report and spun it on top of the pile of others. "We've been at this for hours. What now?"

Stuart opened a file on his computer. "Let's look at all of Moon's photos that she's downloaded from each of the crime scenes and the victim's homes one more time. There must be some clue we can find."

Chief Quinn slid his chair next to Stuart's. They scanned hundreds of photos, from the grassy fields to every possible angle of the bodies, to every single room in each of the victims' residents.

Chief Quinn sat back in his chair and stared at the ceiling. "It's like looking for a specific grain of sand on the beach."

"Hang on. I might have something." Stuart enlarged a photo. "This is a photo from the first victim's closet. Christine Krohmalney had hiking gear."

Chief Quinn sat up and pulled his chair closer to the monitor. "Okay."

"We can see hiking poles, hiking boots, and a backpack. Moon said that Sandra was attacked after she finished hiking in Neversink.

Hiking connects the first two victims in the Catskills."

"It's something." Chief Quinn stood and went to the whiteboard. He wrote "Christine and Sandra—hiking."

Chief Quinn sat back down, and Stuart continued to swipe through the photos. He got to the photos taken in Margaret Bender's apartment.

"Wait." Chief Quinn pointed to the computer screen. "Go back. That one there from Rachel Mariner's kitchen. Look at the refrigerator. What's that under the magnet on the side just above the coffee maker?"

Stuart enlarged the photo. "It's a prayer card."

Chief Quinn ran out of the office and returned with two evidence envelopes in his gloved hand. He removed a plastic bag from each of the envelopes.

"This prayer card was entered as evidence from Margaret Bender's kitchen," Chief Quinn said. "The police gathered objects from Holly Sherman's kitchen countertop as possible evidence. Can you enlarge Margaret Bender's prayer card?"

Stuart clicked and held down the control key and tapped the plus sign. The image expanded across the screen. Chief Quinn pulled out prayer cards from each plastic bag and held them up to the monitor.

"All three cards match," Stuart said. "It's Bannister's Funeral home."

There was a knock on the door frame. Officer Newman held a piece of paper.

"Come in, Newman," Chief Quinn said. "What have you got?"

"I went through all the registered black Dodge Rams in New York State in and around Groverton and Neversink. We got a hit." Newman handed the paper to Chief Quinn. "There is one Dodge Ram just outside Groverton registered to a Seth Woodman. The address is 1550 Groverton Road."

Chief Quinn and Stuart looked at each other.

"Let's go to the funeral home and speak with Mr. Woodman," Stuart said.

Chapter Forty-One

"Hello, Moon." Seth flicked on the light.

Moon squinted. The light felt like two dirty thumbs gouging her eyes.

"Since you already know who I am, I didn't see the need to blindfold you. And bonus for me, I don't need to keep the room dark for us. I had a feeling if anyone would have figured out that I was The Rainy Night Stalker, it would have been you." He laughed to himself. "The Rainy Night Stalker. It has a nice ring to it, don't you think? Did you get a load of the merchandise they were selling outside the police department? Those T-shirts are so soft. I doubt they'll shrink much in the wash. And won't that umbrella come in handy in the rain?"

He walked over to the right side of the bed and stood beside her face. She saw that he was wearing a silk robe. It was burgundy with blue and yellow embroidered flowers that flowed up one side from the hemline. It made her think of a Japanese kimono.

"Now, as to that piece of paper you passed to that detective during the press conference, that bit about me having, what did he say it was, a micropenis?" He untied and opened the robe. Seth's penis was large and fully erect, shiny and pulsing with blood and thick veins. He turned his body, posing from side to side. "Now I ask you, does anything about my penis look micro to you?"

He removed the robe and draped it back and forth across her back. "Don't you just love the feeling of silk against the skin?"

Seth tossed the robe onto the bedpost. He sat on the edge of the bed. He leaned in close to her face and gave her a smile, oily as Valvoline. Seth placed his hand on Moon's back, then spider-walked it down her spine. He cupped her right buttock.

"You know, of all the beautiful women I've had in my life, and I've had quite a few, I've never anticipated having one quite like I've anticipated having you."

He stopped suddenly and took a step back. "Extraordinary. By this time, all the women are crying, screaming, begging me to stop, although I can't quite make out exactly what they're saying—given the gag and all. You? You aren't making a sound."

I won't give you the satisfaction, Moon thought.

He untied her gag and dropped it on the floor. They studied each other for a long moment.

"Thank you for removing the gag," Moon said, licking her dry lips. "I appreciate it."

His eyebrows went way up, and a rapscallion twinkle appeared in his eye. She had a sense that this caught him off guard, but that he was enjoying the civilized banter. "My pleasure."

"Do you mind if I ask you a question?"

"Fire away."

"Who was it that made you feel vulnerable? You're a handsome, talented, intelligent man. What happened to you?"

His smile faded, and he looked at Moon with such confusion and pain. He swallowed and his bottom lip quivered. He looked away from her and blinked.

"Was it your mother? Your father? Sometimes it's helpful to talk to someone. I'm a good listener."

In an instant, his eyes grew cold and lifeless—like a doll's eyes. "That's none of your business."

He stepped out of her line of sight. She heard him go to the foot of the bed and felt the mattress shift as he climbed on. He began to softly hum "Harvest Moon."

Oh my God, she thought, he was right there, watching me and Matthew dance.

The doorbell rang. Both Seth and Moon looked at the door as though whoever rang the doorbell was in the hallway. They heard loud knocking on the front door, then pounding. Whoever was at the door wasn't leaving right away. Seth got down off the bed and knelt next to Moon's face. She felt his hot breath on her lashes.

"If you make a sound, I will kill you. Do you understand?"

Moon nodded.

Seth slipped into his robe and left the bedroom.

Chapter Forty-Two

hief Quinn grabbed his car keys and followed Stuart out the door. They drove, pulled into the funeral home parking lot, and knocked on the door. David Bannister answered and invited them in.

"Chief Quinn, Detective Bauer, how can I help you?"

"We'd like to speak to your assistant, Seth Woodman," Chief Quinn said. "We'd like to ask him a few questions."

"Seth has the day off today."

"Do you know where we might find him?" Stuart asked. "Does he go anywhere special on his days off that you know of?"

"He might be fishing. There's something about fishing that relieves stress for me. For Seth, too. He's a big-time fisherman. He has a cabin in the Catskills where he goes fly fishing."

Stuart shot Chief Quinn a look.

"His home address is 1550 Groverton Road," Chief Quinn said.

"That's right. Can I ask what this is about?"

"Seth may be connected to the murders," Stuart said. "Do you have the address of his cabin in the Catskills?"

"Sure," David said.

David handed Chief Quinn a piece of paper containing both addresses. "His cabins are both in such remote locations. Damned if I know why a person would want to live so far out of town. A place like that would give me the creeps."

Chief Quinn wrote down his cell number on his spiral notebook, ripped it out, and handed it to David.

"I want you to call me if you hear from Seth."

As the two men turned to leave, Stuart tapped Chief Quinn on the arm and pointed to a jar of Skor candy bars on the corner of a desk.

Chapter Forty-Three

Seth opened the front door. Officer Stevens looked Seth up and down, making a mental note of his bare feet and elaborate robe.

"What seems to be the problem, officer?"

"I'm Officer Theodore Stevens with the Clivesville Police. I'm sure you've heard of The Rainy Night Stalker. What's your name, sir?"

"Seth Woodman. Yeah. I saw something about that in the paper."

"We're out here going door to door to see if anyone in the area has seen or heard anything out of the ordinary."

"Nope. I haven't seen anything unusual."

"You see, we understand the killer may have a residence in this area."

Stevens shifted his body to look beyond the homeowner into the house. Seth sidestepped, blocking his view.

"Like I said, I haven't seen anything out of the ordinary. It's a shame about those girls. And what was done to them."

"Yes. It's a shame."

"You're going door to door. Does that mean you're close to catching someone?"

"Yes." Stevens locked eyes on Seth, who stared back for a moment but then averted his eyes to the floor.

"How long have you lived here, Mr. Woodman?"

"Many years."

Stevens shifted his weight again to see into the house, and again, Seth blocked his view.

"You hunt? I noticed the hoist out back."

"Everyone around here hunts."

Stevens looked down at Seth's feet. "Would you say you were a size 11 shoe?"

"That's right. Pretty common for a guy my size, wouldn't you say?"

"You just mentioned that you thought it was a shame about what the killer had done to those poor women."

"Yes."

"What do you mean, exactly? You see, the police haven't given out any information about what had been done to those women. How would you know what the killer had done to them? Do you have anything you'd like to share with me—some information you're privy to?"

"No."

Stevens shifted again to get a glimpse of the interior of the house. This time, Seth stepped forward causing Stevens to take a few steps back. He was six inches taller than Stevens. Seth hovered over him, nose to nose, staring him dead in the eye.

"I told you I haven't seen anything unusual. Now, unless you have a search warrant, officer, I suggest you move along."

Chapter Forty-Four

hief Quinn picked up the radio as he pulled out of the funeral home parking lot.

"Newman, what are you and Patterson doing?"

"We're in the car patrolling the Northside—you know, driving around, flying the flag."

"Bauer and I are headed out to Groverton Road, number 1550. We're going to question a Mr. Seth Woodman. I need you and Patterson to drive out there now. This place is out in the country, so there may be a chance we could go radio dark. We should be there in 15 minutes."

"Roger that. We're right behind you."

Chief Quinn replaced the radio receiver and punched his foot to the floor. His cell phone rang. He swiped it and cradled it onto his shoulder. "Quinn."

"This is Stevens. Detective Bauer asked me to check out the residents and report back if I saw anything suspicious."

The phone slipped from Chief Quinn's shoulder. He caught it and handed it to Stuart. "Stevens, it's Detective Bauer. You're on speaker"

"Okay. Listen, I was just out to a house in Groverton. The address is 1550 Groverton Road. The man's name is Seth Woodman. I didn't get inside to see the house, but he was acting weird. The guy gave me the creeps. I think he's someone you should check out."

Chief Quinn and Stuart locked eyes.

"I need you to turn around and head back out there. We're on our way. And Stevens, that's good police work."

Stuart hung up the phone and tucked it into the cup holder. He looked at his watch. "I'm going to call Moon and let her know."

Chapter Forty-Five

Moon bent her legs and pulled herself off her stomach and onto her knees. Then she felt it. Thunder shook the house. A storm was coming. Seth would be back soon, and when he did, he would kill her. She had to get out of there. She maneuvered her bound hands so that her wrists were no longer crossed one over the other but touching. She balled her hands into fists, leaned forward, and slammed her fists down hard onto her lower back. The zip ties cut into her wrists, but she didn't care. On the third try, she brought her fists down with such force that the ties snapped. She untied one ankle, then the other. She sat on the edge of the bed and slowly stood.

She felt around the bed for anything she could use as a weapon. She heard footsteps coming toward the door. She pushed the soiled mattress aside and grabbed one of the wooden bed slats that ran across the top of the metal bed frame. She wiggled it from under the mattress and stood behind the door. She raised the plank over her head. Her arms shook from the weight of the board, but a steeliness overtook her, and she nodded to herself. She was ready.

She shifted from one foot to the next and took a deep breath. She heard the key as it was inserted into the doorknob. She planted her feet and waited. The light turned on, and the door swung open. Seth stepped inside the room. At the same instant that he realized the bed was empty, Moon brought the board down on his head with all her might. Seth lost his footing and hit the floor. She brought the board down on him again. It connected with Seth's face in a loud crack. The sound of his nose breaking reminded Moon of a barn door slamming.

She stumbled through the door and down the hall. She ran through the kitchen and spotted the sliding glass doors in the dining room. As she rushed toward them, she snatched a flannel shirt that had been draped across the back of a dining room chair. She yanked the glass door open and leapt outside. She grabbed a large knife from the table under the awning and rushed across the courtyard toward the woods. When she reached the edge of the woods, she looked over her shoulder. Seth was standing in the open sliding glass doors with a rifle in his hand. He wiped his face with the back of his left hand. The blood smeared across his cheek like war paint. His teeth were coated in blood as he smiled.

The hunt was on.

Chapter Forty-Six

eth stepped outside the glass doors and placed his rifle on the table. He watched Moon look back at him as she rushed toward the woods. There was no need to rush. He smiled and shook his head. This one was going to be fun.

He reached down and flipped a cigarette from a pack on the table and struck a match. He held the flame to the tip of the cigarette and inhaled. His face was divided by the rippling ribbon of smoke. The hit of nicotine and the thrill of the hunt sent a surge of endorphins to his brain, dulling the pain.

He looped the rope to his belt. She should be near the thicket by now, he thought. I'll give her time to get hopelessly tangled. Her breasts will be the crowning jewels of my portrait.

He took a step out from underneath the awning and glanced up at the smoldering clouds. Lightning flashed across the sky. Everything was falling into place.

He took a step back and leaned against the table. The anticipation of this particular kill thrilled him. He sighed and took another crackly drag.

Chapter Forty-Seven

Moon watched Seth light up a cigarette and knew he was waiting to follow her into the woods. She understood that he planned to stalk her as he did the others. As she stepped into the woods, she desperately wanted to run but forced herself to take a deep breath and clear her mind. She didn't want to alarm the birds. She needed their eyes and ears. She let her breath out slowly and stepped into the woods. She walked steadily over the root-crossed ground, listening.

The wind picked up. Leaves lifted off the forest floor in a small tornado. The storm hung above the treetops, just waiting to happen. She pushed her arms through the sleeves of the flannel shirt and walked on.

The tree branches meshed overhead, blocking much of the light. She wormed her shoulders through the thick brush about fifty yards into the woods. The sharp twigs on the ground punctured the soles of her bare feet. The blood would make tracking her easy. She had been in the woods for about ten minutes when she heard the birds' loud caws. She caught a glimpse of a murder of crows circling above through the branches of the canopy, then swooping down. Seth had entered the woods somewhere behind her. He really must have mistreated them at one point because they continued to caw and dive bomb. She listened to the direction of their alarm calls and walked in a different direction.

The farther Moon pushed into the brush, the more tangled she became, and her hair and the flannel shirt caught in the branches. Whenever she moved her head to free herself, the branches scraped across her face. She became so tangled, she could barely move.

Moon closed her eyes and stopped struggling. She fell to her hands and knees and looked through the trunks of the brush. She noticed just beyond the brush there appeared to be some sort of trail used by wildlife. She ran the knife along the trunk to clear away the brush then wedged the board between two of the trunks. She rotated the board enough to create an opening for her to crawl through. Once on the trail, she pulled the board through the trunks and got to her feet. Moon made her way along the trail until the woods thinned enough for her to see that there was a clearing. As she left the woods, she spotted a cabin in the clearing. Her heart raced. She could call for help. Please, God, let there be someone home, she thought. They've got to have a phone. Please, God, please.

She stumbled across the clearing, but the closer she came to the cabin, she realized it had been abandoned for quite a while. The white paint on the old clapboard had peeled off like the thin, irregular patches of birch bark. Parts of the roof had caved in. Vines had claimed the porch and the front door. All the windows were broken.

The sound of the crows' scolding grew closer. Seth was nearing the clearing. She had to get back into the woods. She backed away from the cabin and ran in the opposite direction of the cawing toward the other side of the clearing. She made it about twenty feet from the cabin when the ground disappeared beneath her.

Chapter Forty-Eight

hief Quinn pulled off County Route 41 and followed a long, winding driveway to the cabin at 1550 Groverton Road. They parked beside a black Dodge Ram and approached the front door. Chief Quinn knocked several times without a response.

"Chief," Stuart whispered. He chinned toward the corner of the cabin, and they went around back. As they rounded the corner into the courtyard, Stuart motioned toward the tree with its hoist.

Chief Quinn pointed to a cigarette butt smoldering in the ashtray on the table. "This was just snubbed out."

"The sliding glass door is open," Stuart said. "There's blood on the door frame."

They drew their guns and approached on either side of the door.

"Seth Woodman," Chief Quinn called into the cabin. Without hearing a response, he nodded to Stuart. They raised their guns and entered the cabin in a semi-crouch. They followed the trail of blood on the floor sweeping their weapons in an arc. As soon as they entered the dining room, they stopped and stared at the large canvas on the wall.

"Holy Mother of God," Chief Quinn said. He reached up to his shoulder and pinched his microphone. The radio crackled. "Newman, do you read me?" He released the microphone. "Of course. No service."

Stuart took a step toward the canvas on the wall. "A self-portrait made from human flesh. Now we know what he's been doing with the missing body parts. How many areolae would say there are?"

"I'd say at least 50. God Almighty, in all my 30 years on the force, I've never seen anything like this."

Stuart nodded at the trail of blood on the floor and motioned Chief Quinn to follow him down the dark hallway. A parallelogram of light spilled onto the hallway floor from the room at the end of the hall. They crept toward the room and stood on either side of the open door. They stepped inside, guns drawn.

"Clear." Chief Quinn motioned for Stuart to follow him back through the cabin to the opposite wing. They entered the bedroom at the end of the hall.

"Clear," Stuart said. He flicked a switch on the wall and a dim overhead light came on. The only furniture in the room was a twin bed and a wooden nightstand. Chief Quinn opened a closet door and thumbed through clothes on hangers. Stuart pulled a photo album from underneath the bed and opened it.

"Jesus. Chief, take a look at this. I assume these are pictures of his victims—a few we know of and several we didn't know." Stuart flipped a page and saw several pictures of Moon, Matthew, Maisie, and himself taken from different vantage points, from the woods outside Moon's house.

"These were taken inside her house," Chief Quinn said. "The bastard even has a picture of Moon sleeping. Did you ever hear back from Moon?"

"No. Are you thinking what I'm thinking?"

"Yes. Let's go."

As they rushed out the sliding glass doors, Stuart felt a chill—not because of the storm coming, but because of the photos. They hurried through the courtyard following the bloody trail into the thick woods.

Chapter Forty-Nine

oon dangled by her fingertips on the inside edge of an antique well. Its lid had been covered with wooden planks that had rotted and had been overgrown with dirt and grass. She clung to the damp sod along the rim of the well. The knife and the wooden bed slat, the only weapons she had to defend herself, had flipped over her shoulder and disappeared into the black pit below.

Her legs bicycled the air trying to find traction along the slimy well wall. She felt a searing pain and saw that the jagged end of the board she had fallen through had impaled her right side. The more she tried to raise herself up out of the hole, the deeper the board dug into her flesh. The pain was unbearable. Her grip on the damp grass was slipping. Rain began to fall, and she could feel the sod loosen.

A strange stillness came over her. She could end the pain. All she had to do was to let go. If she released her grip on the sod, the board would dislodge from her side. She would fall into the well, away from the pain. Death would come quickly. As her father said, it would be as easy as falling asleep. They could all be together again and she wouldn't be alone. All she had to do was to let go.

She looked up at the sky. From inside the well, she could see the dark storm clouds scud across the last sliver of blue sky. That blue. It was the blue sky of her youth in Virginia. In her life before she came to Clivesville. Before her parents' murder.

A sizzle-flash of blue-white lightning flooded the well. Anger suddenly swelled inside her. She locked her eyes on the rim of the well and dug the fingers of her left hand further into the soil until she felt the stone lip of the well. She let go of her right hand and gripped the rotted board, pulled it up and out of her side, and threw it behind her into the well. She found the stone lip of the well again with the fingers of her right hand and pulled up with all her might. Her toes found protruding stones in the well wall. She dug her fingers deep into the wet grass. Inch by inch, hand over hand, she pulled herself up out of the well.

Once out, she got to her feet and turned around. She glanced down into the black pit of the well, then took several steps back. She ran her hands along her side and looked at her bloody palm.

She knew she'd never make it across the clearing to the woods. The wind suddenly blew in low and fast, and a wide curtain of rain tore across the ground. Moon ran toward the cabin and pushed through the front door.

She stood in the middle of a large open room. The wallpaper had passed fading into death. There were so many cobwebs that the air appeared veiled. There was a living room on the right of the grand room. The roof had long caved in above the rain-soaked sofa. Beside the sofa was a wooden end table with a lamp and an old rocking chair. The tattered furniture huddled around a large stone fireplace. Straight ahead along the back wall was a wood-burning stove and a sink. On the left, Moon noticed a partially opened door. She snatched a wrought iron poker from the fireplace tool set beside the hearth and headed across the room to the door. The old wooden floorboards bowed and moaned under her feet. As soon as she pushed the door open, a handful of pigeons flew up at her.

She held the poker in front of her with both hands and took a wary step inside the room. A ruined mattress lay dejected on a dull brass bed that had been pushed against the far wall. Beside the bed, a wooden nightstand held a lamp made from deer antlers. Moon looked up. A large hole had opened in the ceiling above the bed, exposing the rafters. She tied one end of the flannel shirt in a tight knot around the iron poker. She walked toward the bed, leaving a purposeful trail of bloody footprints. She pulled the bed slightly away from the wall and walked behind the bed. She then stepped up onto the bedframe, jumped up, and grabbed a hold of one of the rafters. Moon pulled herself up onto the wooden beam. She got to her feet and walked back across the rafters to the part of the ceiling by the door that was still intact. She pulled the poker from the knot and held it over her head with both fists as though it was a spear. The poker shook in her trembling hands.

She heard the front door creak open as Seth entered the cabin.

Chapter Fifty

"It's no use, Moon. I can see your blood on the floor."

She listened to Seth move through the cabin. Moon watched the door underneath her rotate inward. The barrel of Seth's rifle led the way into the room. He moved slowly below her in a crouched position. Moon focused on Seth's back. She tightened her grip on the poker and leaped down onto him, driving the poker into his flesh. She landed on his back sending him sprawling face-first onto the floor. The rifle left his hands and slid across the room under the bed. Moon stood and drove the poker further into his back. She took a step back and stared at Seth as he lay motionless.

Moon let out a deep, shaky sigh. She did it. It was over.

As she turned toward the door, she felt a hand grasp her ankle. Seth pulled hard and her feet came out from under her. The full weight of her body connected with the floor. She spun around to see Seth get to his knees. He reached around and pulled the bloody poker from his back. He held her ankle with one hand and raised the poker in the other. He cocked his head and smiled as he drove the poker down at her stomach. She twisted her body, and the poker impaled into the wooden floor. Moon spun again to face him and kicked him in the nose. Fresh blood sprayed across Seth's face as his head snapped back.

Moon scrambled to her feet and ran toward the door. Again, she wasn't fast enough. Seth grabbed her by the hair, picked her up, and threw her against the wall. She crashed into the nightstand and lamp, then landed hard on the floor, showered in broken glass and crushed antler bones. Moon felt the wooden floor buckle as Seth took a step toward her. She quickly tucked her body and rolled under the bed. Her shoulder connected with something cold and hard. She watched Seth's feet as he stepped to the edge of the bed.

"You're dead," he said with a laugh.

As soon as Seth flipped the mattress away from the bedframe, Moon pointed the rifle between the bed slats and pulled the trigger. Seth's body spun, but he remained on his feet. Moon aimed at his chest and pulled the trigger once more. Seth fell straight back. His body shuddered against the floor. Moon pushed the bed slats away and stood. She kept the barrel pointed at Seth until he no longer moved. Blood flowed from his mouth and under his body, spreading across the floor.

Moon raised her face to the ceiling and closed her eyes. She let out a deep sigh. It was well and truly over. She had done it. She had stopped Seth from ever harming anyone again. She got justice for all of his victims, especially for Holly. But more than that, for the first time since her parents' murders, she felt an unseen weight lift from her and float away. For the first time since that tragic day when she was twelve, Moon felt free.

Moon's eyes widened when she heard the front door of the cabin swing open. She raised the rifle and stepped into the grand room.

"Whoa, it's us," Chief Quinn said.

He and Stuart stood still with their hands raised. Moon dropped the rifle, and Stuart ran across the room to her. Chief rushed passed them into the bedroom.

"What are you doing here?" she asked.

Stuart shrugged. "Rescuing you?"

He draped his blazer over her shoulders and led her outside. Chief Quinn joined them on the porch. The rain had eased to a trickle just as Newman, Patterson, and Stevens stepped into the clearing.

"Stuart, you and Stevens take Moon to the hospital," Chief Quinn said. "Newman and Patterson will stay with me until the other officers and Dr. Babbitt arrive."

Stuart lifted Moon into his arms and carried her back through the woods. As the three of them passed through the courtyard and the bloody sliding glass doors, they turned their faces away. Stuart helped Moon into the back of the cruiser first, then slid in beside her. As Stevens backed the police car out of the driveway toward the main road, Moon watched the cabin through the front windshield until it disappeared behind a row of pine trees.

Chapter Fifty-One

Moon stared at herself in the hospital bathroom mirror and noted the various colors of her bruises. The side of her face where Seth had struck her while on the kitchen floor was a bright russet, almost brown and haloed in yellow. The raw wounds on her feet were wrapped in gauze. She lifted her white T-shirt to look at the bandages all along her right side. She lowered her shirt and limped back to the bed, slowly sitting on the edge. She wore loose-fitting silk lounge pants and flip-flips, as none of her shoes would fit over the bandages.

An old woman wearing a blue flowered patient gown and yellow hospital socks shuffled past her doorway. She did a double take at Moon, then turned and looked behind her. When she saw that no one was there, she looked at Moon again with her head cocked and entered the room.

"You can see me," the old woman said.

"Yes."

"How extraordinary. I've heard of people like you."

"Is there something I can do for you, Mrs.—"

"Bedingfield. Edna Bedingfield." The old woman smiled. Wrinkles pleated the outer edges of her deep blue eyes. "No dear, there's nothing you can do for me. I was 101 years old. Nearly all of my family and friends passed long ago. The doctors tried everything to save me, but it was just my time. To tell you the truth, I'm relieved. You have no idea how good this feels. I feel eighteen again. Is there anything I can do for you?"

"For me?"

Matthew strode past Edna with a fist full of daisies. "Of course, these are for you. I remembered that they were your favorite."

Edna stepped aside while Matthew sat down on the bed beside Moon.

"They are my favorite—they're so cheery," Moon said.

"I like this guy," Edna said.

"How are you feeling?" Matthew asked.

"I'm fine. Just waiting for the nurse to come back with the discharge papers."

"The doctor is on the phone, but he'll sign them as soon as he's off," Edna said.

Moon smiled at Edna, then turned back to Matthew. "Thanks for getting my clothes yesterday."

"My pleasure. The crime scene cleaners left your dining room and kitchen spotless. You would never know anything happened there." Matthew watched Moon's legs swing back and forth. "You look anxious."

"I'm just ready to go home."

"It's only been two days. The doctors wanted to make sure you were okay. You lost a lot of blood."

"I'm fine."

"You might be fine physically, but it's okay if you're not quite okay emotionally. You've been through a lot."

"He didn't take anything that won't heal."

Stuart tapped a knuckle on the door frame and walked in.

Edna's eyes grew big. "How many suitors do you have?"

As soon as Matthew spotted Stuart, he stood.

"I'll call you later, Moon." Matthew kissed her. As he turned to leave, he nodded once at Stuart as they passed one another in the doorway.

"Shouldn't you be going, too, Mrs. Bedingfield?" Moon whispered.

"Oh, no. I'm enjoying this immensely."

Stuart strode into the room and sat in a chair beside the bed. "How are you?"

"I'll be better once I'm out of here. Is there any news from forensics?"

"Yes. They're testing the DNA of all the areolae from Seth's canvas to see if we can match it with the FBI's Missing Person DNA database. They've already matched seven cases so far."

Edna stepped aside as a young male nurse in green scrubs entered the room. "I have your discharge papers here, Moon. I'll go get a wheelchair and get you out of here."

"I don't need a wheelchair."

"It's hospital procedure. I'll be right back."

The nurse disappeared, and Stuart stood. "I'm going to go bring the car around."

Edna watched Stuart leave. "The first man, the blond one with the flowers, was very nice. Is he your beau?"

"My beau? No. Well, he was a long time ago."

Moon thought about how she felt about Matthew. She guessed that in some sort of primal way, she felt connected to him by something ancient and important she couldn't quite put her finger on. She knew his personality, his laughter, his voice, his smell. To her, Matthew's scent and the memory of him were one and the same. He would always be a part of who she was.

"And the second man?"

"We work together, that's all. He's just a friend."

Edna shook her head and sighed. "Never underestimate the power of denial."

"All right. He's sexy and new and exciting. And I like him very much."

Edna shrugged. "Conundrum."

"Exactly."

The nurse pushed the wheelchair into the room. "Your chariot awaits."

"Thank you." She slid down off the bed and slowly lowered herself into the chair.

Edna walked beside Moon as the nurse wheeled her down the hall toward the elevator. When the elevator doors opened, the nurse nudged the chair into the car and turned it around to face the doors. Edna stood in the elevator doorway.

"So, which man are you going to choose?" Edna asked.

Moon shrugged her shoulders. Edna gave her a thumbs up, and Moon returned the gesture as the doors closed.

While Moon waited for Stuart to pull up to the door, she looked up at the afternoon sky. It was a brilliant blue—the kind that hurts your eyes if you stare too long. There wasn't a cloud to be seen. She closed her eyes and filled her lungs with the crisp, cool air.

Stuart pulled up beside the wheelchair. He got out, held the door open for her, and helped her into the car. He pulled out of the hospital parking lot onto the highway.

"So, what's next for you?" Moon asked. "New York City or D.C.?"

"Chief Quinn called me into his office after I turned in my investigation report."

"And?"

"And he offered me a position on his team."

"You would be working here?"

"Yes."

Moon laughed. "You are completely overqualified."

"True. But I think this will be good for me. I need a fresh start. I'm tired of working 50 hours a week. I've handed in my resignation. FBI approval isn't required to resign, but I still have to tie up a few loose ends with the administrative office at FBIHQ to make it official. Besides, there's nothing for me back in D.C. I feel as though my life up until now has been a little like a scavenger hunt. Every clue along the way has led me here. I'd like to get to know Clivesville better."

"Are you sure you can handle small town life?"

"I have a usual at the diner. It feels as though the season has just turned the page. Yesterday, I saw geese honking in a V-formation across the sky. Fall is just around the corner, and I want to do all the autumn things I can't do in a big city—apple picking, exploring a pumpkin patch, getting lost in a corn maze. I've never done any of that, but I hear it's fun. I've had enough of city life for now. I have a feeling this is where I belong."

"Where will you stay?"

"I've already rented a house on the Southside of town. The house is a little long in the tooth, but the bones are great. It was built in 1830. I love that the house has been around that long. Anyway, the owner is giving me a break on the rent because I'll be helping him with the historic renovations."

Moon shook her head. "You? Don't take this the wrong way, but you don't seem like the fixer-upper type. You seem more the 'pick up the phone and call the super' type. Have you ever held a hammer in your life?"

"No, but how hard can it be?"

"Oh, boy. Tell you what, I'll let you borrow my hammer. And if you can manage that, then at some point I'll even let you borrow my power tools."

"You own power tools?"

"Of course," she said with a nod.

"Deal. You said something that stuck with me. You said that death takes care of itself, and that it's the living that's hard."

"Yeah."

"I think there are times when the living can be easy." He shrugged. "It's just a theory I'm working on."

"Is that so?"

"I'd like to test my theory tonight if you're up for it. We can discuss it over dinner. A do-over of sorts."

"That sounds nice."

Stuart's phone rang through the car radio. "Bauer."

"It's Chief Quinn."

"Hey, Chief. What's up?"

"Where are you? Are you able to meet us outside Savona? We've got one, more than one actually. It's pretty grisly. A couple of forestry students found human remains—several skulls, one with long dark hair still attached. Some of the skeletal remains are still connected by sinew. Others are scattered. It looks as though animals got 'em. We're up Smalliage Road off Robie Road passed the Mud Creek Bison Ranch. Have you seen Moon?"

"I'm right here, Chief," Moon said.

"Do you feel up to coming out?"

"Absolutely." Moon pulled a small notepad and pen from her purse.

"Take I-86 west to the Savona exit. Take a left at the four corners by the Dollar General and hang a right onto Robie Road. Veer left onto Smalliage Road. You'll see the cars about half a mile out."

"We'll swing by Moon's place to pick up her gear and head out," Stuart said, then hung up.

Within minutes, Stuart pulled into Moon's driveway. She opened the garage door with her iPhone. She ran into the house, grabbed the pitcher from on top of the refrigerator, and filled it with water. She dropped the daisies in the pitcher and headed back out the door. In the garage, she opened the back of the van and took a quick inventory of her crime scene and camera gear in her duffel bag, then slung it on her shoulder. She closed the van door and ducked under the garage door as it rolled shut.

They pulled out of the driveway, past the city limits, and back out onto the highway. Twenty minutes later, Stuart pulled onto tree-lined Robie Road. They passed several homey houses, their porches bedecked with vibrant mums and the season's first pumpkins. Colorful scarecrows struck poses in fields. She watched the geese arrow their way across the sky. They drove deeper into the woods. If they hadn't been on their way to a crime scene, they could have easily been out for a lazy afternoon drive through the country hills.

Stuart stayed left onto Smalliage Road and parked behind a line of cruisers. Moon got out of the car and opened her duffel bag. She tied her hair in a loose bun and slipped a hairnet over her head. She pulled the hooded overalls over her yoga pants and T-shirt. She care-fully stepped into her rubber boots and looped her camera bag around her neck. She tucked gloves into her pocket.

"You ready?" Stuart asked.

She clipped a tripod to her belt loop. "I'm ready."

Officer Stevens waved them into the woods. Stuart and Moon fol-lowed him along a dirt trail until they came to the yellow crime scene tape. Moon got out her camera and wide-angle lens. She ducked under the tape and paused. Moon took in the area. The air was thick with decay and the musty smell of rotting leaves and wet mud. In the midst of a thick forest, a natural rock wall rose from the earth. Much of the rock wall's edges were covered in a shroud of kudzu. The vines draped across the top of the rock wall like eyebrows. Broken beer bottles lit-tered the ground. A couple of bottles still stood on the protruding rocks. It looked as though someone had been target shooting. At the foot of the wall, human remains were strewn over a 30-foot radius.

Chief Quinn stood with his hands on his hips surveying the ground. When he spotted Stuart and Moon, he waved them over.

"As far as I can see, it looks as though we have four victims. Hard to tell from what's left of them after the animals came on the scene, but some of the remaining flesh is red indicating the blood's decomposition. Lloyd will pinpoint the time of death, but I'd guess they've been here about 10 days."

Moon lifted the camera to her cheek and started shooting. She took several wide-angle shots of the area. As her camera shutter clicked, she thought of the victims. Who were they? What happened to them? Why were they left here?

One thing was certain—she would help them the only way she knew how. While she photographed the remains, she whispered to them.

"Talk to me. I can hear you. I promise I will get the person who did this to you."

About the Author

Debbie Shannon has an MFA in creative writing from Florida International University. She has published three books: *The Fisherman*, *A Crowded Loneliness: The story of loss, survival and resilience of a Peter Pan Child of Cuba*, and *W.H. Auden, Poetry, and Me: A 102-year-old reluctant poet reflects on life, poetry, and her famous teacher*. *The Rainy Night Stalker* is her latest novel. She lives in a small town in upstate New York. When she's not writing, you'll find her learning to play the cello and searching for the perfect fish taco. You can find out more about her at https://www.debbieshannon.com/.

Acknowledgments

There are so many people I need to thank for helping me with this story. First, I'd especially like to thank Josh Teeter for his knowledge of forests and the birds and their different vocalizations. He was taught how to clear his mind before entering the woods to keep from alarming the birds, a skill I passed on to Moon. He taught me that birds are the sentinels—the eyes and ears of the woods. Because of him and my research, I now have a great love and appreciation for crows.

Many thanks go to my editor, David Pasquantonio, for his insights and encouragement.

A special thanks are due to David Bannister, our local funeral director, for his knowledge of crime scenes, embalming techniques, and protocols. Thank you for letting me use your name and your "Rum-a-Dumb" story! You truly are someone strong and dependable to lean on.

I have to thank nurse practitioner, Christine Krohmalney, for the use of her name and for volunteering to be victim number one. I hope I wrote you well.

Many thanks are due to my dear friend, Reverend Barry Lomax, for his instruction in Catholic funeral masses.

A special thanks goes out to Officer Amber Rightmire. She generously instructed me in police protocols and procedures.

And finally, to my dearest friend, Gladys Dubovsky, who passed away peacefully in her bed on November 10, 2023, at the ripe old age of 108. I am filled with gratitude for her love, her encouragement, and her faith in me.